PRAISE FOR THE NOVELS OF ROBERT RODI

Fag Hag

"A hilarious tale—bitchy without being savage—I adored every word."
—Quentin Crisp

"A fun romp of a book."
—*The Atlanta Journal-Constitution*

"A camped-up *Fatal Attraction* . . . Rodi's comedy is over the top,
his chills are on target."
—*Lambda Book Report*

Closet Case

"A hilarious follow-up to *Fag Hag* . . . Rodi fans should rush out and
buy this novel immediately!"
—*Out* magazine

"A joyride of a book . . . Infectious . . . Hard to put down."
—*The Boston Phoenix*

"A book for Gay and Lesbian Pride Month . . . Roars to its
much awaited finale."
—*The Advocate*

Drag Queen

"Rodi is the gay Molière . . A smart, funny, and
terrifically entertaining tale."
—*Kirkus Reviews*

ROBERT RODI is the author of *Fag Hag, Closet Case, Drag Queen,* and
Kept Boy, all available in Plume editions. In his spare time, he writes
the comic book series *Codename: Knockout* for DC/Vertigo, about sexy
superspy Angela Devlin and her hunky gay sidekick Go-Go Fiasco. Mr.
Rodi lives in Chicago.

ROBERT RODI

Bitch Goddess

A NOVEL

a plume book

PLUME
Published by the Penguin Group
Penguin Putnam Inc., 375 Hudson Street, New York, New York 10014, U.S.A.
Penguin Books Ltd, 80 Strand, London WC2R 0RL, England
Penguin Books Australia Ltd, 250 Camberwell Road, Camberwell,
    Victoria 3124, Australia
Penguin Books Canada Ltd, 10 Alcorn Avenue, Toronto, Ontario, Canada M4V 3B2
Penguin Books India (P) Ltd, 11 Community Centre, Panchsheel Park,
    New Delhi—110 017, India
Penguin Books (N.Z.) Ltd, Cnr Rosedale and Airborne Roads, Albany,
    Auckland, New Zealand
Penguin Books (South Africa) (Pty) Ltd, 24 Sturdee Avenue, Rosebank,
    Johannesburg 2196, South Africa

Penguin Books Ltd, Registered Offices:
Harmondsworth, Middlesex, England

First published by Plume,
a member of Penguin Putnam Inc.

First printing, March 2002
10 9 8 7 6 5 4 3 2 1

 REGISTERED TRADEMARK—MARCA REGISTRADA

CIP data is available.
ISBN 0-452-28310-8

Printed in the United States of America
Set in Sabon

PUBLISHER'S NOTE
This is a work of fiction. Names, characters, places, and incidents either are the product of
the author's imagination or are used fictitiously, and any resemblance to actual persons,
living or dead, business establishments, events, or locales is entirely coincidental.

BOOKS ARE AVAILABLE AT QUANTITY DISCOUNTS WHEN USED TO PROMOTE PRODUCTS OR SERVICES.
FOR INFORMATION PLEASE WRITE TO PREMIUM MARKETING DIVISION, PENGUIN PUTNAM INC., 375
HUDSON STREET, NEW YORK, NEW YORK 10014.

FOR JEFFREY

senza in quale la vita non varebbe niente

With thanks to Christopher Schelling,
a staunch character

and to Laurie Horowitz,
who strives for bitch but achieves only goddess

Bitch Goddess

... Is it running? Is it running now? ... I don't see the needle jumpi— Oh, there it is. ... Is it jumping too much? *Hello! Hello!* Look at how much it's jumping. *Hello!* ... I don't want my voice distorted ... Don't bother with the controls, angel, just tell me. I can modulate. I'm an actress.

Okay? All set? ... Right, then. Where shall I start?

My name is Viola Chute. But of course you know that. What you may not know is, I had a different name when I was born. Back in Cornwall. The original one, angel—in England. Never *mind* when. I was the daughter of a very handsome claims adjustor, David Tregothan, and his bride of two years, Rowella. They named me Violet. My mother died when I was very young. I have no recollections of her beyond the stories my father would tell. And of course some old photographs ... I had one put into a locket that I always wear around my neck. Look here ... oh, the clasp. Can you ... ? Thanks. So difficult with these nails, luv. But there—my mother. Beautiful, isn't she? Much more so than I, don't you think? ... Oh, you old kiss-ass. Of course I'm not. Not nearly. But thank you for saying so.

Anyway ... How's your water? Ready for a refill? ... Whiskey, then? Something else? ... Well, just speak up when you do. Dominique will fetch you anything you like. Within reason—a*haaa*-ha! Where was I, then? Oh, my father, my father. Well, he was a very cultured man, despite his station in life. On weekends he'd play phonograph records, you see, and hold me in his lap, and we'd just rock—this being on a rocking chair, angel—we'd rock, rock, rock while listening to the most glorious music. I remember hearing Nellie Melba sing Violetta in *La traviata* on my father's lap, and oh, that changed my life!

I

"*Sempre LI-bera degg'io folleggiare di gioia in GIOI-a . . .*"
Well, you might try not to wince so *frightfully* evidently. Anyway, after that, as I said, my life was changed. I wanted to become an opera singer, a great soprano. Great mezzo, more like, with my voice as it is now—hell, great *tenor*, a*haaa*-ha—but that was then, luv, and my tones were quite ringingly bell-like. You'd have wept to hear them. The purity of innocence . . . Anyway, my father didn't have the cash, did he, for such an education—I mean an opera singer's education. So I decided to become an actress instead. The stage was really the thing . . . anything, so long as I could be *up* there. And while I couldn't teach myself to sing, I could teach myself to *act*. I started attending amateur theatricals. Lots of Shakespeare, luv. Reams and reams of it. I remember the first time I saw *Twelfth Night*. The plot was absurd—cross-dressing nonsense with long-lost twins—but I adored it. Such felicitosity . . . felici . . . what's the word I want? . . . *Felicitousness*. Thanks, angel. I even changed my name to Viola, after the lead. Funny, isn't it, how many of my heroines have names close to the one I was christened with. Violetta, Viola . . . I suppose a Freudian would say that's *why* I admired them. But if that's the case, why didn't I take up the violin? . . . Hm? Luv? . . . Or a life of violence, yes, exactly! A*haaa*-ha. Clever bastard. Although there's at least one photographer in town who'd probably say I've done just that. No, let's not talk about *him*.

Mind if I smoke? . . . Oh, come on, now. I'll only have one. Just hold your breath . . . Got a match? . . . Just teasing, luv! My God, what a fucking sourpuss. They're *my* lungs, you know.

Anyway . . . where was I? Oh, yes; so that's the story behind the name Viola. The Chute came from my first husband, Regnal. A real-estate magnate, many years my senior . . . Never *mind* how many. Look, do you want this fucking job? . . . Kidding, angel, kidding. Anyway, I first met Regnal when I was . . . um, nineteen, and performing in a harvest festival pageant in Illuggan. I was Britannia, and a great honor it was. Great woolen costume, smelt of every fat cow who'd worn it all those years before me—don't use that bit—and despite it I was thrilled. Anyway, Regnal was in town, buying up vast tracts of land to put ugly buildings on—don't use that bit, either—going to have to watch my mouth with you, I can tell—and Regnal . . . where was I? . . . Oh, Regnal was buying up vast tracts of land, and he stopped in Illuggan to see if there was anything else he could pick up on his way back to London, and settled on me. Whisked me off to the capital, which didn't take much whisking, believe me. Because first of all, he was drop-dead gorgeous, and second . . . well, have you ever seen Illuggan?—Don't you dare use that bit. I may have to go back there someday.

Anyway, this was just two months before my father succumbed to a respiratory infection and died. Never really forgave myself for deserting him. I think, in fact, it was the guilt that ruined my marriage to Regnal, who was a perfectly lovely man. I look back now and think what a loss that was . . . but I was so *very* young, angel. And it seemed to me, however absurdly, that my marrying Regnal had somehow *caused* my father's death. No relationship can withstand the injection of just a drop of that kind of poison . . . it spreads, doesn't it. Long story short, I soon found myself seated in a solicitor's office wearing a Chanel suit and trying not to look afraid, signing almost anything they put in front of me. As luck would have it, Regnal died before he could sign anything himself. A lorry in Earls Court—right through the intersection. Not much left of Regnal . . . except for a vast and dazzling fortune. And there I was, free as a bird, and possessed of every last shilling of— Oh, there's the phone. Be a darling and answer it? And listen: I'm not in to *any*one . . .

Who was it? *Peter Grace?* Oh, Christ, luv, why didn't you say so? Got to call him back at *once*. Would you be terribly crushed if we had to continue this tomorrow? . . .

SUBJ: aargh
DATE: 97-6-2| 23:25:55 EST
FROM: emanfr@ysa.net
TO: nbcasem@bot.ubsm.edu

you have no idea what i'm going through. ok remember the 1st interview i did with viola chute—the one in prismen way back when i
could still get a job from a national rag. it was the interview that
helped kickstart her comeback remember. she was a totally foul-
mouthed politically incorrect old shrew maybe because she didn't
have anything to lose. all i can say is now that she's a big star again—
bigger than ever pulling down 125 gs per ep—suddenly she's turned
herself into jackie kennedy. no lie you should hear this crap version of
her life i'm getting—me her supposed biographer. starting with her
how artistic her insurance salesman father was listening to opera with
baby viola in his lap for christ's sake. then there's the part where she's
swept off her feet by her 1st husband and i mean i've seen the news
footage of that pageant where she met him. she's this dewy young
thing—cute as nails is the phrase that comes to mind—with a grip on
his arm like a bear trap and he has this look like omigod what can i
do. funny really—self made industrialist pig finally meets a superior
will and it belongs to this eyelash batting girl. though i think she
must've been in her 20s when this happened. she says 19 but what
was i born yesterday.

anyway she's right in the middle of this story about how they filed for
divorce for some crap emotional reason—like i haven't heard the rumors about what really happened—when suddenly she dumps me
to take a call from peter grace who is only her agent which shows me
where i fit on the scale of things. even the damn dogs come first. i
know what you're saying i'm lucky to have the job. which reminds me
did you see the review of mincing in urania that ran in the times. i got
a copy from one of my less well bred intimes. you know gay men live

4

for this kind of thing. oh you haven't seen the times review how lucky i have one here in my backpack laminated with the best parts high-lighted in pink. and there i am suddenly staring at phrases like attempts to make a virtue of fatuity and the 1st novel at its most highfalutin. but hey i laughed it off swear to god. took 2 years of my life to write the freakin thing—a 2 year hiatus from paying assignments no less—and everyone in the developed world goes and trashes it. so now i find myself having to ghost a whitewashed biography of a b movie queen just to stay alive. surely you can see the humor in this can't you. oh god just let me die.

actually i have to admit viola is pretty fabulous despite the bullshit. she looks great i mean i know she must've had a facelift or six but damn if i can spot the scars. and what a body, crosses her legs and you expect the shockwaves to knock out the nearest wall. dresses to kill too—only versace and vivienne westwood she says they're the only designers who understand her as if that's one of their big considerations when they design which for all i know it is. but truth i think it's just because they start with v. she's the kind of woman who creams over magazine captions being alliterative that way—vivacious viola vibrates vermilion in versace. there's an ancient life magazine cover framed on her wall with her looking totally pouty and sex-ready and the headline is va va va viola. i think she burns incense and prays beneath it. i'm pretty sure i saw cinders in the carpet.

you can see what's happening here can't you. bemoaning my fate my aborted journalist career my stillborn literary career my descent into movie star ghosting and all the while it's viola this viola that va va va viola the other thing. yes of course i've fallen under her spell just allow me to pretend otherwise for wounded dignity's sake.

write and tell me what's new with you. skin cleared up yet. thought you botanists were supposed to be immune to that kind of thing why weren't you wearing long pants. isn't that rule one when traipsing about in the wild. don't tell me there's some sort of right stuff thing you field researchers have. my sister is an avian zoologist at a big chicago zoo and she had her lower lip bitten off when she was trying to handle a wounded vulture. i said don't you guys have wire masks for jobs like that. she gave me this horrified look like yes but only a geek would actually wear one.

lip was reattached btw. good as new in fact better it's like she's had a collagen injection that never wears off. i wish you equal good fortune in your injury.

smooches
harry

NOTED BUILDER FILES FOR DIVORCE

London Daily Herald
April 2, 1964

The solicitors of Mr. and Mrs. Regnal Chute have announced that the couple have separated and intend to divorce as soon as proceedings will allow. Mr. Chute, a successful commercial land developer and builder, is the plaintiff, citing withdrawal of affection as his justification for the suit, and further claiming that Mrs. Chute has vacated the couple's South Kensington address and taken up semi-permanent residence with a clarinetist in Cheapside. Mrs. Chute's solicitor insists that the musician is merely a close friend, while Mrs. Chute herself adds that "Regnal wouldn't know friendship from love anyway, the dried-up old cow pat." Mrs. Chute, the former Violet Tregothan, wed Mr. Chute six months ago in a civil ceremony three weeks after the couple met in Mrs. Chute's native Cornwall. Mr. Chute is divorced from a previous wife.

INTERVIEW WITH VIOLA CHUTE

by E. Manfred Harry

(Excerpt)

Homophile, July 1993

HOMOPHILE: Are you familiar with the term "outing"?

VIOLA: What, as in "we're going on one"? A picnic, you mean? Like that?

HOMOPHILE: No, no—I mean like shoving someone out of the closet.

VIOLA: Oh, angel, is that really done?

HOMOPHILE: All the time, these days. We figured, you've been in the entertainment field for quite a while, you must have worked with some gay actors . . .

VIOLA: *(laughs)* No, never! Not a one. *(laughs harder)*

HOMOPHILE: Well, we figured, it's 1993, maybe you'll talk.

VIOLA: Oh, luv, what a temptation, but no. Bad manners. Some of those people are still my friends.

HOMOPHILE: What about the ones who aren't?

VIOLA: Don't be silly. Everyone adores me. *(laughs)*

HOMOPHILE: Okay, what about the ones who are dead?

VIOLA: Just that: they're dead and gone. Don't look back, that's my motto.

HOMOPHILE: Okay. Just one, then. I wanted to ask you in particular about Klaue Werther—

VIOLA: Oh, I might've known you'd ask about Klaue.

HOMOPHILE: —your costar in the first *Agrippina* movie.

VIOLA: Oh, Klaue, Klaue! He broke some hearts, I can tell you that.

HOMOPHILE: Women's?

VIOLA: Men's! Men's, angel. Klaue was straight as an arrow. I should know.

HOMOPHILE: What . . . you and Klaue?

VIOLA: Me and *everybody*, luv. Lots of down time on those shoots. Anyway, Klaue . . . well, he was a god, you know. Chiseled from marble.

HOMOPHILE: But that voice . . .

VIOLA: I know. Sylvester the Cat. And the way he moved! The directors rode him like a horse, didn't they—forced him to butch it up. But off the set he minced like pudding.

HOMOPHILE: So, you're telling me his marriage to Loretta Colby wasn't a sham?

VIOLA: Good old Larry! She was quite a fella.

HOMOPHILE: Wait a minute! . . . Klaue Werther was straight, but his wife was a dyke?

VIOLA: Oh, Christ, yes. Loretta was as lesbian as you could get without actually coming from the island.

HOMOPHILE: I'm sorry. You've just boggled me.

VIOLA: You boys today—such little pigeonholers! Trust me, Hollywood back then—especially *my* Hollywood, where the people who weren't *quite* in the top tier lived and worked—well, that was just a great big fuck machine, wasn't it? Women like Loretta . . . they sometimes screwed men because men were all that was around. She didn't *really* like it . . . I mean, Loretta was—I saw her beat up a teamster once. I swear.

HOMOPHILE: I don't get your point.

VIOLA: Sex was in the air, angel. Everyone fucked like rabbits. Men fucked men, women fucked women, everybody fucked everybody. It wasn't an identity thing like it is today; you know, "I am a lesbian." No one said that. It wasn't about identity. It was about fucking.

HOMOPHILE: Okay, then. Did Klaue Werther fuck other men?

VIOLA: I don't know that he didn't. But he was so handsome, I doubt there was a moment when women weren't available to him, so my guess would be no. But if he did, it wouldn't mean he was gay.

HOMOPHILE: That could be argued.

VIOLA: Anything can be argued. You'd still be wrong.

HOMOPHILE: Fine, let's talk about you, then. You ever fuck any women?

VIOLA: Does the pope dream of zebras?

HOMOPHILE: What's that supposed to mean?

VIOLA: It's for me to know, angel, and you to find out.

MINCING IN URANIA
by E. Manfred Harry
Chapter 16: The Rigors of Illusion

Julian, alas, had nothing to say in response to Anton's heartfelt plea. "Ennui," he explained as he reclined on his chaise longue and popped a dried fig into his perfectly formed mouth, "is my armor. It excuses me from both duty and reproof." He smiled, and as he did so the dazzling row of ivory sentries he called teeth appeared, as if taunting Anton by refusing him entrance.

Anton balled his fists and called on a heaven in which he did not believe. "My God, Julian," he said, frustrated passion pulling his vocal cords taut, like a bowstring, or a piano wire. "I've just placed my heart on a platter before you, and you've callously stabbed it with a shrimp fork."

"Shrimp forks aren't *quite* big enough for stabbing a human heart," said Julian as he pushed back an already perfectly manicured cuticle. "I may have punctured it, at best. If, as you insist, I did anything so energetic. I, for my part, maintain that when presented with your heart on a plate, I did nothing more violent than utter a polite 'No thank you.'" With his long, golden fingers, he plucked another fig from the crystal bowl and dropped it on his tongue like a lozenge.

Anton gazed at him longingly, at his sculpted chin, his flaxen hair and ice-blue eyes, and he thought: "Cruelty: before me is the corporealization of that abstract concept. Can I have truly loved him—loved him as I had thought, believed, insisted I had? Or is it the mere fact of his maddening beauty that drove me to such an extreme? Is it my desire for his flesh that persuaded me to adore his tyranny? Can I have been so shallow? Is this love, which I deemed epic, nothing more than ambition—greed—lust?" And even as he asked this, he denied it—cast it aside. He had proven his integrity by posing the question; now he reaffirmed it with his answer: "No. There is something in Julian that is good, that is just, that is worthy and noble and human. It is that I see, beneath his silken eyelashes and voluptuous lips and tawny chest hairs. It is his soul I desire; his body is merely the pathway by which I might reach it. That he battles me so fiercely is nothing more than evidence of his own fears—fear of passion, of intimacy, of the paralyzing notion that love, once realized, might dissipate, like the haze at dawn or the last ringing note of an exquisite aria."

But even as Anton massaged his dejection with these epiphanies, Julian was ringing for his valet, the mute but expressive albino, Pietro, who entered the room and bowed before his master, revealing even through his trousers a pair of buttocks the shape of fresh cantaloupes.

"Pietro," said Julian without once looking at his majestic manservant, "Mr. Gideon was just leaving." He raised one earth-shattering eyebrow and added, "Show him the door, please. And make certain that the next time he calls, the door is *all* he is shown."

With what appeared to be an almost empathic sadness, Pietro laid his massive hand on Anton's shoulder, and with a firmness that lacked any hint of coercion, he escorted the failed suitor out of the salon and into the long, narrow, shadow-shrouded corridor that led to the mansion's great hall. There, at the massive oaken door, carved with scenes from cautionary tales from the Old Testament that could provide Anton, in his despair, with no moral he might put to use, he turned to the sorrowful-faced Pietro and made a desperate attempt to explain his apparent love of punishment, to beg some scrap of understanding as might make his errand here somewhat less a defeat than the smoking ruin it appeared.

"You see," he said, a tear slipping from his eye like an emissary from Olympus, "I love him."

Pietro astonished him by taking his face in his hands and mouthing the words *I know.* And then he began kissing him; kissing him as he had never been kissed before—roughly, with such urgency as might arouse the dead—as indeed, Anton's heart, a dead thing, now flared to renewed and brilliant life.

There was no more need for words; he understood, then, that all that was good in Julian was housed in Pietro. The humility of one muted the arrogance of the other; the consideration of one softened the contempt of his corollary. It was a virtually symbiotic relationship: authority-servitude, yin-yang, Dionysos-Apollo. Were they lovers, the two of them . . . and did it matter? As Pietro's useless tongue explored the roof of his blistering mouth, Anton thought, "There is a place for me here . . . a place betwixt and between . . . a nether-place, a place of fluctuation and upheaval . . . and there, only there will I find ecstasy."

You have reached the office of Peter Grace. No one is available to take your call. After the tone, please leave your name, the time of day, a number where you can be reached, and a detailed message. Thank you.

Peter, it's Viola. Returning your call yet *again*. I swear, I phoned back not ninety seconds after that dullard ghostwriter of mine stupidly hung up on you. You must have put down the receiver and immediately leapt out a window. Very frustrating on my end, luv. Such a lot to talk about, and where the bloody hell are you? I was so upset I had to cancel dictation for the day. Couldn't look at that horrid little man a second longer after he'd made me miss you, angel. I said to him, *distinctly* I said, "Find out if it's Peter Grace. I must speak to Peter Grace." What does one pay these people for? I suppose he's a decent enough writer—he just came out with a book; nothing you could work with, angel, too full of steamy gay sex. Gave me a signed copy of the thing. One has to pretend to be honored by these gestures, you know. Can't bloody well say, "Oh, thank you for the autograph, but luv, I've screwed the brains out of four Pulitzer winners and sucked dry at least one Booker short-lister, so exactly how excited am I supposed to be about your 'To Viola with greatest admiration'?" But the thing is, luv, I've actually read a few pages of the thing and it's not bad. The kind of style I'd have, if I could spare a bloody moment between being me and—well, whatever it is I do when I'm *not* being me. Sleeping, I suppose. From exhaustion. *Ahaaa*-ha.

Anyway, I didn't call to run on about the goddamn gho—

You have reached the office of Peter Grace. No one is available to take your call. After the tone, please leave your name, the time of day, a number where you can be reached, and a detailed message. Thank you.

Very tiresome, luv, your machine cut me off. Give it a good thwack for me. Anyway, as I was saying, I'm phoning because I assume you need to talk about my contract. And I've decided— well, first let me say, have you seen the new issue of *Celebrity,* luv? The annual "Best and Worst Dressed" issue that every Walmart-clad cow in the country studies like the Koran? Don't know if it's on the racks yet, but guess who's front-and-center, angel. I'll give you a big hint: me, me, me, me, *me!*

Now, that got me thinking. I mean, Barbara Walters comes begging for my presence on her next special like some kind of papal supplicant. Two perfume manufacturers come calling with offers to give me my own scent. And now I'm the centerpiece of the *Celebrity* "Best and Worst Dressed" issue. And I'm thinking, all right, this isn't exactly *The Glass Menagerie* in summer stock. This is celebrity on its grandest scale. Far grander than I ever had in the seventies. And so I think we should capitali—

You have reached the office of Peter Grace. No one is available to take your call. After the tone, please leave your name, the time of day, a number where you can be reached, and a detailed message. Thank you.

Angel, I'm quite sure it cut me off far sooner that time. It's indecent. I'm your biggest client, you know. And if that wasn't true yesterday, it's true today. Oh, God damn it, there's call waiting. I'm ignoring it, luv, this is more important. As I was saying, I'm very, very major league right now, aren't I, and as we both know from bitter past experience—oh, go away!— not you, angel, the bloody insistent little terrier on call waiting. *Please just die.*—There. Gone. Might I now *finally*—

You have reached the office of Peter Grace. No one is available to take your call. After the tone, please leave your name, the time of day, a number where you can be reached, and a detailed message. Thank you.

I think this is called the law of diminishing returns, angel. Who programmed this bloody instrument of torture for you? Hm? I'd better be quick, then: I've changed my mind. I want five hundred thousand an episode. I know the gorgon makes eight, and that would put me second after her, but bloody hell! She may get her name before the title, but *I'm* the goddamn star of the sh—

You have reached the office of Peter Grace. No one is available to take your call. After the tone, please leave your name, the time of day, a number where you can be reached, and a detailed message. Thank you.

FIVE HUNDRED THOUSAND PER EPISODE, ANGEL! AND GET A FUCKING SECRETARY!

... Topping our annual best-dressed list is a new entry, but a familiar—and lovely—face: Viola Chute, lately emerged from obscurity for a socko comeback in UBN's primetime soaper, *The Winds of Wyndhamville.*

"Now here's a woman of a certain age who's definitely learned the score," says top designer Francisco Nives. "You look back at the kind of thing she was wearing in the late Sixties, early Seventies ... disastrous. Clingy little shredded-fabric numbers and hip-boots. Of course, it's hard to find anyone who dressed well in the Seventies. Even so, Viola's emergence as one of the most stylish women in Hollywood is something of a one-eighty in terms of a come-around. She's in fantastic shape, and she shows it off in with very simple, elegant lines and a minimum of jewelry, usually gold. A classic look for a very classy lady."

"A complete success from head to toe," agrees *Les Jeunes* fashion director Margot Plaice. "Here's a woman who knows that real beauty merely needs framing, not augmentation. And all her clothes are designed to show off her tiny waist and legendary breasts. She never, ever overdoes it, and best of all, even when she's caught by paparazzi in nothing more than a blouse, sun hat and sandals, she looks effortlessly gorgeous, as if she's unaware of her clothes. That's her real secret: she wears her clothes, they don't wear *her.* A very, very rare trait."

Effortlessly gorgeous she may be, but there's nothing else free and easy about Viola Chute ... as one paparazzo has found, to his peril. Currently, a suit for $10 million has been filed against Chute by Berry Leyton, a Dallas journalist, who claims his right eye was irreparably injured when Chute struck his camera while he was sneaking a shot of her on holiday in St. Lucia earlier this year. Chute dismisses the suit with characteristic drollery: "Injured his eye? Have you seen his photos? It's obvious he's never *had* one."

Of course, the possibility of a good right hook is unlikely to swerve the press from Chute's scent. *Winds of Wyndhamville* was hotter than ever last season, due largely to her phenomenally popular recurring role as Grand Duchess Samantha, introduced at midseason in a desperate gambit to shore up the series' flagging ratings. It seemed an unlikely bid; Chute had never achieved more than B-movie fame in her long career. She was best known for such cult classics as *Passion on the Nile* and *The Private Life of Agrippina,* before a career slouch reduced her to TV game shows.

But against all odds, she achieved instant superstardom as Samantha, a former royal from an Eastern European country who languished in a gulag through the fall of Communism (somehow managing to maintain a gorgeous hairdo through it all). Samantha was rescued and wooed by the ambitious industrialist Drake Wyndham (the show's major villain, played by Jameson Legge), who took her to America, intending to marry her for her title, then use his millions to push forward her claim to her country's throne—all in an attempt to get its valuable petroleum rights. Samantha was saved from that scheme by Wyndham's political foe, Summers St. Simon, the handsome conservationist congressman (played by another midseason recruit, Belgian heartthrob Alain Thill), who promptly fell in love with her.

The series really hit the ratings stratosphere when Samantha was kidnapped by one of Wyndham's enemies and given a post-hypnotic command to murder him, triggered by the word "darling." What the villain couldn't know, of course, was that Summers St. Simon, not Wyndham, was now the object of her affections. In the season-ending cliffhanger, Samantha was released by her captor and reunited with St. Simon on a suspension bridge over a river. He embraced her and said, "I can't tell you how my soul rejoices to see you alive, *darling,*" at which she promptly went berserk and pushed him over the side.

How does all this sit with *Wyndhamville*'s nominal star, the legendary Georgia Kirkby, who plays Drake Wyndham's ex-wife Jocasta—and who for the first time in the show's five seasons did not figure into the cliffhanger subplot? She isn't commenting publicly, but rumor has it there's no love lost between Kirkby and the midseason upstart who has virtually taken over the show. Apparently the two-time Academy Award winner is less than thrilled that the vehicle designed for her is now a showcase for a refugee from old historical potboilers. And if the adoration Viola Chute receives almost daily isn't enough . . . well, this nod as *Celebrity*'s Best Dressed Woman is scarcely likely to improve matters. Hold on to your hats . . . the real *Wyndhamville* fireworks this season may occur *off* the small screen! . . .

From
THE WINDS OF WYNDHAMVILLE
EP 30040G—"Her Oil Highness"

INT—WYNDHAM INC. BOARDROOM
The board is in session; the chairman, Prescott, rises and addresses the members.

PRESCOTT
Gentlemen, as you know, Mr. Wyndham has just returned from Boravia and has asked us to assemble so that he may inform us of an acquisition he made there.

BOARD MEMBER #1
An acquisition? In Boravia?—Don't be absurd.

BOARD MEMBER #2
The country's a disaster—a ruin. No industry, no commerce, just post–Iron Curtain rubble.

PRESCOTT
I appreciate your skepticism, gentlemen, but I suggest you allow Mr. Wyndham to answer your assertions himself. Gentlemen, our CEO.

Drake enters with Samantha on his arm. All rise at the sight of her; she smiles dazzlingly, but is clearly nervous and anxious. Drake takes the podium and waves the board members down. Samantha stands at his side.

DRAKE

Sit down, gentlemen; sit down.

(beat)

I'd like to thank you all for coming here this afternoon. I'm afraid I was having a bit of fun at your expense when I mentioned a Boravian "acquisition." As you know, I went there in search of Terence Tyrantt, the villainous bastard who so brutally murdered our beloved founder, my father, Gareth Wyndham.

BOARD MEMBERS

(murmurs of assent)

DRAKE

I'm happy to report that Mr. Tyrantt was taken off our hands by a neo-Nazi gang leader known only as Sieglinde the She-Wolf, whom he had the poor instincts to cross in the matter of a weapons deal. So I don't think we need to worry about seeing *him* again anytime soon.

BOARD MEMBERS

(appreciative laughter)

DRAKE

It was not until I was certain that Tyrantt had been taken out of Boravia for trial and execution, that I made my plans to return, and discovered in the meantime a precious treasure long hidden in a Boravian prison cell.

He extends his hand to Samantha, who takes it with winning shyness.

DRAKE *(cont.)*

Members of the board . . . my good friends . . . I introduce you to the former Grand Duchess Samantha of Boravia, the niece and only surviving relative of that country's last king, Magnus the Third.

(to Samantha)

My dear? Would you do us the honor of saying a word or two?

SAMANTHA

What? . . . Oh, no. I couldn't possibly.

DRAKE

Of course you can.

(to the Board)

She speaks perfect English, you know. Educated at Oxford. How about it, fellas?

The board erupts into applause. Samantha demurs a moment, then tentatively takes the podium.

SAMANTHA

Well . . . I . . . don't know exactly what to say. I . . . I know that all during the years of my captivity, I dreamed of America, the land of the free. And I dreamed of rescue by a gallant knight. But I must say it is very humbling to have both these dreams come true in so wonderful a fashion. I thank you so much for your welcome. I only pray I can be worthy of it.

The board members are completely won over by her; they burst once again into applause, and Samantha, abashed, beams at them. Drake mounts the podium with her, takes her hand, and smiles.

DRAKE

That's not all, gentlemen. I'm happy to announce that in Samantha I have found the one woman above all others whom I desire to be Mrs. Drake Wyndham.

(to Samantha)

That is . . . if she'll have me.

SAMANTHA

But . . . Drake, this is so sudden . . . and so soon!

DRAKE

Just say yes, darling . . . say yes . . .

The board members leap to their feet and roar their approval. Overwhelmed by this acceptance, Samantha relents.

SAMANTHA

Oh . . . ohhh . . . yes, my darling! Yes, *yes!*

They kiss, and then board members rush forth to meet and congratulate Samantha, who basks in the warmth of their approval. Prescott takes the opportunity to pull Drake aside.

PRESCOTT

Drake . . . listen. Are you mad? You've only just met this woman!

DRAKE

I know what I'm doing, Prescott.

PRESCOTT

But what about your ex-wife, Jocasta? She's still our majority shareholder! And you know she only hangs onto that stock because she's hoping for a reconciliation! Can we risk angering her like this?

DRAKE

You just leave Jocasta to me. And as for Samantha, stop a moment and think about it: she's the only surviving member of the Boravian Royal Family. Now that Communism has fallen there, it's highly possible that the monarchy will be restored . . . and Samantha is the only candidate available.

PRESCOTT

So, if she becomes queen . . .

DRAKE

. . . her husband becomes king. Or as good as.

PRESCOTT

But . . . Drake, why would you *want* to be king of a smoking ruin like Boravia?

DRAKE

I wasn't just chasing Terence Tyrantt in Boravia, Prescott. I had a research team with me. And they discovered that Boravia is staggeringly rich in crude oil. Pockets of the stuff virtually everywhere.

PRESCOTT

My God.

Cut to Samantha, accepting handshakes and congratulations from the board members.

DRAKE *(VOICE-OVER)*

And as soon as I set eyes on this naive little bitch, I knew she was my ticket to every last ebony drop of it.

COMPLAINANT'S DEPOSITION

My name is Berry Leyton. I am a freelance photographer covering entertainment and show business for a number of publications, including several national magazines. In April of this year I was sent by the newspaper *Weekly Inquisitor* to the town of Soufriere on the island of St. Lucia to get photographs of the actress Viola Chute, who was on holiday there. Ms. Chute had rented a villa in the hills above the town, and every day I left my hotel and drove up there and parked outside the gate of the villa. At no time did I drive or step foot on the grounds of the villa. At no time did I leave the public road to trespass on private property. I endeavored to take all my photographs from within the cabin of my Jeep, with a telephoto lens. I had not had much luck, but on April 11, Viola Chute and a man unknown to me appeared in the front of the villa and began picking mangoes from the trees overhanging the gate. I got out of my Jeep and went to the front of the gate where, while standing on the public road, I began to take pictures of Ms. Chute. When she noticed me, she began to swear and threaten me, but as I was not on private property, I saw no reason to pay any attention to her threats. She grew increasingly angry while I stood my ground and continued to shoot, even though her male companion was trying to calm her down. Then all at once she raced over to the gate, flung it open, and ran over to me, with her face twisted up with more rage than I have ever seen in a civilized human being. She swung her arm at me and hit my camera, causing extensive damage to that very expensive instrument and also ramming the lens into my left eye, which resulted in ruptured blood vessels and a great deal of pain, plus an almost total lack of vision in that eye. Ms. Chute then left me clutching my eye on the road while she went back and shut the gate behind her. The last I saw of her, she was withdrawing into the interior of the villa. I was in great pain and completely incapacitated, so I could not drive, and I had to wait more than three hours for a native farmer to stop and take pity on me and drive me back to town in his truck. Since returning to the States my eye has worsened, resulting in a drastic loss of income and also of my ability to simply enjoy life. I have not had so much as an apology from Viola Chute, who is a very wealthy woman.

DEFENDANT'S DEPOSITION

My name is Viola Chute and on the day in question I was on holiday from my first grueling season on *The Winds of Wyndhamville*—UBN, Tuesdays at eight—and I was enjoying myself tremendously until the houseboy, Charles, and I went to pick some mangoes to use in daiquiris from the wonderful mango trees on the estate. We were picking and laughing and having a good time till I noticed that horrible man up in a tree above us, taking pictures. The tree-trunk is outside the villa but the boughs of the tree overhang the gates so he must have climbed up there from outside. I threw a mango at him and it hit him and he fell out and that's when he damaged his camera. He got up and said "If this is busted you're in big trouble you bitch," yes, "you bitch" if you please, so what could I do but strike him? Unfortunately it was just as he looked into the camera to check it out. Well, what can I say, he threatened me and I reacted. Then he went running away howling and Charles was kind enough to open the gate for him. I'm sorry if I hurt him, but there it is. Actually, I'm not sorry. I mean, how dare he?

11 December 1983

My Dear Helena—
I hope this card finds you in time for the holidays—
May yours be filled with joy—All here is as always—
Be assured that you are well missed—

Fondest regards—
Beva

```
FAX MEMO TO:    Viola
FROM:           Peter
SUBJECT:        Contract demands
DATE:           6/24/97
```

Met with Franco Kreiss today to discuss your salary for next season. Kreiss unfortunately was unreceptive and made repeated attempts to economy-lot the whole issue. I continued to influx him
with our rationales until he realized we aren't back-downable.
Then he switched tactics and happy-faced the rest of the meeting
without giving me any definitives. My take is that he knows he's
rock-and-a-hard-placed and is trying to massage the network for
more $. We've definitely bulleted this issue and I will follow
through with serious potentialization efforts at the next round,
which is with both Kreiss and Sandy Asher next Thursday. Sit
tight.

Con amore furioso—
P.

. . . My first film? That wasn't in Hollywood, angel . . . Mina!
Sedgwick! Get down! Leave Uncle Harry alone . . . *Dominique,
il faut summoner les chiens* . . . *Dominique?* . . . Sorry, angel, I
don't know where she's got to. Just ignore them for now.
They'll go away eventually. Where were we?

Oh, yes. My first film was in London. Having been left a
rich widow, I didn't have to worry about working, so I was
free to do whatever I wanted. Imagine that—and me only
twenty-f—twenty. *Just* twenty. Erase what you just wrote. . . .
Bullshit. I *saw* it, Harry. And I said *twenty*.

Now, it happened that I was a bit notorious at the time, because it was well known that Regnal and I were in the midst of
divorce proceedings, but that Regnal had died before signing
on the dotted line so I got all his money anyway. He had a first
wife—some old Welsh cow—don't use that bit—who made
what Americans would call a "stink" about it. She tried to get
the money for her children by saying that I'd signed the divorce papers, which was true, but all we had to say in reply
was, "Tsk, tsk. Regnal didn't."

In the end, you know, I put both the little angels through
school. They took what I handed out, oh, yes, but I never got
a thank-you, did I? Even the girl, Judith, who graduated Cambridge at my expense! . . . What? . . . Oh, no, I haven't heard
from them in years. They haven't wanted anything. A*haaa*-ha.

So I had this notoriety, then. Especially since the police had
to investigate Regnal's death—just as a matter of course—and
you'll remember it was from an auto accident with a lorry
driver. The tabloids got hold of the news that there was an investigation, and suddenly for a week or two I was "the Cornish Black Widow" in all the headlines, and it was reported

that the lorry driver was my lover and had run over Regnal at my instigation. One snapshot of that smelly old urine-soaked fish should've squelched the rumor, but no, people thought it too delicious. Still, it put my name and face in every household. And once the police closed the investigation and the tabloids went into a sulk about it, I decided I'd better do something, because in a fortnight everyone would have forgot about me, and I didn't want that. See, what I discovered during the whole three-ring circus is that I *liked* the spotlight. And I'd had a smattering of acting experience . . . that's how Regnal and I met, remember? The first mention of me in any London newspaper was of "Viola Tregothan, a Cornish actress . . ."

So I put out feelers, and within a few weeks I was invited to read for the role of a money-hungry prostitute in a small art film being produced in a rented studio in north London by an artist named Jackie Slipper. That was his name, I swear it; he was quite the thing back then, although no one remembers him now. Painted vast, tatty swatches of color; not my cup of tea, but I'm a Philistine, what do I know? I do know that it was Jackie's first film, and it was sort of like his canvases, because there was no plan, no script; he made the story up as we went along, and we improvised our lines. I think he might have had a thing for me, because he shot three separate rape scenes for my character—a*haaa*-ha—but only one ended up in the picture . . . What? . . . Oh, don't be such a Puritan. It wasn't an *actual* rape. It was just pretend . . . Hm? Harry, you sanctimonious old queen! Get down off your high horse. Pretend rape doesn't incite real rape, any more than pretend murder incites real mur— . . . Oh, I see, you believe that too. What a morally stark little world you live in! You make Cotton Mather look like Donahue. Well, luv, I was raped on camera and enjoyed it; damn me if you dare. May I go on now? . . . *Mina! Sedgwick! Out* . . . See what you did? You made me raise my voice and that always sets off the girls. Harry, will you do me the favor of remembering, please, that you're not here to save my soul? You're a fucking *employee*. You're the *help*.

. . . All right. *May* I go on now? *Thank* you . . . Oh, Dominique, there you are! *Champagne pour Monsieur Harry, s'il tu plait.* He needs to loosen up a bit . . . There, now. You may be the help, but don't say I don't treat you right . . . I don't care if it's only four o'clock, angel. I don't want to drink alone, so you're having one with me. Or just pretend. Hold the bloody flute in your hand, just *humor* me . . . You do *want* this job, don't you?

So . . . where were we? Oh, yes, Jackie Slipper. Well, the film was finally cut—*barely* cut, I should say. I think it has a grand total of nineteen edits. Jackie had lost interest by then. It was a mess. Today, I hear, film students think it's brilliant, but if you ever saw it . . . Fortunately, the master print was destroyed when Jackie torched his warehouse, and incidentally himself, back in '79. But he was quite the smart set's darling back then, and it was his first film, and the notorious Viola Chute was in the cast . . . ah, thank you, Dominique . . . *cin-cin* . . . mmm, delicious . . . so all of London's gay and glittering rushed out to see it, and my reputation was made. I was rather good in it, you see. I'd found my calling, and I knew it. Something about the camera being turned my way . . . what can I tell you, I came alive. I could feel myself *becoming* Travesty—that was the character's name. One of the great turning points in my life.

You don't have to take my word that I was good, either. It was just days after the premiere I got a call from Zim Lovsky, who's still alive, believe it or not; he sent me a birthday card last year. Must be a hundred and eight . . . *Zim,* not *me,* smart-ass. Anyway, Zim was at the screening, and was bowled over by my performance. He was on his way to Los Angeles to do a quick six-week shoot of a script about the life of Joan of Arc. He asked me, on the basis of my portrayal of a prostitute in a film where I made up my own lines, to play the great Saint Joan. So that rather speaks for itself, I think.

You've worn me out, Harry, you really have. If you're really not going to drink that, would you pass it over? . . . Thanks. And now that your hands are idle, would you be an *absolute* angel and massage my feet a bit? . . .

JACKIE SLIPPER'S *TRAVESTY, MY LOVE*
An appreciation by Mark David Sewell
American Film Journal, Winter 1992

In assigning a proper historical place to *Travesty, My Love,*
one must examine the work's historical context. It was 1964;
the avant-garde movement in London had not extended much
beyond what I like to call the inert arts—painting, sculpture,
verse—to the living arts—theatre, film, song. Andy Warhol's
experiments with film were still a few years away; in fact, one
might even conjecture that Warhol, also a painter, was influ-
enced by Jackie Slipper's maiden effort.

It certainly seems like his kind of film. The grainy, black-
and-white 16 mm provides as much *mise en scène* as texture.
In its grinding repetition it recalls the Surrealists—whose
moment was ending just as filmmaking was becoming an art
form—and anticipates the punk movement. What's more, in
assembling a freak-show cast of nonactors, including the enormously fat Ruby Cary (the night charwoman of the studio
Slipper had rented), the perpetually hiccoughing Herman
Smeel, and the disgraced socialite Viola Chute (who went on
to become something of a fixture in American B movies), Slipper set the tone for later directors such as Warhol, David
Lynch, and John Waters. (It is notable, in this respect, that
Slipper claimed an affinity for the work of James Whale.)

There are only six scenes—six set pieces, really—in the
film's 68-minute length, and almost no internal editing within
those scenes, which results in a kind of hypnotic, insistent
rhythm. The film's rawest, most unflinching, and most studied
scene is, of course, the fourteen-minute rape of the prostitute
Travesty (played by Chute) by the unnamed hiccoughing bur-
glar (Smeel, of course). The scene is, to be sure, awkwardly
staged and amateurishly acted, with almost no dialogue what-

soever. Chute's only lines during the entire scene are slightly modulated repetitions of "You bastard, you bastard, you bastard," punctuated only once, at the eleven-minute mark, by "God damn it, I broke a nail." As for Smeel, his sole line comes at the very top of the scene, when he grabs Chute and snarls, "You're a romantic lemming!" (No one has ever been quite clear on what he means by this. Indeed, the distinguished critic Jeremy Paul is convinced that the line is actually "Your aromatic lemons," but that seems even less helpful.)

Yet all of that is beside the point. What *is* the point is that during this scene the camera itself becomes the principal player—or rather players. First as Viewer, then Voyeur, then Judge, then Chorus, it stares fixedly on the atrocity being committed before us. It does not blink; we do. It does not turn away; we do. It represents moral courage and rectitude in the face of the unfaceable, and it is the supreme moment in all of Slipper's (admittedly limited) oeuvre.

The scene following that—the final one in the film—initially begins weakly, providing a denouement only by virtue of its ultimate position. Travesty, in her kitchen, fries bacon and eggs for her rapist while speaking on the phone, summoning the police to arrest him. A wasp flies into the frame, and Travesty shrieks, curses, then drops the phone and flees. We are left gazing at the empty kitchen, listening to the hiss of the griddle. But Slipper holds this shot for a full four and a half minutes, bringing the scene to a startling and provocative finale: in staring at an empty kitchen with the same intensity as he has regarded the rape, Slipper is commenting on the subjectivity of our moral imperatives.

In later interviews, Chute has commented that the wasp was an accident that genuinely surprised her, that she broke character and fled due to fear, and that Slipper let the camera roll simply because he was off urinating in the makeup-room sink and wasn't aware of what was going on. Perhaps so; but his decision to *use* the film as it was shot is a clear example of a director recognizing what fate or karma or simple happenstance has given him. It makes *Travesty, My Love* one of the few complete artistic experiences of the mid-sixties underground film scene.

MEET THE ARTISTS: VIOLA CHUTE
(Excerpt)
London Film Journal, September 1964

INTERVIEWER: Miss Chute, I hope you don't mind my asking a rather delicate question.

MISS CHUTE: I shan't know that till I hear it! *(laughs)*

INTERVIEWER: It's been reported by members of the *Travesty* crew that you were asked by your director, Mr. Slipper, to perform a certain scene in the nude . . .

MISS CHUTE: Yes, the rape scene.

INTERVIEWER: . . . and that you refused him.

MISS CHUTE: Yes, I did.

INTERVIEWER: I wonder if you might tell us your reasons for that refusal.

MISS CHUTE: My goodness, I should think it obvious. I'm a lady. I may *play* a woman of easy virtue in the film, but appearing starkers in the role would be rather akin to *becoming* one, wouldn't you say?

INTERVIEWER: Indeed; and may I add you've answered just as I imagined you would.

MISS CHUTE: Thank you.

INTERVIEWER: I certainly never meant to imply otherwise. I would never impugn the honor of a widowed lady.

MISS CHUTE: Thank you. But there's really no need for apology.

INTERVIEWER: I'm sorry.

SUBJ: poor you
DATE: 97-6-30 14:15:03 EST
FROM: emanfr@ysa.net
TO: nbcasem@bot.ubsm.edu

what a shame about your fungus you're really not having a very good summer are you. how long are you out of work. is it infectious. does it hurt. wish you'd stop putting on a brave face and let me know what's really going on. i didn't know field botanists had to be so stiff-upper-lip. admit it didn't you ever once on the job come across a big ugly bug and scream.

that said if you need me to be there for you just say so and i'm on the next plane. i'm serious about this but so should you be if you ask because my viola chute gig is going great and i'd hate to bail on it just now. we've sort of glossed over her childhood and her 1st marriage and now we're at the beginning of her career which is maybe faster than i'd like to take things. but she's talking about her admittedly brief experience in the underground film scene in london in the 60s so who can resist. i can always fill in the childhood and 1st marriage stuff later.

been spending lots of time with her just basically hanging out. she's on summer hiatus from the show so she's kicking up her heels. and i get to tag along because she says she never knows when she'll remember something important and when she does there's no telling how long she'll retain it so i have to be there at the time to get it all. hey long as she's paying.

two days ago i got to be her date to a party at mitchell main's. you're a cultural ignoramus so i suppose i have to explain that mitchell main is the guy who produces all those prestige movies based on edith wharton and george eliot novels. the one who won a golden globe last year for mrs. warren's profession. it was really exciting to be there among all those stars and power-brokers well at least all that money. meryl streep and jodie foster were there i know you say they're the same person but now i've seen them in the same room so there.

but let's not mince words what was really adorable was that viola was so excited too. she was hiding it well but face it this is a woman who hasn't made a movie in over 20 years and in the ones she did make she was usually wearing a toga. so for her to be not just accepted by a crowd like this but sought after well let's just say she was a tad giddy.

and everyone really was seeking her out. she's basically the queen of tv now and besides half the people there grew up watching her old movies on the late show so she's like this legend. it was all pretty amazing even though i myself got shunted aside and spent most of the party wandering around mitchell main's house going hey whoa at the expansiveness of it. even his master bathroom could double as an airplane hangar. i checked out the medicine chest but the only thing in it were a hairbrush and two full bottles of equalactin. hollywood people are so weird where does he put all his stuff. i mean everybody needs a freakin toothbrush.

then i got cornered by this woman named clarissa or clarice or some-thing who had badly permed hair and glasses that must have weighed 4 pounds. i think she was the only other person at the party no one would talk to so it was inevitable we ended up together. i forget ex-actly why she was there she's a pr flack or something i think at disney. she was wearing an ellen t-shirt at any rate which seemed to appall people. it even appalled ellen. i was so desperate for conversation i allowed her to corral me in a corner where she uptalked at me for i swear forty minutes and it was only near the end i noticed this hot bartender was actually cruising me something that doesn't happen every day need i remind you. and there i was trapped by clarice/clarissa who wouldn't stop telling me in excruciating detail how she got ripped off 85 bucks by her shiatsu masseur whose name btw is jinx. who would trust a shiatsu masseur with the name of a car-toon cat.

i tuned her out whenever possible and checked out viola just to see if i could get any material from what she was saying. but she's mastered the art of party conversation lively witty shallow. she completely charmed everyone without saying a single word of substance all night.

the only thing i got that was even close to a scoop was i saw georgia kirkby glare at viola from across mitchell main's cherrywood-frame aquarium. no love lost between them did you know that—gk is SUPPOSED to be wyndhamville's star. i hadn't noticed her before which can only mean she and viola had been making a conscious effort to circulate in different rooms. but as gk passed on one side of the aquarium when viola was mingling on the other she shot viola a look that could've frozen anti-freeze. almost stopped my heart but i don't think viola saw it.

hmm. occurs to me that viola may know gk from before wyndhamville. have to ask her about it next session.

what a wonderfully deep human being i am eh—viola this viola that. next time i promise not to bore you too much with superstar gossip instead i have some theories about fractal geometry i'd love to share. plus there's this cracker of an ontological argument i'm just dying to lob your way. see made fun of myself before you had a chance to. life's unfair get used to it. just concentrate on getting better and write when you can. fungus-foot.

smooches
harry

GEORGIA KIRKBY'S FIRST ACADEMY AWARDS ACCEPTANCE SPEECH
Best Actress, *Lie Down with Liars*
March 1977

Oh, my word. This is very humbling. Very humbling indeed. You see, I'm accepting an award that honors my performance, but the performance in question is the result of the talents and gifts of so many more persons than just myself. I was directed every step of the way by my brilliant mentor and friend, Fred Solomon. And I owe an unreciprocable debt of gratitude to my dialogue coach, Caren Macy. Not to mention the man who provided the dialogue to begin with, our masterful screenwriter, Lido Barney. And our wizard of an editor, Margaret Church, who cut every scene so as to render my readings so much more pointed and brilliant. And, oh, too many others to name. Every hand that touched this picture, formed my performance. I was merely the grateful vessel. On their behalf, I accept this honor with the greatest pleasure.

GEORGIA KIRKBY'S SECOND ACADEMY AWARDS ACCEPTANCE SPEECH
Best Actress, *The Serum House*
March 1983

My husband, Paul, and I recently traveled amongst the people of the Kalahari. And it astonished me and moved me to witness that even among those people, so ill-served by nature and hard-pressed by history, not to mention perpetually worried by the corrosive play of power across a troubled continent ... even among such a people, the urge to create is yet both omnipresent and unquenchable. I left them with their songs echoing in my heart and their tales swelling my soul, and a greater understanding than ever of the need for stories, for expressions of our lives and how we live them . . . in short, for the nourishment of art. To me, this award signifies that I have, in some small way, been able to supply some of that nourishment, and I thank you from the bottom of my heart for conferring it upon me.

Lisa, Julie, you can go to bed now!

From

THE CULT COLLECTOR'S CATALOG
Spring 1993

Brand New Exclusives!
We're proud and excited to offer our customers five first-time video releases starring that glamorous gal of genre moviedom, Viola Chute—a.k.a. Viola the Vivacious Vamp! These classics have been remastered from pristine 35 mm prints and look *incredible*. SPECIAL BONUS: Order all five, and we'll throw in *FREE,* a special video, *Viola Speaks!*, featuring vintage clips from Viola's TV appearances on the Johnny Carson, Dinah Shore, Mike Douglas and Merv Griffin shows—with each tape case autographed by Viola Chute herself! (Offer expires 9/15/93.)

VC00831   *Passion on the Nile* $19.95
Viola stars as Hatshepsut, the Egyptian princess who dares to assume the Pharaonic throne. The film was clearly inspired by the Elizabeth Taylor/Richard Burton *Cleopatra,* but with fewer zeros in its budget. Don't miss the scene in which Mike Sweringen, as boy-toy architect Senmut, gets his linen shift caught on a prop statue and keeps on walking, essentially disrobing himself. Co-starring Brian Culpepper and Regis Mason. 1966

VC00832   *The Many Loves of Mary Queen of Scots* $19.95
The tragic history of the Scottish monarch's disastrous marriages and affairs. Especially beloved by cultists for the beheading scene, in which the queen's noggin falls from the chopping block and actually bounces out of frame like a basketball. With Hugh Mackerly, Donald Donovan and Gregory Peigh. 1967

VC00833   *Big Man on Campus* $19.95

One of Viola's few non-costume roles finds her looking ravishing as Maria Free, a young graduate student torn between completing her degree in Nuclear Physics, and taking to the streets with her fiery student-protestor lover, played by a clearly-in-his-thirties Kevin Lyle. Cultists love the fact that the film's three separate student riots are represented by the same two minutes of grainy stock footage. 1969

VC00834   *Agrippina II* $19.95

Viola had one of her biggest hits in the original *Private Life of Agrippina,* as the noble widow of a Roman general who defies (and is famously raped by) the corrupt Emperor Tiberius. Five years later, she tried to repeat that success in this sequel, where she portrays the daughter of the original Agrippina, this time a degenerate villainess who sleeps with both her brother (Emperor Caligula) and son (Emperor Nero). The film today is best remembered for the immortal line, "No more imperial legions . . . I've got a headache," but there are others just as good. Co-starring Harold Meyerbee, Conrad Kempt, Virginia Lesley and John Allen Porter. 1970

VC00835   *Madame Frankenstein* $19.95

Viola's last big-screen appearance to date is an early attempt at feminist revisionism. She plays a Victorian-era lady scientist who builds her ideal man from spare body parts. Of course, he turns on her; and when you see what the makeup man did to him, you won't blame him for being surly. The film was a bomb, but has made the midnight-movie rounds ever since; here's your chance to own it! Co-starring Hayward Lott, who manages to portray the monster without ever convincingly seeming dead *or* alive. 1977

FAX MEMO TO: Viola
FROM: Peter
SUBJECT: Contract demands—Round 2
DATE: 7/2/97

As promised, met with Franco Kreiss and Sandy Asher today to hard-copy terms. Clear from the start they'd agreed to good-cop/bad-cop—Kreiss blue-skying, Asher hitting click-undo. Kreiss afterwards: "What can I say? Listen, let me work on him. I'll message you." Me: "You see this?" Stuck last week's *Celeb* under his rhinoplasty. Kreiss: "Oh, yeah, it's great. We love her." Me: "Good. Then there's no problem."

Now we need to chrysalis a crisis scenario. First, you do nouvelle with Alex Wylie. It's already initiatived—Spago, Tuesday, 1:30. He's developing a series for Eureka—"The Sultans of South Beach." Look interested. Wet your lips. Before they're dry, Kreiss'll know. He'll have his people torrent your phone lines. But *do not answer*. Unplug your fax. Demobilize your mobile. We've got to blue-ball the Dimmer Twins.

Con amore furioso—
P.

42

7 December 1984

My dearest Helena—
May this card find you well—All here is as always—
Emily who you didn't know had to be sacked because she
had a baby with no father—(She took Edith's place)—The
first great scandal since you—Despite which be assured
you are still remembered fondly and well missed—

Fondest regards—
Beva

43

. . . After the failure of *Joan of Arc,* I actually feared I might never work again. The reviews were *scathing,* Harry. But I knew they would be, once I started seeing the rushes. You know how sometimes you can hire a crew of top professionals, and things can still go all wrong? . . . I think the basic problem was that while we were all doing good work, it just didn't *cohere.* And for that you can only fault the director—in this case, Menachem Bolonik. Don't worry if you haven't heard of him; I'd worry about you if you *had.* Anyway, here's an example for you: in my performance, I gave Joan an ungainly English accent. My thinking was, she's a young French provincial girl, so of course her English will be awkward at best. I also thought it was a good way of stressing her alienness, her *other*-ness, when she was before her English judges. But no one else in the film followed my lead, so my performance seemed out of tune with everyone else's. Bolonik should have been able to perceive and correct that. I'd have suggested it to him, but I was so young and inexperienced—I was afraid of stepping on his ego. Anyway, I later learned that English was his second language, so let's give him the benefit of the doubt.

Still, never mind all that, luv, because in every other sense I knew what I was doing. See, once I'd had a gander at the script, I could tell it was sky-high melodrama, and I pitched my performance accordingly. Ask any good actor, he'll tell you you should never be any better than your material. And oh, angel, you should see my Joan; I'm proud to say she makes Lillian Gish look like a sleazebag . . . And wasn't I right, in the end? Within a year, *Joan* became one of the first college-campus cult hits. There was, in fact, a certain Ivy League fraternity—I heard this years later from one of its old members—who would rent that film every month or so, and talk back to it, like teenagers did later with *The Rocky Horror Picture Show*. It was all thanks to my deliberately over-the-top performance, luv. Well . . . that, and the way Menachem kept having the English soldiers rip away my tunic to reveal my breasts. And possibly the hilariously anachronistic sets—which I later learned Zim got secondhand from the Italian outfit that used to make those Steve Reeves *Hercules* epics. Dear Zim, he said he went to Europe to get "inspiration" for the picture, but all he really brought back was some old bits of *Hercules* and me.

Well, on the basis of this kind of cult notoriety, I got an agent—Wally Novo. He did me a lot of good; he was *very* connected. Not with the best people in the business, but with the kind of people who could guarantee me constant and steady work. Two months after I signed with Wally, I was on the set filming *Agrippina*. Darling Wally. He really gave me my career. He also embezzled nearly five hundred thousand dollars from me, but I think you have to take the bitter with the sweet, don't you agr— *Mina! Sedgwick!* . . . Can you see what it is they've got there, luv? . . . It isn't alive, is it? . . . Oh, bloody hell. Where *do* they dig these things up? . . . Would you be an angel and take care of it, angel? Dominique is off, and I can't even look. I'll be in my room . . .

GUILTY PLEASURES
Film Critics Recall Their Inexcusable
Favorites
Pelican Books, 1989

When I was at Stanford, living at the Kappa Theta Mu house, we had a tradition of renting a projector and showing bad movies every Thursday, and just drinking our way through them, shouting obscenities at the screen. For this reason, I have an undying fondness for that terrible old Viola Chute historical bomb, *The Trial of Joan of Arc*. Everything about it is a disaster, but nothing more so than its star. She's a calamity from head to toe . . . literally! I mean, Joan is one of the few medieval personages whose hairstyle we know beyond doubt, yet along comes Viola with a totally mod sixties perm. And that accent—! You can tell she's trying to shape her native Cornish vowels to what she perceives as BBC standard, but it comes out sounding like she's burned her tongue on rice pudding or something. Some lines are so garbled you can't even make out what she's saying—and the look of panic in her eyes makes you think she doesn't know, either. Give the girl credit, though: she is in dead earnest all the way through. She's like a Chihuahua trying to pull up a tree stump—you know there's no hope, but you admire the persistence.

There's one scene in particular, where Joan is in an English prison, being tortured. It's this big stone dungeon with manacles hanging from the walls—like something out of a goddamn Hercules movie. Of course the first thing the torturer does is rip off her tunic. Then he makes her bend over a kind of sawhorse thing and starts whipping her back with a very long lash. Well, the director—Menachem Bolonik; never heard of him before or since—decided to shoot this scene from in front of

46

her, presumably so that you could see the exquisite agony that plays across Joan's face with every lick of the whip (never mind that Chute's expression is more akin to someone trying to puzzle out a difficult crossword clue). Unfortunately, because of the way the shot is framed, you can't really see that the torturer is wielding a whip, and the audio mix is so bad that the whip-snapping sound effect gets buried in the music; and as a result, all you see is Joan moaning in agony, and a male torso somewhere behind her, busy doing *something*. And I swear it looks for all the world like she's being sodomized. At least it looked that way to me and my fraternity brothers, who would watch this scene over and over, while yelling repeatedly, *"Just ONE more inch! Just ONE more inch!"*

Karl Ogerman
Washington Free Press

WALLY NOVO, AGENT TO THE STARS

MovieScope, October 1965

When Darryl Pierpoint was faced with the end of his career following the financial flop of *Dancing Desperadoes*, to whom did he turn to reignite his dimming star? None but Wally Novo!

When Florence LaFleur bottomed out after the box-office bomb *Whither Wilhelmina*, whom did she trust to put her back in the pantheon? None but Wally Novo!

Now that both Darryl and Florence are steaming up the screen in the summer's romantic blockbuster, *Calvacade of Kisses*, whom can they thank for making it all a reality? None but Wally Novo!

Mr. Novo, who despite his diminutive frame and rather ample proportions is facially so handsome he might pursue a career on the silver screen himself, is the latest sensation in Hollywood's behind-the-scenes movers-and-shakers set. In the six months since Mr. Novo came west from New York City (where he ran the distinguished Patricia Leahy Talent Agency, introducing many fine stage actors who brought luminosity to the Broadway boards), he has taken Hollywood by storm, becoming the actors' representative most sought after—and most lucratively rewarded—by the movies' most elite corps of thespians, and by those who aspire to that august rank.

Take Mr. Novo's latest acquisition: the lovely young ingenue Viola Chute. Since coming to America from England, Viola has made only one film—Menachem Bolonik's Grade-B programmer *The Trial of Joan of Arc*, which was reviewed in *Variety* under the headline JUST SHUT UP AND BURN HER. "It was *not* an auspicious beginning to my American career," understates the kicky ingenue, who turned pert and perky at the mention of her hero. "Wally knew how to build on it, though.

I've just been offered a part as the famous Roman heroine, Agrippina! Back in England, I was trained for the classical stage, like Shakespeare, so this is much more up my alley."

For his part, Mr. Novo is equally smitten with his newest client. "I attended the screen tests Miss Chute made for *Agrippina*," he says with quiet pride. "Believe me: there is an Oscar in her future. You haven't seen acting like this since Kate Hepburn or Miss Bette Davis." Asked how much he snagged for the future star from Summit Pictures, Mr. Novo only smiles: "No comment."

As for Darryl Pierpoint and Florence LaFleur, they speak on behalf of the many, many actors now flocking to Mr. Novo's prestigious Beverly Hills office in search of similar mid-career miracles. "Without Wally, we'd be a pair of has-beens," says Florence. "He believed in us, he took charge of our careers—he's done everything for us."

"He's even taken over handling our finances," beams Darryl.

In an age when the names of star actors play on everyone's lips—with an occasional star director making the grade (hello, Mr. Hitchcock)—it is unusual, if not unheard-of, for an agent to ascend to that celestial berth. Gentle readers: Watch the stratosphere for the clients of Wally Novo. And for Wally Novo himself!

LETTER TO *MOVIESCOPE*
Dated October 3, 1965
(unpublished)

Dear Sirs:

I am writing with regard to the article in your October issue, "Wally Novo: Agent to the Stars" (page 54). In presenting his *curriculum vitae*, you credit Mr. Novo with running "the distinguished Patricia Leahy Talent Agency, introducing many fine stage actors who brought luminosity to the Broadway boards."

Not only is this demonstrably false, it is in fact the opposite of the truth: which is that Mr. Novo only worked for me for seven months in the capacity of an assistant, during which brief time he caused the *departure* of three of my biggest talents, before departing himself with more than twenty-four hundred dollars from our petty cash and client entertainment funds.

My advice to Mr. Novo's so-called "clients" is to clamp shut their wallets and bar their doors. They have made a deal with the devil.

My attorneys have advised me to say nothing more.

Sincerely,
Patricia Leahy
New York City

May 3, 1997

Dear Miss Chute,
I just saw your first episode of "The Winds of Wyndhamville"—
thank God it finally aired here in England! And I just wanted
to say how much I enjoyed it and how amazing I think you
are! I'm especially proud because I happen to live in your
hometown Illuggan! I know you can probably barely remember
it after having traveled all over the world and seen and done
so much but you're definitely the most famous person ever to
come from here! And the most fabulous as well!

I think I am your biggest fan! I have videos of all your old
movies (well all the ones they've released anyway—I keep
writing the manufacturers asking for more!) and I even have
some of them memorised! If I had to choose a favourite I think
it would be "Passion on the Nile" because you look so gorgeous
with brown skin! I read you took a bath in coffee to get it that
way is this true?

I think it would be brilliant if you would come back to
Illuggan! I would love to show you my collection of clippings
and scrapbooks and I would be delighted to host a dinner in
your honour with all my friends who are adoring fans as well!
I would even put you up in my house I know you're probably
used to staying in only the best hotels but unfortunately as
you know Illuggan doesn't have any! (Haha!)

It would be wonderful if you could write back and let me know
if you ever think of coming back to Illuggan! I am a struggling
actor myself also so any tips you have on "making it" would
be brilliant!

I look forward to hearing from you!

Your number one admirer,
Andy Trebliss

INTERVIEW WITH VIOLA CHUTE

by E. Manfred Harry

(Excerpt)

Homophile, July 1993

HOMOPHILE: You have a very large gay fan base.

VIOLA: I know, angel. Isn't it wonderful?

HOMOPHILE: To what do you attribute that?

VIOLA: I couldn't say. I don't try to understand it. My father was an illusionist, you know; he'd pull things from his sleeves, make them disappear in his hands . . . card tricks, that sort of thing. And as a girl I'd beg him, "Show me how you did it." And he'd always say, "Very well, but if you know how I did it, it won't be magic anymore." I've always remembered that. If something is magic, don't analyze it too much, or it might just evaporate.

HOMOPHILE: That's a sweet story.

VIOLA: Thank you, luv.

HOMOPHILE: But you must have some idea of why you appeal to gay men.

VIOLA: Oh, you hard-nosed journalists! Very well, if I must hazard a guess—and a guess is all it is—I suppose the appeal of women like me, and by that I mean strong women, women who refuse to be dominated by men, who in fact do the dominating, as I did in a number of my most successful movies, and certainly in my real life—well, we sort of subvert the accepted sexual order, don't we? We make the world go topsy-turvy, and create a sexual environment in which up is down, and down is up. Which is the only possible environment in which gay men can thrive, you see. So women like me and Marlene Dietrich and Bette Davis, we become sort of symbols of that ideal world, and gay men love us for it.

HOMOPHILE: You appear to have done some thinking about this.

VIOLA: Nonsense, it's all intuitive. I'm a great intuiter. *(laughs)*

HOMOPHILE: The fact is, though, you haven't always been strong in your movies. When you played Catherine the Great, or the Egyptian queen—

VIOLA: Hatshepsut, yes.

HOMOPHILE: —you dominated all the men, sure. But as Agrippina, as Mary Queen of Scots, as Maria Free—

VIOLA: Maria Free! I can't believe anyone even remembers that dreadful bomb!

HOMOPHILE: My point is, in those roles, you were ultimately subjugated by men.

VIOLA: So were all the great heroines of literature, angel. And of the stage. And of the opera. But gay men still love them. You say they weren't strong: bullshit. They were strong. They just weren't successful. Nora, Aida, Tosca, Anna Karenina . . . all of them, every last one of them, struggled like men. They *fought*.

HOMOPHILE: Against patriarchy.

VIOLA: Oh, that word!

HOMOPHILE: What about it?

VIOLA: It's such a convenient label, isn't it? None of my characters would have recognized it. Catherine the Great didn't struggle against patriarchy. She loved men. She didn't want to topple men's power; she just wanted to join them in wielding it.

HOMOPHILE: So, in a sense, she was attempting to alter her gender.

VIOLA: No, she was attempting to *augment* her gender.

HOMOPHILE: That flies in the face of generally accepted understandings of sexual politics. There are lots of people who have spent their lives examining these issues, who would argue against you.

VIOLA: The people who examine the magic too closely, yes.

HOMOPHILE: They would say that men suppress strong women . . .

VIOLA: Nonsense. Women are weak. Because of our bodies, our hormones . . . it's nature that keeps us weak, not men. Occasionally a woman will have what it takes to fight nature, and to fight men's quite natural expectations of what a woman can do, and those are the women we call great. Those are the strong women who turn the sexual scales.

HOMOPHILE: Well, I must tell you, I can produce a whole auditorium filled with scholars and thinkers who disagree with you.

VIOLA: Oh, yes, what do you call those kind of people . . . "politically correct," isn't that the term?

HOMOPHILE: Well, the term certainly exists.

VIOLA: Yes, yes! The "politically correct." Well, angel, as far as I'm concerned, all those "politically correct" scholars and thinkers can line up right here and suck my big black dick.

SUBJ: curiouser and curiouser
DATE: 97-7-7 15:11:14 EST
FROM: emanfr@ysa.net
TO: nbcasem@bot.ubsm.edu

sorry it's taken me this long to write and say how bad i feel about
your foot. :-(there i made an email face which i swore i'd never do. i
figure the least i owe you is a token gesture of humiliation to make
you feel better if nothing else. :-) that's 2 god help me what if i start
to like them.

anyway the foot thing. well at least they caught it in time. sure you'll
be out of commission for a while but think how much worse it
could've been. yeah you'll be bedridden but i promise to help make
the hours pass quickly by supplying you with witty and diverting info
on my life with viola chute. to wit.

i'm in nyc right now. viola is being wooed by the producers of a new
show all about sex and sleaze in miami beach. it started out she was
just going to take a meeting with them to make the wyndhamville
producers start sweating blood. but although they must've heard
about it by now they haven't called to up the ante which has her way
pissed. so she's started listening more seriously to these new guys
cause she'd be the star of the series—a fabulously beautiful hotel
owner in south beach around whom will swirl intrigue and passion
and gorgeous wickedness. she likes the idea of being the star especially since we're pretty sure georgia kirkby is the one putting the ki-
bosh on giving her any more money for wyndhamville. peter grace
her agent is sure they're just stalling and they'll pony up eventually no
matter what gk says. but viola's take is she saved that fucking series
how dare they toy with her when they should be jumping at the
chance to give her anything she asks.

so anyway they flew her out here to take some more meetings and she insisted her biographer come along which i think she did not so much out of affection for me as for the calculated effect it will have on these network types.

this is where i used to live so you'd think no big deal right. but the wild thing about manhattan is you can live here for years and right next to you on the sidewalk is someone else who's also lived here for years but who's basically living in an entirely different city. suddenly I'M THAT PERSON. viola's manhattan is a place i don't even recognize. on streets i thought i knew suddenly there are these doors i never noticed before without any names or numbers on them and they just open when she shows up and suddenly we're engulfed by beautiful people and waiters offering us tons of drinks and food and sometimes even drugs and i can only await the wonderful day they start offering us other waiters.

yesterday for instance. long as we're in town viola agreed to tape a little tribute to sir david cole who's being honored by some film society or other. so she drags me across town to what i think is going to be some crummy video studio with a bunch of propellerheads blistering lights and no bathrooms where i'll sit on a folding chair while she does 17 thousand takes of her speech because the lighting keeps not being right or whatever. instead we end up in a private room at the metropolitan museum by the temple of dendur. spread of food larger than any wedding i've ever been to and celebrities crawling out of the woodwork. taping happens behind some little scrim in the corner where viola takes all of 8 seconds to reel off her line—david darling i met you before you were a knight but i was already a dame—then we're off for a full evening of schmoozing. i end up spending 40 minutes listening to that blue eyed hottie matthew garrish—you know him he does the this much dirt even i can't handle commercial—as he explains in agonizing detail how he's renovating the top floor of his new brownstone. i know for a fact i'm getting jaded hanging around with viola because i can't wait to get away from him. a month ago i'd have paid cash money to lick his pants cuffs now i've got his full attention and all i want to do is flee.

plus i look around there's calvin klein there's bernadette peters there's yoko ono lily tomlin pavarotti. sure it's dazzling but in half an hour all i'm thinking about is where's the guy with the tray of smoked salmon and capers and what else is there to drink. i was even carrying my ratty brown backpack and wasn't embarrassed about it. viola says she's going to get me a new one—coach she promises—because she thinks this one is such an eyesore but how bad can it be if ethan hawke comes up and asks where'd you get it.

anyway i was going to say there are only two incidents from this particular little bash that bear reporting. 1st of all that acid lounge singer you like harrison beverly was there which i couldn't really understand because what possible connection could he have to sir david cole. but he's absolutely smashed and he's wearing these sheer silk trousers. and he corners this blonde actress i can't remember her name she's on that tv show about zany office workers and their pitiful love lives you know the one. anyway harrison beverly corners her and in about 20 minutes there's this kind of buzz about him in the room. so i look over and lo harrison beverly's silk trousers are barely concealing one all beef whopper of an erection. it's causing an absolute sensation all these women getting their ears whispered into then looking over squinting their eyes and turning back with a gasp covering their mouths and laughing. and viola well you know she's completely fearless she waits till everyone in the room has noticed harrison beverly's distended trousers then she gets this look in her eye and asks me for the little cocktail jacket i'd been holding for her. i say sure are we leaving she says no no just give me the jacket. so i do and she makes a beeline for harrison beverly who still has this actress practically pinned to the wall. when viola reaches him she says really loudly excuse me harrison luv but do you know of a place I can hang my jacket. and everyone in the room suddenly has to turn away and start coughing really hard but harrison beverly is so smashed he just says no and goes back to the blonde completely sans clue.

admit it that made you forget your foot.

the other thing to report is georgia kirkby showed up about 40 minutes after we arrived and when she saw viola her face just went rigid.
viola of course fluttered her fingers at her and said oh how lovely
which is partly taking the high road and partly doing her best to irri-
tate the shit out of her. so gk goes behind the scrim to tape her tribute to sir david and she's in there for i swear 15 minutes so viola
starts joking oh she's just telling davey about her adventures among
the headshrinkers of paraguay and how they made her reconsider
the subjectivity of the artistic imperative. everyone's cracking up. and
of course just as luck would have it gk comes out from behind the
scrim as a whole clutch of people are laughing wildly at something
viola's said and she gets this look like she knows it's about her. so
she signals her lackey agent husband whoever he was—little man in
a powder-blue jacket with a combover—and they head for the door.
it's perfectly obvious she's leaving because being in the room with
viola is something she can't stand for even 1 more second. and i think
viola's done with her mischief for the night but no gk gets about three
feet from the stairs she can almost taste her freedom and that's when
viola calls out oh georgia angel have you met tony hopkins. and she
puts her hand on anthony hopkins's shoulder in the most amazingly
proprietary way and gk does this niagara falls move—you know
slowly i turned—and says in a voice just loud enough to carry to the
spiral arm yes many times. then she nods at hopkins and sweeps up
the stairs big print dress flowing behind her.

as i write this i can tell you are appalled that such a tempest in a
teacup has assumed for me such mythic proportions. but as i recall
when we were in college i was the one who kept dragging you to ing-
mar bergman movies when all you wanted to see was orca the killer
whale so you clearly have no sensibility for this type of drawing room
dramedy. just trust me there's meat there. i asked viola if she knew gk
was going to be at this event and she said why no in a way that made
it perfectly clear she did. then i said do you really know sir david cole.
because gk has played everything from shakespeare to shaw with
him. and viola says oh we did a bob hope special together once and
of course fucked several times. this type of thing has ceased to stop
me in my tracks so i press on asking what is the big hairy deal be-

tween you and gk anyway. viola: why don't you ask her. me: i just might do that. viola: you do and you're fired.

i decided to leave it there because i know i can get her to spill. she clearly wants to. and we're just now getting into the kind of dull stretch of her career when she was spending 10 months of the year working endless hours in one costume melodrama after another giving basically the same performance whether as boudicca or sacajawea or whoever it didn't seem to matter. so the actual movie stuff has become less interesting and it's her personal life that's getting hotter. haven't had much luck getting her to talk about it yet so give me until next time.

till then keep that foot elevated. i'm keeping my fingers crossed for a full recovery. or barring that just the slightest limp.

hugest of smooches
harry

FAX MEMO TO: Viola
FROM: Peter
SUBJECT: Update
DATE: 7/7/97

Franco Kreiss confirms: it's Kirkby, not Sandy Asher, who fiascoed our handshake. Apparently she krakatoaed over the $. Franco is eager to conserve a dialogue, but I downstated that in view of your potentializing Alex Wylie. My sources say Asher is doing a Depends over Wylie privately, but is zipperlocked for the record. (I can believe it: *Wyndhamville* shutters are set to bug again 8/18.) Let me just caveat: don't overplay South Beach—unless it's trajectoried past Wyndhamville? Advise aysap.

Con amore furioso—
P.

SERIES PROPOSAL
The Sultans of South Beach
Chris Waller, Robert Lane & Avery Kellerman

The sunlight. The sizzle. The magic. The muscle. The glitterati and the paparazzi, the drag queens and the drug lords. There's no place in the world like South Miami Beach, scene of a million melodramas every day, from the beachfront to the back alleys to the boardrooms. *The Sultans of South Beach* is designed to deliver the essence of this magical, almost mythical playground/war zone.

At the crux of the series are two hotels. The venerable, decades-old Maximilian is run by **Jonah Ives,** the patriarch of the powerful but waning Ives dynasty. The Maximilian is past its glory; once visited by statesmen, captains of industry and living legends, it is now a haunt for package tours from Iowa. The newly influential and powerful flock instead to the Orpheum, run by **Victoria van der Wheyde.** A beautiful entrepreneur, Victoria has taken the decrepit old hotel and turned it into South Beach's most dazzling, of-the-moment locale.

Victoria is supported in this venture by her ex-husband, **Connor,** and her son, **Pierce.** Connor, however, is secretly many hundreds of thousands of dollars in debt to the evil Cuban drug lord **Raul Caballé.** Caballé, unbeknownst to everyone but Jonah Ives, is also the majority shareholder in the Maximilian, having taken nearly all of Jonah's shares after a botched business deal in the 1980s; Jonah, a tragic figure, is being kept on as a figurehead, with even his own family thinking he's still really in charge. Looking after his investment, Caballé is now pressuring Connor van der Wheyde to supply him with information on the running of the Orpheum, so that he can bring down Victoria and restore the Maximilian to its proper primacy and prestige.

Complicating this is Jonah's daughter, **Haley,** who hates what she sees as Caballé's influence on her father and who is also having an affair with Victoria's son, Pierce. She is not quite "on" to Caballé's plans yet, but she and Pierce still plot against him. Unfortunately for her, Caballé has an offspring as well: a handsome, amoral son, **Reynaldo,** who is wildly in love with Haley, and who has threatened to kill any other man who as much as looks at her.

In the meantime, the Maximilian has become part of a complicated drug-trafficking chain that has been so successful it requires new warehousing facilities. Connor has been "persuaded" to provide space in the Orpheum. This occurs just as Victoria is beginning a new romance with a crusading television journalist, **Dack Ackerman,** who is in town ferreting out drug routes for his hit documentary series, *Action Man.*

Projected highlights from Season One:
- Victoria's evil sister, Veronica, makes a guest appearance and becomes romantically involved with Raul Caballé;
- Reynaldo discovers Haley and Pierce making love on the beach, and subsequently kidnaps Pierce, whom he keeps drugged and bound in a suite at the Maximilian;
- Dack Ackerman, investigating mysterious noises in the basement of the Orpheum, discovers a cache of cocaine and concludes that his new lover, Victoria, is secretly a drug lord;
- Jonah and Connor get into a fistfight over their mutual loss of honor to Caballé, which is overheard by, and brings into the cast, a beautiful blackmailer, Sirina Cleyderman, who seduces them both;
- A massive tidal wave threatens the entire cast and both hotels, and closes the season on a cliffhanger.

Casting suggestions:
Every prime-time drama series depends chiefly on its villains and its women, so the lynchpins for *Sultans of South Beach* are definitely Raul Caballé and Victoria van der Wheyde. *Raul:*

Must ooze sex as well as danger. Test Julio Iglesias (can he act?) and Kris Kristofferson (can he play Latino?). *Victoria:* Must be larger-than-life, equal parts glamour and virtue. Recommended: Jane Fonda (if she'll agree to dye that ratty gray hair) or Viola Chute (if we can steal her from *Winds of Wyndhamville*).

ACTRESS SUED FOR ASSAULT

Los Angeles Herald
July 9, 1997

LOS ANGELES COUNTY—A court date of September 4 has been scheduled for the assault charge brought against television actress Viola Chute by Berry Leyton, a freelance photographer.

Mr. Leyton charges that on April 11, Ms. Chute, best known for her recurring role on UBN's *The Winds of Wyndhamville,* accosted him as he shot photographs of her while she was vacationing in the British Virgin Islands. The actress, however, maintains that Mr. Leyton was trespassing on the gated property she was renting on the island of St. Lucia, by climbing out on a tree limb that overhung the villa's perimeter. According to Ms. Chute's own testimony, she threw a mango at him and he fell from the branch, sustaining damage to his camera and an injury to his eye. Mr. Leyton, who filed suit against Ms. Chute in May, is asking for ten million dollars in damages.

The photographer has retained the services of Powers Keenlyside, a partner with the law firm of Derringer, Morse & Hayek, to represent him. At a press conference yesterday afternoon, Mr. Keenlyside told reporters, "My client is eager to go to trial, and we have every reason to hope for success. By her own admission, Viola Chute is responsible for the injuries sustained by my client. Furthermore, Viola Chute is a public figure; she has no right to claim that the professional interest of my client in her was in any way prurient, invasive, or untoward."

Neither Ms. Chute nor her attorney, Gretchen Ojan, were available for comment.

You have reached the law offices of Gretchen Ojan. Our hours are Monday through Friday, eight-thirty a.m. to six-thirty p.m. After the tone, you may leave a message for Ms. Ojan or her assistant, Kevin Putnam. Thank you.

Gretchen, luv, it's Viola. Will you explain to me, please, how it's possible for that horrible little bush-league bastard to file suit against me in *May,* for God's sake, and not get a court date till *September fourth,* which is just a few weeks after the new season of *Wyndhamville* starts filming? There are a lot of complicated location shoots planned, and I really can't have this odious little legal charade preventing me from being on site.

Honestly, angel, it's either going to have to be before August eighteenth, or he'll just have to wait another seven months till the season wraps.

Of course, there's a rather large chance I might not re-sign with *Wyndhamville,* but the contemptible little cretin doesn't need to know that.

Make him go away, please.

If you need me, I'm still at the Pierre.

... Honestly, luv, I wish I could understand this mad obsession you seem to have with Georgia Kirkby. Granted, the poor woman deserves *some* kind of attention, but I'm thinking more of the psychiatric kind. But since you ask, yes, we *had* met before I was hired to play Grand Duchess Samantha. Just once. Oh, Harry, will you turn that silly thing off? This isn't for the book ... but it's such a horrid little story that I just can't bear not to tell you ... Is it off now? ... Angel, you wouldn't lie to me, would you? ... Forgive me, luv, this asshole business turns the best of us into paranoids.

Well, then. This was ... oh, Christ. I want to say '77. I'd just finished shooting *Madame Frankenstein*, which was to prove the end of the line, as far as my film career went. Angel, it was *putrid*. It was putrid and I knew it, I knew it every day on the set, and so did everyone around me, but we were sort of ... I don't know. Becalmed by inertia, I suppose. There was always a big overseas market for no-budget B-movies like these—I say B, but I think this was around the time the phrase "Grade Z" was invented, and if it was, *Madame Frankenstein* certainly applied. But, like I said, the market was there, in places like Taiwan and the Philippines, so we knew however dreadful the movie ended up, it was still a money-making proposition, and in those days you just didn't get too upset if you were at least working. Plus, I was in heated negotiations to play the heroine in a musical version of Sylvia Plath's novel *The Bell Jar*, which was going to premiere in Atlanta and tour for a few months before settling in on Broadway, so I had my head in the clouds over that. I really didn't care much if my movie career ended, because I was going to be making my sparkling stage debut. And I ... hm? ... Oh, Harry. Please be serious. I do not acknowledge my Cornish credits as real stage experiences, and *certainly* not playing Britannia in that woolen fright suit Regnal Chute first saw me in. Don't interrupt if you can't at least be intelligent about it.

. . . Where was I? . . . Oh, angel, there's the door. I ordered up a little room service. Just brunch. Would you mind? Here's a twenty for the tip . . . No, it's *not* too much. This is the goddamn Pierre. And whose money is it, exactly? . . . Thank you . . . Hmm-mmmm . . . Hmmm . . . *Chill that champagne, will you angel? The bucket's in the bath. They did bring ice, didn't they?* . . . Hmm-hmmm . . . five . . . one . . . six . . . one . . . eight . . . Hmm-hm-hmm— Oh, hello! . . . Yes, luv, it's Viola. Listen, I can't talk long. Got my bloody ghostwriter here; man's an absolute albatross. But I did get your message this morning and I've decided . . . Don't be a pain in the ass, angel. It *is* my decision to make. I don't know why you have to make such an unpleasant business of this. I really hold no grudge, and you shouldn't eith— what? . . . Well, honestly, you haven't half turned into a poisonous old wretch, have you? . . . You're making me angry, now . . . Don't tell me what I can afford to do or not do! . . . All right, let's calm down a moment. Shall we just? Hm? If you insist on conducting this . . . *transaction* as though we're in some ridiculous film noir, so be it . . . Oh, but listen, I have to go; the scribbler is nigh. Do you know your way around New York? . . . Then take a cab! You can afford it. Eight o'clock. And given your choice of attitude, I'll want you out by eight-fifteen . . . Why, you disgusting littl— *must dash!*

Ah! Harry. There you are. And you found the crystal, clever boy! Where'd they hide it? . . . Mm? Nothing's wrong, angel! What are you talking about? . . . I'm *not* upset! Honestly. You're imagining thi . . . The phone call? . . . All right, I admit it. I have a stalker . . . A *stalker*, Harry. Surely you've heard of those. A not altogether unflattering type of psychotic. Anyway, he found out I was staying here, and somehow the hotel allowed his call through. I'll have to have a good scream at them later . . . Well, it only rang once, maybe that's why you didn't hear it. But none of this is *your* cross to bear, luv. Par for the course in the life of a star. Look, I'm utterly recovered now . . . No, angel, I *don't* want to talk about it. Forget it . . . I said *forget* it. Who's paying whom, here, Harry? . . . Who can fire whom, here? . . . Thaaat's right. Clever, *clever* boy . . . wouldn't do to have you unemployed again, would it? . . . And unless you treat vengeful Viola with kid gloves, guess who's not walking away from this assignment with any sort of reference? . . . Yes, as a matter of fact, angel, it *is* a threat. I've had just about enough of your pissing about on this project when you're paid to *co-operate*. If I say forget the stalker, you job is to *forget the fucking stalker!* . . . Don't tell me to calm down! That's not your job either! . . .

What? . . . Oh. Yes. I *would* like some champagne . . . Thanks, angel . . .

Mm . . . Better now . . . Ready to work, then? . . . Well, where was I? . . .

Oh, yes. 'Seventy-seven. My film career had just ended. And even though I had *The Bell Jar* ahead of me, that wasn't a done deal yet, and besides, it was Broadway, which might as well be Mars for all that Hollywood cared about it. All that mattered was that my film career had limped to a close. I had the stink of death all over me, you see. No one in this town would as much as *talk* to me. I'm not kidding, Harry. I wasn't even looking for a job, and people were still avoiding me. It was dreadful; I'd been working nonstop since I arrived, twelve years before, so I didn't know what it was like for people when the work dried up. Isolation, alienation . . . it was awful. I was so miserable that I contacted an acting coach in New York, Victor Cywzyrk, and I arranged to go and spend the spring and summer studying with him, even though I didn't know if I had *The Bell Jar* or not. The thing was to get out of Los Angeles.

Anyway, I made arrangements to stay in Manhattan; I took over Delia Wishman's apartment, do you remember her? Stage actress; used to guest-star on *The Mimi McCoy Show* a lot. She was in London doing . . . oh, Christ, I can't remember the name of it now. Her biggest hit, too. But she was an old friend, and she'd had her agent feeding her cat, which hadn't been going very well—he was allergic, apparently—so she highly approved the idea of me moving in and collecting her mail and feeding Sir Pouncealot. See there, I can remember the name of the bloody cat, but not her hit show. This may explain why I've had career trouble. Pass me that ashtray, will you, luv? And top off my glass while you're at it.

So, there I was, all packed up and ready to go. Now I don't think I've mentioned this before, but I'd once had an assistant, Claude . . . back in the early days, when I was still learning the ropes. He was such a darling—handled my calendar for me, saw to it that I was driven where I needed to go, took all my calls . . . *everything*, really. He was the one, in fact, who figured out Wally Novo was embezzling from me. I forget exactly when I had to let him go, but by '77 he hadn't worked for me for quite a while. Even so, we'd remained friends, and bless his heart he ended up marrying well. He became lovers with Leonard Beckwith, who at that time was Georgia Kirkby's manager . . . You're grinning. You can see where this is going, can't you? Clever Harry! Just let me fill in the details.

Well, it's exactly five days before I'm scheduled to fly off to Manhattan, and no one in town has even spoken to me for what seems an age. And what should happen but I get a phone call from Claude! "Oh, hello, Viola, Lenny and I are having some people over for drinks tomorrow to celebrate Georgia winning Best Actress." This was just after the Oscars, luv. Well, of course I accept, *gratefully* I accept—I mean, Claude knew what my situation was, and it was so like him to give me this chance to leave town on a high note, with my chin up and my dignity intact. Of course, he'd cleared it with Lenny. But Lenny made the mistake of not clearing it with the apocalypse beast herself.

So, picture it: a balmy, breezy Los Angeles evening. I'm actually nervous, angel; me, who's never intimidated by anything! That's how much this party means to me. I have to have a brandy or two just to bolster myself. I hire a car to drive me up to Claude and Lenny's place in the Hollywood Hills. The invitation is for six o'clock, and it's six-fifty, which I think is just about right. But then, as I may have mentioned, I was never quite A-list Hollywood, and it turns out that in A-list Hollywood, fifty minutes late is just a bit on the prompt side. So I arrive at Claude and Lenny's house and ring the bell. There's a bloody doorman admitting people. I come in, and the house is all quiet, I'm obviously the first to arrive. I begin to feel uncomfortable, but suddenly there's Claude rushing up and hugging me, telling me I look fabulous. Which I do, of course. My career may have been kaput, but I had a little dosh from *Madame Frankenstein,* and I spent some of it on a spectacular Oleg Cassini. Lavender, in honor of Claude and Lenny. And we're standing there chattering away, when who should appear at the top of the stairs but the Best Actress of 1977. Who's that? she thunders. Claude shrinks; he visibly shrinks. "It's Viola Chute," he says, "a dear friend and former employer of mine, and your fellow actress." I think it was that last part that did it. She knew exactly who I was, see; and she also knew I had no career left. And here she was, the single actress at the top of the Hollywood heap, basking in all the glory she must have always believed was rightly hers. There was no place in that bloated, roiling, cruise ship of an ego for an admission that *my* cinematic endeavors had *any* relation at all to hers.

I'll spare you the ugly details. Let's just say that five minutes later, I was on my way back home. Pity poor Viola—all dressed up and nowhere to go. But I'll tell you this much: before I left, my eyes met Georgia's, and something passed between us—a kind of understanding. It was as though we were communicating telepathically, angel. In an instant, I managed to convey to her that she should enjoy this little triumph while she might. And she, for her part, conveyed to me her infinite disdain—"Do your worst" is how she might have put it in words.

Well. Here I am, all these years later, doing my worst. And isn't it delicious!

Of course, when we met again, at my first read-through for

Wyndhamville, we both pretended to have no memory of that day. But neither one of us was fooling the other.

Anyway, Claude called me the next morning, mortified and apologetic; I'm sorry to say I was rough on him. I called him spineless for not standing up to her. It was *his* house, after all; I was *his* guest. I never spoke to him again. He died in '82—a year after Lenny; they were two of the first—and I've regretted it ever since. If I'd known, I'd have rushed to his side and forgiven everything. But I'd been . . . well, out of the country for a while . . . Never mind where. I only found out about Claude when I got back . . . Never *mind* where, Harry. It's not *important.* Anyway . . . regrets, regrets . . .

But none regarding the gorgon. What she did was . . . well, looking back on it, it may not seem like much. She turned me away at the door, that's all. But it was my friend's door. She wielded her power against me when I had none to defend myself, and made me unwelcome in a place where I had always found open arms . . . What can I say, except that I hope soon to show her just how that feels.

Funny thing, though. In a way, the gorgon *did* do me a kind of favor. I've told you how important the party was for me, as a means of reclaiming some dignity. Well, in affronting my dignity so very directly, Georgia actually *did* help me reclaim it . . . her attack on me was so unwarranted and so vicious that I was able to go away with my head held high, recognizing that if nothing else I was *her* moral superior. And that's what gave me the patience required to wait decades for a turnaround, angel. I knew I was better than she was. And I was content to trust in God, or fate, or karma, or what have you, to provide the opportunity for proof. Vengeance as such never entered my mind.

Not that I don't take satisfaction in how things have worked out.

Top me off again, there's a luv.

THE PRIVATE JOURNAL OF
CLAUDE PERRY ASHE
(Unpublished)
Property of the estate of Lawrence Beckwith

April 2, 1977—Rung up Viola this morning to see if she's all right, which turned out to be a mistake. She accused me of calling to gloat, as though that's something I'd ever do. She must know it's not, deep down, but her anger and shame won't let her admit it. I think this breach is the final one. She's never forgiven a humiliation before and this may be the worst she's ever suffered. I must've been crazy, inviting her to a party in Georgia's honor. I still think maybe it would've come off all right if she hadn't arrived fifty minutes early. What was she thinking? Me barely finished shaving, and Lenny still in his boxers! . . . Also if she hadn't arrived stone drunk. That was the kicker for Georgia—this tawdry B-movie actress in her clingy Oleg Cassini gown stumbling across the threshold smelling like a distillery and treating Georgia's husband like a goddamn doorman. Mumbling incoherent congratulations and just generally tarnishing the pure silver shine of Georgia's victory. And I mean, Georgia's self-regard—I wouldn't say this to Lenny—has swelled to brontosaurus-like proportions since the Oscars. I think if Princess Margaret had shown up drunk she might *just* have been able to get away with it, but certainly no one lower on the social scale.

Also if Viola hadn't stupidly dismissed her car. Of course in this case I *know* what she was thinking. She was thinking she'd hook up with someone at the party and find a place in *his* car (not to mention his bed). Perfectly reasonable assumption, it's what she's always done. She just didn't count on being forced to leave the party before any eligible candidates had a chance to arrive. Of course she was too angry and proud to accept my offer of a ride. I can just picture her, hiking the Oleg Cassini up above her knees as she gingerly trod back down the hills. Cursing me all the way, no doubt. Rehearsing some of the blue streak (and I do mean blue) she let fly with on the phone this morning.

I also think things wouldn't be *quite* so bad if she hadn't passed out by the side of the road and been picked up by the LAPD and charged with vagrancy. And if I weren't the only person in the world she could think of to come fetch her. Me, the source of her humiliation, now the source of her rescue, too. She was so mortified and appalled she couldn't speak to me. Except to blame her blackout on sunstroke. Sunstroke, at 7:30 P.M. Then she just sat there in my car looking dirty and disheveled and with vomit on her chest, staring out the window and not offering up word one.

That's certainly no longer a problem as of today. She really let me have it, as only Viola can. "I never thought *you'd* turn your back on me, Claude, not after I plucked you from the street and dusted you off and turned you from a white-trash chicken hustler to a goddamn A-list faggot with a string of slobbering sugar daddies." Her exact words. I wanted to say, What do you mean no gratitude, I came and got you from the police station. But I knew bringing *that* up would be a tactical error no matter how I put it.

She also told me—God help me I can't *ever* let Lenny hear this—that she'd brought a tab of acid with her for later. Again, not an unprecedented thing for her to do. But after Georgia slammed the door on her face and she was forced to turn away from the house and make her humiliating retreat, Georgia's little bichon frise started yapping ferociously at her through the fence. Which I guess was the final straw. She told me—practically bragged! "It's my revenge," she kept repeating—that she took the tab of acid and fed it to the dog. She must have known it was Georgia's constant companion. Well, I suppose she was driven to it, and I certainly have no fondness for the little beast, but still. An innocent dog. Of course later on when the party got into full swing Georgia decided she *had* to have

73

the mangy thing by her side, and didn't it just go berserk in front of everyone and start savaging the guests. Petra Solomon bitten on the ankle so hard you could see bone! Georgia herself got a pretty bad bite on her cheek when she tried to grab the little cur and calm it down.

Of course I didn't tell Viola any of this, wouldn't give her the satisfaction of knowing she had her revenge all right. The rest of the party had a pall on it after that. Fred Solomon insisting over and over again that the dog be put down. Georgia throwing a drink in his face. I suppose he'll sue now. Over Petra's ankle, not the drink.

Maybe it's better that I don't see Viola again. That phrase everyone's using all of a sudden—"loose cannon"—could've been invented for her. Course the cannon's got a lot less ammo now that her career's a smoking ruin. All that pathetic boasting about a new career on Broadway—does she really expect anyone to believe it?

So sad when friends go to seed. But what can one do . . . ?

AT HOME WITH GEORGIA KIRKBY
High Style, September 1977

Georgia Kirkby is a collector.

She collects roles: Lady Olivia in *Post Haste,* Inger Woolf in *Zuider Zee,* Saint Alicia of Bodmin in *The Silence of Blood,* Joanna Dexter in *Isidro and Joanna,* and her latest acquisition: the tormented yet dignified Mrs. Heath in *Lie Down with Liars,* for which she was earlier this year awarded the coveted Academy Award for Best Actress.

She collects life experiences: among her recent travels, she has spent two weeks in the Australian outback, living for a time among the region's aboriginal people; she has gone behind the Iron Curtain to perform in a diplomatically arranged season of classic theatre in Prague (including the role of Nora in Ibsen's *A Doll's House,* which she learned in Czech); and, thanks to special dispensation from His Holiness Pope Paul VI, she also spent an autumn as an unofficial extern in a convent of cloistered nuns in rural Belgium (she speaks fluent French), which she undertook both as study for an upcoming role and "for spiritual reasons, which I prefer to keep respectfully private."

Georgia Kirkby also collects accolades. *Time* has called her "one of the century's splendid chameleons"; *Life* christened her "a godsend to intelligent audiences"; *The Atlantic Monthly* dubbed her "one of the premier exponents of the classic repertoire in this half-century"; and *The Illustrated London News* declared that "she is proof one can be an actress and a movie star concurrently."

And upon entering her Beverly Hills home, it becomes abundantly clear that this habit of collecting extends to her personal surroundings. In her spacious drawing room, which displays elegant spareness and restraint in the Oriental manner, hangs her collection of original Japanese woodblock prints. The vivid yet fragile works of such masters as Hiroshige, Hokusai, and Kokunimasa are among her prizes. "I love them for their passionate *there*-ness," she says, regarding a print of a scowling, pop-eyed demon. "It's why I keep so little else in the room; they occupy it so fully already."

The beloved actress sweeps down a rich rosewood corridor to her impeccably appointed dining room, where she proudly displays what she is reasonably certain is "the largest and most historically significant collection of Lalique crystal in the Los Angeles area," which means, of course, the largest and most significant in the western United States. "And we use it all, too," she declares with a touch of the defiance she has displayed in some of her greatest roles. "They're rare enough to be museum pieces, some of them, but that's too unkind a fate." She removes a breathtakingly lovely goblet and allows its many facets to catch the light—and this writer wonders if she is deliberately trying to plant a metaphor in his head for the many facets of her talent as immortalized in her enthralling body of work. But the look on this famous face is too ingenuously rapturous; no, she is merely finding joy in the beauty of the crystal.

Up a flight of stairs—one can't help thinking of her descending it later, in a shimmering evening gown, to greet a complement of smart yet submissive dinner guests!—to her study, where she removes a folio of Moroccan leather from atop her surprisingly simple oaken desk, and unties it to reveal yet another collection—this one of 18th-century autographs. It is perhaps a relief to discover that this woman, who is capable of reducing even the most jaded cosmopolitan to abject awe, is in a way quite "starstruck" herself! As she carefully turns over the priceless documents, revealing the correspondence and other personal documents of such luminaries as Denis Diderot, Thomas Jefferson, and Queen Christina of Sweden, her voice grows hushed, suffused with respectful wonder. Pride of place in the folio goes to a short note written by Voltaire to Catherine the Great; the epistle resides in a special acid-free mylar envelope, to ensure its survival. It is, Georgia sighs, one of her great regrets that she has not been able to track down the empress's reply, nor even determine whether she *did* reply; and indeed, the absence of any document in that imperial lady's hand is a signal omission from the collection, one which the determined actress vows to correct. In fact, so decidedly does she recite her oath to capture Great Catherine's autograph, that I am moved to ask her whether she has ambitions to capture this monumental heroine's *character,* on film; certainly she has reached a point in her career at which she can be said to have acquired the requisite stature. Georgia Kirkby frowns. "I'd like to, but it's nearly impossible to mount a costume drama that doesn't smother itself in the costumes. Catherine the Great was an autocrat who helped foster the Enlightenment—think of the delicious paradox in that!—but there's never been a film about her that hasn't reduced her to a hideous cartoon."

We are interrupted by the appearance of the great actress's most constant companion, her bichon frise, Clothilde—named after her first Oscar-nominated role, in 1970's *Every Lover's Every Favour.* The adorable canine wags its bit of tail and leaps into its mistress's lap, provoking a delighted laugh from this writer—till it turns, quite sharply, grabs the Voltaire letter, and runs with it, snarling ferociously. With cries of alarm, we give chase, and at last rescue the precious document from certain ravaging. Fortunately, it has not been damaged; the only teeth marks are to be found in the mylar envelope—and, alas, on this reporter's hand. Georgia Kirkby apologizes profusely (there is no need; her mere presence incurs a debt no mishap can eradicate). "Clothilde hasn't been the same since I won the Oscar," she says by way of explanation. And looking into the wild eyes of the now-restrained animal, I realize that there are two more things Georgia Kirkby collects: the rapt, devoted attention of everyone she encounters—and the resultant jealousy of anyone who had claim to her previously, even the creature closest to her heart!

THE VIOLA CHUTE INTERVIEW
(Excerpt)
Playboy, April 1973

PLAYBOY: Now I'd like to tackle one of the more persistent rumors about your career.

CHUTE: I can't even imagine which one that might be.

PLAYBOY: It concerns the filming of *The Passions of Catherine the Great* . . .

CHUTE: Say no more. For the record—and I hope this will be the last time I have to answer this question—no, we did not film the scene with the horse.

PLAYBOY: Well, there's a legend that the footage was scooped from the cutting room floor by a crew member, and has been making the rounds at private screenings ever since.

CHUTE: Ridiculous. It was never even in the script. The story of Catherine and the horse was probably just invented by her enemies to sully her name. It's completely ahistorical, and we never even considered using it.

PLAYBOY: I wondered about that, in view of your famous refusal to do nude scenes.

CHUTE: Especially with a horse. *(laughs)*

PLAYBOY: You've appeared partially nude in the past, though.

CHUTE: Only for brief moments. I refuse to allow the camera to linger over my flesh.

PLAYBOY: Why not?

CHUTE: Acting is a very naked profession, as it is. I need to hold something in reserve, some element of myself that I don't offer up to my audience, that I keep just for me . . . and for the men I love. My body serves that function. Whenever I'm naked, I feel a thrill of privacy and intimacy . . .

feelings I'm certain I'd lose forever if I accustomed myself to romping naked in front of a film crew.

PLAYBOY: May I just say, then, how much I envy the men in your life?

CHUTE: You old flatterer! You may. And I accept the compliment.

FAX MEMO TO: Viola
FROM: Peter
SUBJECT: Urgent request
DATE: 7/12/97

Kreiss & Asher are tenterhooked re: Alex Wylie. Are we having sex yet? Is Wylie spongeworthy? Say the word, and I'll requiem *Wyndhamville*. Or, if Wylie's wily, I'll keep Kreiss & Asher wind-twisting. But *advise*. And sign nothing I haven't fine-toothed first.

Con amore furioso—
P.

24 November 1985

My dear Helena—
May this card find you in good health this holiday—
I am sending early as my extra duties leave no time—
Old Jenny you remember her the part-time seamstress,
well she finally died two days before her 97th—
Poor thing a lorry hit her while picking raspberries—
Now all her work comes to me and me with my arthritis—
Otherwise all here is as you remember—Be assured you
are well missed—

Fondest regards—
Beva

SUBJ: the plot thickens
DATE: 97-7-13 15:11:14 EST
FROM: emanfr@ysa.net
TO: nbcasem@bot.ubsm.edu

so guess what i think viola is being blackmailed. last session i had with
her she told me to turn off the tape recorder so she could tell me
the secret behind her feud with georgia kirkby—which i dug hearing
at the time but now by comparison seems like no big deal. because i
didn't turn off the tape i only pretended. then room service arrived
and i went to greet them and while i was off doing that viola made
this phone call to someone. listening to the tape later i thought at first
it was a dealer and she was trying to score some blow but the more
i heard the more i was convinced she was talking to a blackmailer. i
didn't know about any of this at the time of course or i wouldn't have
come back in the room so soon forcing her to hang up. story of my
life i even get in my own way.

anyway before she hangs up she tells this mysterious caller to come
by the hotel at 8. we usually have dinner together and do a show or
a club or something but that night she pleads a headache and is all oh
harry don't be disappointed but i just have to get over this bad head.
i say okay because i know she just wants me out of her hair for this 8
o'clock meeting and i want her not to suspect me of showing up for
it. so i tell her it's the perfect opportunity for me to look up some old
friends in town. oh harry you're so good to me so understanding. this
despite the fact that on her tape she calls me an albatross. which i
suspect she didn't mean and was only saying to show off but even so.

anyway i show up at her room at 10 after 8 and i've got a bouquet
of flowers and a heating pad i bought at a drug store. and i knock and
there's this long silence and then hello who is it. i say it's harry i just

82

wanted to check on you make sure you're okay. another pause and i swear i can hear whispering. i'm fine harry thanks but i really am too fagged to come to the door. i think about making a joke about the word fagged but nothing comes to me. so i just say but i brought you something to help you feel better. which is like magic because viola can't resist little gifts and tributes so she's like oh all right just a minute. then a lot of hushed voices and she opens the door about four molecules wide. yes harry what is it.

i give her the flowers and she's like oh how sweet and then the heating pad i say use it on your neck it'll work wonders. oh harry you're such a luv i wish i could ask you in. but i'm no fool i planned for this. so i'm like gosh viola i'm sorry you're in such a state but if you don't mind i just need to dash in and get my notebook from the desk. i want to put some of my notes in order tonight cause i haven't had a chance to do that yet with our hectic pace. she gets this look of total panic. oh harry does it have to be tonight i thought you were seeing your friends tonight. i say yes i was but on 2nd thought i thought this project was more important and it'll only take a second for me to grab my notebook i know exactly where i left it i won't disturb you and then i'll be out of your hair and you can go back to resting.

she knows when she's beaten so she says really loudly WELL ALL RIGHT YOU CAN COME IN FOR JUST A MOMENT and sss-looowly opens the door like she's giving someone time to hide. and she's all dressed to the nines and even has high heels on so clearly this is not a relaxing evening for her. i slip in and see two glasses on the bar both with ice in them so obviously there's someone else here. but i don't say anything i just grab my notebook and as i'm heading back to the door i'm thinking hard what else can i do what else can i do. but nothing comes to me and i'm forced to leave. on the way out i say be sure and use that heating pad and she says oh you're such a dear while practically shoving me out the door.

i go to the elevator and press the button but then i double back and try to find a place to hide. of course there's no place because it's the pierre and i mean it's not like there's going to be a little room off the hallway for a coke machine. then i think okay i'll just lurk by the elevator and i can see who comes out. but then i think what if viola comes out too then i'm fucked. so i go down to the lobby and i think okay i'll just wait here watch the elevators and when one goes up to the 11th floor i'll see who gets off when it comes down again. although this isn't foolproof i think maybe intuition will tell me who was in viola's suite.

i may have to wait all night so i settle in. twice the elevator goes up to 11 and stops then comes down carrying couples so i know that's not who i'm looking for. but about ten minutes later it goes to 11 then comes down again and it's just this little old man in a tweed jacket with a pocket hankie—looks about 80. he gets off the elevator and i see he's walking with a cane. everything about him drips of breeding. somehow i know this is the guy—i just get a tingle at the back of my neck when he walks by which tells me yeah. i follow him out of the hotel and there's a car waiting for him. i take down the license plate but i haven't had it tracked yet.

who is this man and why is he blackmailing viola chute. plus excuse me but how is it even possible to blackmail somebody at the end of the 20th century. what possible secret can viola have that is so bad she'd prefer to shell out money to keep it hushed rather than go on oprah and publicize it. i went through the whole list in my head and there isn't one thing that she couldn't turn into a big p.r. boost for her—incest adultery lesbianism prostitution even a lover who was a nazi. i even consider that she might have once been a man which is plainly ridiculous because i've seen the news footage of her in cornwall and those breasts are the real mccoys. then i think well okay maybe it's murder or manslaughter or something. maybe she committed some terrible violent crime and the attorneys for that photographer who's suing her have found out about it and they're after her to settle out of court or they'll go public. it's a long shot because i've spent a lot of time with viola and she just isn't a violent woman except of course for her tongue. but it's all i've got to go on. so now i have to do a little cautious interrogating at our next session and see if i can get something from her even if it's just body language. i'll keep you in the loop wish me luck.

oh and hey how's the foot.

hugest of smooches
harry

You have reached the office of Peter Grace. No one is available to take your call. After the tone, please leave your name, the time of day, a number where you can be reached, and a detailed message. Thank you.

Peter, angel, it's Viola. Thank you for all the very informative faxes; I'm so sorry for not calling back sooner. So much to think about, but I've come to some decisions.

Sultans of South Beach is very tempting and darling Alex is being so considerate, but to my way of thinking, I'm already in a hit show, so why take a chance on something new? That's why I'll stay with *Wyndhamville* provided they meet my terms. Alas, though, my terms have changed, because as I think you'll agree, giving up my own show is the kind of sacrifice that really ought to be compensated.

One million dollars per episode, angel.

That's a one followed by six zeros. I know it's twice what I was asking before—twice what they said *no* to before—but then, naughty Alex has offered me seven-fifty. Plus, have I mentioned that he has a commitment from Eureka to air *South Beach* opposite *Wyndhamville*? So diabolical; I scolded him, I really did.

A million an episode, Peter. Otherwise, I'll just have to say yes to Alex.

I'm still at the Pierre. Let me know what darling Franco and Sandy have to say.

CHUTE: WORTH A MILL TO *WYNDHAMVILLE*?

The Week in Entertainment
July 15, 1997

Contract negotiations between Viola Chute and the producers of *The Winds of Wyndhamville* have stalled over the actress's requested salary of $1 million per episode. Chute joined the UBN serial drama in December 1996 as Grand Duchess Samantha, for a reported salary of $125,000 per episode, and is largely credited with rescuing the show from cancellation (at the time of her first appearance, it ranked 54th among prime-time network series; by the conclusion of the season, it had shot up to #8). As such, her million-dollar request might seem warranted; but the figure is a highly provocative one because Georgia Kirkby, the Oscar-winning actress who is the nominal star of the show, is paid only $800,000 per episode. "The fact is, Jocasta Wyndham [Kirkby's character] is still the heart and soul of the series," says executive producer Sandy Asher; "for all her popularity, Grand Duchess Samantha is still very much a supporting character. We just can't pay Viola Chute a salary above and beyond everybody else's." When asked whether he hoped to reach a compromise agreement with Chute before the new season of *Wyndhamville* begins filming next month, he admits, "We have to consider that the season might have to begin without her." A difficult proposition, given that the previous season's cliffhanger involved Grand Duchess Samantha pushing her lover off a bridge.

"They're crazy to balk at this," says Chute's agent, Peter Grace. "So she's asking for more than the star? Fine. Make Viola the star, then pay up. No one was watching the show before she came along, anyway. And no one will watch it if she moves on to other projects." Grace refused comment on what those "other projects" might be, but an industry source reports that Chute is currently in New York, being actively courted by producer Alex Wylie *(Las Vegas Legionnaires, Dorrie & Dixie)*.

None of the other cast members of *Wyndhamville* would offer comment for the record; but one member of the show's staff privately speculated that Chute's astonishing salary demand might have something to do with her fear of being forced into a large settlement with Berry Leyton, the Dallas photographer who is suing her for assault to the tune of $10 million. When this reporter reached Chute at her suite at the Pierre Hotel, she laughed off the suggestion; "I'm not running scared from anyone, and certainly not from that cretinous little picture-taker. It's just that my career has had ups and downs before, and I've always promised myself that when the ups came again, I'd make the most of them." When asked if she might have overplayed her hand, she replied, "We'll see, won't we?" She declined to comment on any alleged talks with Alex Wylie.

A representative for Georgia Kirkby had only this to say: "A year from now, no one will even remember this woman. Haven't you people got anything better to write about?"

MEMO TO:	S. Asher
FROM:	B. Engel
SUBJECT:	Cliffhanger resolution
DATE:	7/18/97

Sandy:

As requested, Nick, Susan and I have come up with some possible ways to resolve the cliffhanger without Viola's participation. In my order of preference:

1) We open on Summers St. Simon falling to his death; but when the camera arcs up to the bridge again, Grand Duchess Samantha is gone. The mystery of her disappearance from the scene can be delayed as long as it takes to either (a) reach agreement with Chute or (b) replace her. Which leads to:

2) Replace her right away. Hire another living-legend actress who still looks good, put her in a Viola Chute wig, and make her Grand Duchess Samantha. There are two ways to accomplish this: (a) Incorporate the change into the story, i.e., have Samantha fall off the bridge as well, requiring massive reconstructive surgery on her face; or (b) Just make the switch and brazen it out.

3) Ignore the cliffhanger; have the other *Wyndhamville* characters continue with their storylines, occasionally wondering whatever happened to Samantha and St. Simon. This, again, gives us time to negotiate with Chute, and we can pick up on the Samantha story whenever and however negotiations are resolved.

4) After St. Simon falls to his death, we return to the bridge, where Samantha is in the process of ripping a rubber mask from her face, revealing Sieglinde the She-Wolf, the neo-Nazi gang

leader Drake Wyndham met in Boravia last season. We then reveal that there never *was* a Grand Duchess Samantha; it's been the She-Wolf all along, playing this elaborate ruse on Drake for a reason we frankly haven't figured out yet. This is by far the most bizarre solution to the Viola Chute problem, but I think our viewers will be looking for something bizarre, something that really cuts the cord with Viola and sends a clear, confident message that we never really needed her. Plus, Angie Ashe-Tippett was a real hit as the She-Wolf last season, and would probably jump at the chance to return to the role on a recurring basis. (Although we'd have to play down, if not completely abandon, the neo-Nazi aspect of her character.)

Look forward to your & Franco's thoughts.

Biff

NEW YORK
7/20/97, 3:03 P.M.

. . . Where were we? . . . Oh, yes, Manhattan, angel. Right where we are now, isn't that funny! I'd say something about coming full circle, but honestly, my first stay in Manhattan was *nothing* like this. As I think I said, I was living in Delia Wishman's flat, looking after her cat while she was off in London doing—oh, I remember the show now! *Force of Will.* Terribly earnest bit of business about a quadriplegic learning to take charge of his own life. Delia played the inspirational nurse who ends up being the wife. *Raves,* darling. Delia's biggest hit. Too bad it was such egregious shit. Delia used to call it *Farce of Swill.* But in those days, nobody dared criticize a play about crippled persons triumphing . . . Hm? Oh, *terribly* sorry. *Disabled* persons. Mea fucking culpa.

Anyway, the play kept Delia in London for the whole summer, so I was able to live rent-free on the Lower East Side. But her place, angel . . . *such* a dump. Every trite joke any standup comic ever made about New York apartments being cramped and the size of the rats—just don't even *start* me, I'll repeat them all. And Delia's taste was dreadful. She called her decor French provincial, which is pretty accurate, except for the French part. It was almost like I'd gone through a time warp and was back in Cornwall. Only with cockroaches in the sink and the jackhammers outside.

Now, as I think I mentioned, the whole point of my being there was to hone my stage abilities for *The Bell Jar,* which was going into rehearsal in Manhattan in June, then opening later in Atlanta with an eye towards bringing it to Broadway. Unfortunately, this was just about the time Andrew Lloyd Webber started making his presence known in town with things like *Jesus Christ Superstar* and *Evita* and all those wonderful, high-concept shows . . . what, you're scowling. Don't you like them? . . . Oh, Harry, you little hidebound elitist! I *looove* Sir Andrew. He's a dear friend as well . . . Anyway, his kind of blockbuster was transforming what Broadway audiences expected of musicals, so by the time we opened here our little effort never really had a chance. People *adored* us in Atlanta and Knoxville and everywhere else we'd gone. I know New Yorkers still talk about the show as though it were a huge disaster, but it's just that it wasn't fashionable, angel. We were guilty of bad timing, nothing more. Someone ought to revive that show. There was a lot of merit in it. And if I may be allowed to say so, my performance was quite good. With better luck, I could've had a whole new career.

Anyway, I'm getting ahead of myself. Let's go back to when I first arrived in town. Victor Cywzyrk had agreed to take me on, which was quite a coup. I'd take the crosstown bus every day to study with him. Now the thing about Victor is, I realized at once that he was a complete charlatan. But I kept up with him because I was meeting the most delicious people in his class. Acting royalty, luv. Helen Teague. Brian Ireland. Lawrence Army Dell. Cywzyrk had everyone in New York fooled for about a season and a half. The theatre was in a kind of post-Stanislavsky, post-Strasberg funk, you see, and actors were perpetually on the lookout for the next genius guru, as though one was going to just show up every few years, like a new congressman. People in the arts aren't quite rational, are they, angel?

Anyway, this is kind of a low point in my life, luv, I don't know what else I can tell you. I worked hard to reinvent myself as a stage actress, taking whatever I could from Cywzyrk, which wasn't much . . . his system was called "primality," if you please, and you weren't supposed to inhabit your role, you were supposed to *transcend* it. Utter, stinking shit. And the *money* he charged . . . ! Depleted the last of my savings. But it was noticed that I was there among his students, and that gave me a certain cachet that helped place me in some of the right circles. I did my damnedest to live up to it, to become a serious thespian; I stayed at home most nights—me, the original party girl!—reading books on theory, and doing Cywzyrk's exercises in a mirror. You should've seen me, one hand propping open Eugene O'Neill, the other gesticulating wildly. Oh, I must've been *quite* a sight! And you know, for all that work, the first thing Cam Jeter did—Cam was the director of *The Bell Jar,* the one who auditioned and hired me in Los Angeles—the first thing he did was stop me in the middle of my initial read-through and say, "Whoa, little lady! What the hell happened to *you?*" And he made me start acting like a human being again—those are his exact words. "Like a human being." So much for "primality."

Fortunately, rehearsals began in late summer, so I started getting paid again. It had been getting pretty precarious, being broke in Manhattan. By the time my first paycheck arrived, I'd been reduced to fixing every moldy box of Minute Rice or pancake mix that Delia had abandoned in the back of her cupboard for however many years. In fact, Sir Pouncealot's food was beginning to look awfully moist and appetizing, and I think another week might have found us in a pitched battle for the Friskies.

Well, it was difficult for me, wasn't it, because I had this reputation as the infamous British widow-slash-heiress, and in the popular imagination I was still a very wealthy woman, who was just toying with acting because it amused her so. You know, once the public makes up its mind about you, it doesn't ever change it; the way they see you at first is the way you remain. So to keep up appearances, I found it necessary to get dressed up every now and then and fling myself into Manhattan's night life—yes, luv, in fact, I *was* at Studio 54—but the only way I could do it was to hook up with a man who would pay my bills for the night, and allow me to repay him in my own medium of exchange, if you know what I mean. Don't put that part in. But alas, off the record, that wasn't as easy as it sounds, because in those days—and I think this has been documented somewhere—*every man in Manhattan was gay.* So, while I had no trouble attracting male attention when I went out, it was always the wrong kind of male attention—all these pretty boys who had seen *The Private Life of Agrippina* ninety-seven times on late-night TV and acted out the rape scene with their Barbie dolls. Eventually, I just stopped going out, and . . . hm? . . . More about Studio 54? . . . Oh, luv, I wish I could oblige. I was only there a few times, and I think cocaine has wiped that chalkboard clean. Don't put that in, either. Anyway, I was never very interested in being part of the whole Liza-Halston-Bianca crowd. The truth is, for the duration of my summer in Manhattan, I was a starving artist. I was the cliché. True, I did get pulled into the swirl of the club scene now and then, but I resisted, angel, for my art. And while it didn't necessarily pay off in *The Bell Jar,* the lessons I learned, the experiences I garnered, have served me well in later projects. But alas, such was the monasticism of my life at the time, there's really no more about those days I can tell. It was all study, study, study. And no money.

. . . What, angel? *Anger?* . . . Well, no, I'm not angry about it, of course. As I said, it all bore fruit. And it wasn't as though my predicament could be placed at anyone's door. It's just the career trajectory of the working actress isn't it; sometimes you're up, sometimes you're . . . I'm sorry? . . . Victor Cywzyrk? Now, why would I be angry at him? As I said, his class enabled me to make some very valuable connections. And it gave me a shred of credibility that I badly needed. Plus, Victor's dead now, why would I . . . No, not *murder,* luv! *Aneurysm.* What kind of deranged line of questioning is this? . . . Well, fine, I can understand your disappointment that there's not more . . . *passion* in my Manhattan summer, but angel, it's probably no more than a chapter at best, right? Just play up the starving artist angle. The starving artist with occasional Studio 54 dates. After all, anger and violence aren't the kinds of passion I historically prefer. I've always been a lover, not a . . . I'm sorry, angel, I really have to stop you here. You're beginning to frighten me. All this talk of anger and retribution . . . Fine, fine, I can appreciate that a biographer has to strive to get to know his subject. But keep in mind, Harry, you're *not* my biographer, you're my ghostwriter. You're here to tell my story in my own words, with just your polish to make it readable. You're emphatically *not* here to discover my "dark" side. Though if you keep pestering me like this, you'll discover it soon enough, and God help you when you do. Now, gather up your things, I've had it with you today . . . *Hurry,* Harry, I mean it, I want you *out* . . . I really think you ought to try to get laid while you're here, it's obviously a dire need . . . the tape recorder, too, I don't want anything of yours here reminding me of you . . . Just pick it up and turn it *off* . . . You've given me a fierce little headache and I need t—

PRIMALITY
From Victor Cywzyrk's Course Materials

What do I mean when I say PRIMALITY? . . . I mean that as an actor your responsibility is twofold: to create a PRIMAL emotion in your audience, and to make that emotion the audience's PRIMAL REALITY.

How do you do this? Do not think it is easy! It will take WORK. But I will show you how to STRIP AWAY years of damaging adherence to the THREE M'S: method, modulation, and mannerism.

What will I leave you with? . . . PRIMALITY!

I will give you an example from one of the first classes you will attend: When you portray a character whose mother has died, you DO NOT portray a character whose mother has died. You portray GRIEF. You DO NOT portray someone fixed in time and space whose feelings are particular to his or her small, insignificant life. Is THAT how YOU feel when you lose a loved one? Do YOU feel, "I am experiencing an emotion that is unique to myself, that I convey in a manner appropriate only to me"? YOU DO NOT FEEL THAT! What you feel is PRIMAL. You tap into a wellspring of keening, insurmountable GRIEF that has been in existence since the world began! What you feel becomes your PRIMAL REALITY. It wipes from existence all other traces of your character!

PRIMALITY establishes that DICHOTOMY OF IDENTITY for the stage. When you act, you are the CHARACTER until the character FEELS; then you are the FEELING that has POSSESSED the character. And just as it has possessed him, it must possess YOU; and just as it must obliterate the character, it must obliterate YOU; you must give way to it, not try to shape it nor channel it nor focus it nor alter it. PRIMALITY allows you only your lines . . . the eggshell-thin VENEER of control over raging EMOTION . . . lest theatre become AN-ARCHY.

These are fine lines that I have drawn, yes. Are you prepared to explore JUST WHERE they are drawn? . . . And how to DRAW THEM YOURSELF? . . . Then YOU, scion of the stage, child of Bacchus, are ready for PRIMALITY.

Your life, and your art, will now transform FOREVER!

THIS "BELL JAR" CRACKED

The New York Times, May 30, 1978

These are not happy times for the Broadway musical, and certainly no one should be discouraged from pursuing provocative measures in the hope of resuscitating this worthy American art form. Yet one wonders not at the moxie, but at the incompetence of Campbell Sorrell and Mark E. Vance, who produced, respectively, the book and music for the adaptation of *The Bell Jar* now running at the Ilka Chase Theatre. Surely only a hand as seasoned as Stephen Sondheim's could have hoped to wring a valid work of theatre from Sylvia Plath's 1963 novel, in which a young woman recounts in unflinching terms the slow disintegration of her mind. (Miss Plath, who killed herself in the same year the novel was published, based it on her own mental breakdown; it was originally published under a pseudonym.)

Mr. Sorrell, whose only major credits to date are two successful off-Broadway revues, *Stinky Feets* and *Behold the Traipsing Pachyderms,* would not have been my first choice to make such an attempt, and while he has said in interviews that he has an abiding appreciation for Miss Plath's poetry, one finds none of her jagged, crystalline brilliance in his lyrics; instead, what we find is doggerel. Take, for example, the early scene in which the heroine, Sylvia Greenwood, is assaulted by the woman-hating lothario, Marco. Sylvia (whose first name has been changed from the novel's Esther, presumably to reinforce the connection between author and character) sings, "I know your sort / I've seen you before / You think we are yours for the taking / You flatter and flirt / Just to get up our skirt / And proceed with your wriggling and shaking." Which is bad enough (even as doggerel; since when does "sort" rhyme with "before"?) without being followed by Marco's "Cease your prattle, college beauty / Be my slut, my saucy cutie." This serves Miss Plath's original narrative about as well as Richard Wagner's *Ring of the Nibelung* is served by Bugs Bunny's.

Compounding the damage is Mr. Vance's score, which is bright and tuneful where it ought to be dark and operatic. I doubt the producers desired their audiences to leave the theatre gaily humming "I see death's head / The skull descending / A pool of blood creeping ever outward / My life in my hands, now ending." But such is Mr. Vance's apparent obtuseness to the meaning of the lyrics that he has set them to a melody as catchy as "Mairzy Doats."

Mr. Sorrell and Mr. Vance are not alone in their indemnity, though. Significant blame for the show's failure can be laid at the feet of its star, Viola Chute, who is, incredibly, making not only her Broadway debut but her American stage debut in *The Bell Jar*. One wonders what in the world can have given the director, Cam Jeter, such great confidence—or any confidence at all—in her. Miss Chute has built a film career out of playing both chalk-white virgins and hissing villainesses without much attendant variance in her performances; she has absolutely no resources on which to draw when trying to create a character as complex and dynamic as Sylvia Greenwood, whose mental deterioration can only be charted by watching the set of Miss Chute's jaw. After the electroshock number ("A billion bumblebees, a million mantises / Barrel through my veins / Am I on fire? / Am I aflame?"), her chin drops to her chest and largely stays there, which is only fair, as the audience's have all long since done the same.

Even more lamentable is Miss Chute's voice. One can just about tell that she is attempting to sing, because she regulates her recital of the lyrics in a way that somewhat matches the rhythms of the music; she also alternates her repertoire of bleats, shrieks and grunts in a manner that leads one to conclude she is attempting to make some tonal sense out of them. Despite her efforts, this critic could think of nothing during her solos but the recent documentary film concerning a pair of anthropologists who have spent several years vainly attempting to teach a chimpanzee to speak.

Completing the disastrous production is the staging, by Mr. Jeter and one Hugo Patty, whose name I have never encountered before and which, if I am vigilant, I never will again. Characters zoom about the stage, sometimes dropping in by wire, sometimes popping up through trap doors—I suppose in an effort to duplicate how random and senseless the world seems to Sylvia Greenwood. But the effect is less illuminating of madness than just plain maddening, and when, at critical junctures, the bell jar actually descends—for here the image is not poetic, but concrete; an enormous, fifteen-foot, bell-shaped plastic cone actually lowers onto the stage, entrapping our heroine—the audience cannot understand her complaint. Miss Chute runs around the jar's inner perimeter, pounding it with her fists, as though desperate to get out. But if the musical *Bell Jar* is going on outside it, clearly the bell jar is the only safe place to be.

Presuming, of course, that it's soundproofed.

INTERVIEW WITH VIOLA CHUTE
by E. Manfred Harry
(Excerpt)
Homophile, July 1993

HOMOPHILE: So, tell me a little about your retirement.

VIOLA: Oh, angel, what's to tell?

HOMOPHILE: Well, by my estimation, from the time *The Bell Jar* closed in 1978, to five months ago, when you made those Lean Cuisine commercials, you were effectively out of show business.

VIOLA: That's not entirely true, you know. About a decade ago, I spent a season as a regular on *Double Dutch*.

HOMOPHILE: The game show?

VIOLA: Yes, luv. I was quite popular with audiences, too, because I had an uncanny sense for just how far one could push a double entendre on daytime TV.

HOMOPHILE: So this was . . . what, 1982?

VIOLA: Yes, '82. I remember it distinctly, because about two months after I left the show, I married Michael Winger.

HOMOPHILE: The home-spa entrepreneur?

VIOLA: Yes, lovely Michael . . . miss him still. Then, in May of '83, our daughter, Patricia, was born. So for a few years afterward, I was just a housewife and mother.

HOMOPHILE: Forgive me, it's hard to see you in that role.

VIOLA: Well, I've had better ones. But it was what it was. Alas, Michael died in '86; he'd sold his company to a multinational conglomerate about a year before, and while it made him rich as Croesus, it left him with nothing to do, and to this day I think he died of a broken heart. That company was his real wife.

HOMOPHILE: So you were left a rich widow.

VIOLA: Oh, yes. That was a role I played *much* more zestfully. *(laughs)*

HOMOPHILE: Yet a year later, you remarried.

VIOLA: You *have* done your research, luv. Well, what can I say. We all make mistakes.

HOMOPHILE: Tell me about it.

VIOLA: Oh, you know, he was a rich man on the lookout for a trophy wife. Corrigan Hume, the publishing magnate. Newly divorced after forty years; I think I met him on the very day he signed the papers. He thought I was just the right thing for him—never one to shop around, Corgie. Anyway, it had been a while since I was actively courted, and I rather liked it, so I allowed him a little more liberty than I should have. Before you know it, there was a ring on my finger. Give him credit, though; he's a dutiful father to Patricia. He adopted her, you know, and after we divorced, he kept custody of her.

HOMOPHILE: That seems . . . odd. You being her natural mother.

VIOLA: Well, you know, the two of them . . . from the moment we came together and formed a family, it was like they were in league against me. No, that sounds paranoid . . . not "in league," per se. It was more like they formed a little support group of two.

HOMOPHILE: So the marriage didn't last.

VIOLA: Alas, no. We divorced when Patricia was seven. I've only seen her intermittently since then. She's just turned ten, so I really should make an attempt to hook up with her. Ten is about the time a girl starts to loathe her father's authority.

HOMOPHILE: So, that brings us to your much-publicized engagement to Senator Lawley. Which brought you back into the public eye.

VIOLA: *(sighs)* Oh, yes, I know just what you're going to say. "Wasn't it manipulative of you to agree to marry Dennis Lawley during his reelection campaign, rake in all that publicity as Minnesota's glamorous senatorial-spouse-to-be, then dump him right after he lost." Well, it wasn't like that at all. First of all, people forget how much money I poured into Dennis's campaign. I very nearly went broke, and what return did I get on that investment? Hm? More importantly, one of the things I loved about Dennis was his energy, his positivity, his hopefulness. When he lost the election, all the air seemed to go out of him, like a punctured tire. He wasn't the same man. I couldn't reach him anymore. So I walked.

HOMOPHILE: Yes . . . right into a career comeback.

VIOLA: Oh, no! Is that how people see it? . . . The election was last year, angel, and my "comeback," as you call it, didn't really begin till only recently, when the Lean Cuisine deal came through, and when a majority of my old films were rereleased on video as *The Viola Chute Collection*. And, yes, both of those windfalls were probably the result of all the press I got as Dennis's fiancee, but they were still a long time coming. In fact—you call it a "comeback," but believe it or not, this is the first interview I've been asked to do since Dennis's campaign. Believe me, it's been a dry spell, this last year. But then, I've had my share of dry spells.

HOMOPHILE: Speaking of which, we seem to have covered your entire history, except for the years between *The Bell Jar* and *Double Dutch*. What were you doing from 1979 to 1982?

VIOLA: Resting, mainly. I'd spent so much of the previous year on the road with *The Bell Jar*—playing Atlanta, Nashville, Chicago, Philadelphia, you name it—that by the time it flopped in New York, I was completely exhausted. So I just laid low for a year or so.

HOMOPHILE: A *year* or so? Certainly you must've had *some* characteristically Viola Chute adventures during that time.

VIOLA: Honestly, luv, if I did, I can't remember them.

SUBJ: revelations
DATE: 97-7-21 15:11:14 EST
FROM: emanfr@ysa.net
TO: nbcasem@bot.ubsm.edu

viola chute is oh so very full of shit. i can just see you raising your eye-
brows—oh my no harry not really you must be mistaken. go ahead
and gloat. i mean i knew when i got into this that i wouldn't be getting the unvarnished truth but the piles of manure she's been shovel-
ing at me lately are making me doubt the veracity of everything she's
ever told me. fortunately i am on the case. oh yes yes yes i am.

see viola is painting this picture of herself as a starving artist in new york
in the late 70s because it suits her to be thought of that way. still there's
the problem that she also can't bear not being thought of as the center
of the known universe during any given year of her life. so she insists that
of course she visited studio 54 a few times and would have gone back
more often if only that were her kind of thing and if she hadn't been so
busy working on her acting in an unfurnished concrete cell. but aha as
luck would have it a friend of mine on the west coast found an old book
about the 70s club scene written by somebody i never heard of and
sent it to me because it has a chapter on viola. turns out she was seen
at studio 54 quite a lot that summer—or at least outside it because apparently she didn't always get in which must have galled her in a huge
way. but the exciting thing about the chapter is that it reveals why she is
now pretending to have been too lofty for the place. apparently she totally humiliated herself there one night in front of andy warhol and
never had the guts to go back. i'll tell you how she did it someday but it
has to be in person because i want to see your face when you hear. certainly puts a different spin on her oh that wasn't my scene line of crap.

anyway i thought maybe this could be what viola was being blackmailed about but then i thought no it's a silly incident hardly worth a

million dollars. which is what she's asking for in her new contract did i mention that. her agent flipped out when she told him said there's no way in hell they'd rather see you dead. viola said well then i'll go with the other offer—the miami series remember—and her agent was like well i'll do my best but i make no promises.

anyway i'm totally convinced the million bucks issue comes right out of this whole blackmailer thing. one week she's asking for five hundred thou and isn't even close to getting it—then the next week instead of dropping her asking price she gets a mysterious phone call that i fortunately have on tape and all of a sudden she's asking for a million. blackmail blackmail blackmail i tell you.

i also strongly suspect that murder may be the secret here or at least some kind of manslaughter. at our last session i very carefully questioned her about any past violence in her life but unfortunately she saw right through me and of course she denied everything. which doesn't mean she isn't lying and in fact she very revealingly blew her top at the idea. cussed me out and booted my ass out the door. she really frightened me i was half expecting her to bean me with an ashtray or something. a violent woman then, yes no doubt.

so murder it is. it has to be. it only makes sense because really what else could there be. there are no other scandals left in the world none nada zilch. everything even the very worst things that once would have dashed a person's reputation to smithereens now seem to just be the kind of thing you write a book about which then gets made into a tv movie and wins you an emmy. unless there's a body buried somewhere.

so on with the investigation. i have I other clue which is also in that book my west coast friend sent me. the chapter on viola mentions that she disappeared off the face of the earth—author's exact words—and i got to wondering about that. also i checked my old homophile interview with her and at one point i specifically asked her about a period of her life—1979 to 82. she pretends she can't remember anything that happened then. i was curious so i pulled together all my notes and put together a chronology of viola's life and except for those three years i can account for virtually every move she ever made. so i now think that's where the secret is lurking. i wonder if it'd piss her off if i added to my research by talking to certain people like old producers ex lovers her daughter anybody. what am i saying of course it would piss her off. i guess what i mean is can i do it behind her back and get away with it. i tell you it's just too goddamn bad this isn't an unauthorized bio because i'm on to something here and with a little freedom i could nail it.

actually i have just been handed a little freedom to do some investigating. last night viola jetted off to milan for the funeral of gianni versace the fashion designer who was just murdered in miami—i'm sure even you heard about it on the news, shot by a gay serial killer so of course all the news media are practically creaming in their pants. anyway versace's sister was trying to get hold of viola in l.a. not knowing she was in new york and finally traced her here last night. viola had her bags packed and was out the door like a shot so i figure i've got about 3 days of peace to do a little snooping.

in fact i already started this morning. remember the dapper little man who i'm convinced is her blackmailer well i had the plates of his car traced and guess what they're from the british consulate. they weren't diplomatic plates though which to me means someone who really rates in britain came over to this country and was able to throw his weight around and get the consulate to supply him free use of a car. so i pretended i was a journalist and called the consulate and you'll love what i did. i knew they'd never tell me who had the car so i said i was calling because of a report that they were playing politics by lending cars to members of parliament from one party but not the other. and this receptionist was like oh no that's not the case at all we would never discriminate and in fact the only member of parliament using a car right now is from the house of lords and not even affiliated with a party. and i said who would that be and she said chester viscount killwall. so i went and looked up killwall on a map. turns out it's this tiny little county in scotland. now I know viola is british but she's from cornwall that's not even anywhere near scotland. plus if the dapper little man really is chester viscount killwall, what's he got to do with viola anyway. after all he's a hereditary peer and she's just cornish trash who made good in america. i did some preliminary research into british newspapers and turned up no evidence of viola being in scotland or anywhere else in britain during the years 79–82. so the maddening question remains what possible connection can there be. the whole idea of viola chute swanning about with scottish aristocracy is faintly ridiculous.

i'll be in touch. meantime keep that foot elevated.

hugest of smooches
harry

SUCKING UP IN THE SEVENTIES
Confessions of a Club Climber
by Rodney "Zinger" Eaton
Nova Caledonia Press, 1982 (out of print)

CHAPTER 4

We now come to the Viola Chute incident of 1977, which was legendary for about three weeks during Studio's first historic year. It's perhaps necessary to fill you in on who this fine lady was. Miss Chute was a British actress in her thirties whose film career had just ended (and was never much to write home about, anyway). She'd come to New York because she was beginning a new career—she'd been chosen to star in a musical play about Sylvia Plath. This particular bit of miscasting astounded everybody—what next, Joey Heatherton as Virginia Woolf? Apparently Miss Chute was hired based on a plaintive, yearning song she sang in an old costume drama; the song was a favorite of the play's director, one Cam Jeter. What Miss Chute didn't bother mentioning was that her singing voice in that particular film was dubbed—and by the time Mr. Jeter discovered that her actual singing voice was something like a cross between Carol Channing and Scooby-Doo, it was too late . . . Miss Chute had already gotten to the show's producer, one Hi Inchman. This Mr. Inchman had a predilection for a certain sexual act that almost no ladies of my acquaintance have ever been willing to perform, under any circumstances. But it turned out that this particular sex act was one of Miss Chute's specialties. (I will say no more, except to note that it begins with "r" and rhymes with "imjob.") Needless to say, she almost immediately had the money-man wrapped around her . . . well, tongue, and her starring role was secure. When confronted with his star's lack of vocal acuity, Mr. Inchman told Mr. Jeter to have the show rewritten so that the other members of the cast sang more than Miss Chute.

But the star clearly retained some self-doubts (borne out—the show became a legendary bomb), and for that reason was eager to resume her film career. And she'd decided Mr. Andy Warhol was the key to this rebirth. So she'd show up at Studio night after night, sometimes getting in, sometimes not. It depended on who else showed up who was more famous, or . . . well, younger. When she was admitted, she was a favorite of Mr. Rubell, because she teased him. She had an annoying affectation: she called everyone "angel" (someone once asked her why, and she said, "Because compared to me, everyone is"), yet she cannily made an exception for Mr. Rubell, whom she called "devil." He seemed to get a kick out of this. But, sad to say, the lady was often such a mess—apparently blow had played a serious game of rugby in her brain—that many times the gentlemen at the door wouldn't let her in. She was always desperate to get to Andy, though, and whenever she made it past the sentries, it was always, "Where's Andy? Andy wants to meet me." It's true, he had once expressed such a desire, because apparently she got her start in some avant garde British film that was one of Andy's favorites. Everyone else who's seen it says it's unwatchable, but that's Andy. Someone, however, warned him that Miss Chute was ready to sink her teeth into him and not let go, like an ever so much prettier pit bull, and that frightened him off her; she was always kept away from him, by whatever means necessary.

On the night in question she came into the club hanging, half-drunk, off the arm of a gentleman of the escort variety—you know the type: twenty, buff, shirt unbuttoned to his pubic patch. Apparently she'd escaped Mr. Inchman for the evening. As I happened to be there that night, I said hello to her, and asked her how she was doing. She told me she was wonderful, she'd been making such amazing strides studying with some acting coach whose name I forget—actually, I didn't even recognize it at the time, but Miss Chute seemed pretty impressed with him, kept calling him a genius. Then, the inevitable: "Where's Andy?" I said I didn't know, and bolted.

It turns out Andy *was* at the club that night. He and some friends were holed up in a corner, watching a quartet of young gentlemen dancing together. And as the music got louder and hotter, these gentlemen kept shedding more and more clothing, till they were naked but for little leather jockstraps, which seemed to me an indication that their striptease wasn't quite as spontaneous as they had pretended. Most gentlemen of my acquaintance do not don leather jockstraps for an evening out if all they're planning to do is quietly discuss *quattrocento* frescoes over cognac.

Andy was really enjoying the show these four gentlemen were putting on, and it was so rare to see him smile or appear involved in anything, that word spread through the club about the sheer novelty of it, and our friend Miss Chute must've heard this and decided it was her big chance. So, without even a moment's hesitation—this was *not* a lady much afflicted with shyness—she disrobed, emerging entirely nude but for her high heels and her necklace. She left her escort holding her clothes while she danced into the midst of the four gentlemen, making wild, come-hither eyes at Andy. As for the four gentlemen, at the first sight of her mound of Venus, they retreated in horror, not being at all enamored of that kind of thing, which left Miss Chute dancing happily alone, in the spotlight at last.

Now, there is a rule about appearing naked in public that all my esteemed readers should know, and it is the same rule that applies to appearing clothed in public: before you let yourself be seen, check your fine self in a mirror. Since Miss Chute had famously refused to do nude scenes in her movies, she perhaps never had any reason to learn this. Which is a pity, because if she *had* checked herself in a mirror, she just might have noticed that there was a rather visible bit of *papier du toilette* dangling from her otherwise most attractive posterior. And while all sorts of shocking things had been seen at Studio before, this one caused an unprecedented sensation, because unlike all the others, it was clearly, unarguably, and beyond any doubt, unintentional.

Let's spare the lady the details of her humiliation: but she was indeed serenaded out of the club by the most sustained laughter I ever heard there, before or since. And she did *not* meet Andy Warhol and she did *not* return to try again, ever. In fact, she was seen precious little, if at all, anywhere on the club scene for the remainder of the summer. Now, I was of the impression that Miss Chute was the kind of lady who could brazen out a little embarrassment like that, but apparently such is not the case. I am always amazed to discover which of my fellow beings are in fact secretly sensitive souls. Perhaps the lady would have felt better had she known she'd started a trend; for a few weeks afterward, any time anyone at Studio went bare-assed—and there were always a few—they'd inevitably stick a little Charmin appendage into their butt-cracks and waggle it around while dancing. It was one of Studio's first "in" jokes.

While writing this chapter, I tried to contact Miss Chute to inform her, however belatedly, of her moment in Studio history, but she seems to have fallen off the face of the earth. No one, neither family nor associates, has any idea where she may be. With a lady like Miss Chute, there is no telling: she could be the kept woman of an Arab sheik, doing dinner theatre in Mishawaka, or resting dismembered in a trunk at the bottom of a river. Wherever she is, I hope she is able someday to read this and learn of her brief legacy. For while Viola Chute has no doubt enjoyed greater tributes, none, I think, was more sincerely felt.

From
BERESFORD'S *PEERAGE*

Killwall, Viscount (7th). Chester Robert Louis Marian
Alderton-ffiske, K.G., K.C.M.G., K.C.B., O.M., P.C. Born
1926. Educated at Gordonstoun and Christ Church College,
Oxford. Late Major in 1st Life Guards, Knight of the Order of
the Holy Roman Empire. 1st son William, 6th Viscount Killwall, and the former Edith Elizabeth Casenove, 3rd daughter
of Herbert, 11th Duke of Castershire. Married in 1944, the
late Jane Arabella Everlegh, 2nd daughter of Sir Richard Everlegh. No issue.

STAR-STRUCK PHOTOGRAPHER
STRIKES BACK—
FOR HIS CAREER AND FOR JUSTICE
AmeriScene, July/August 1997

Berry Leyton is an unassuming-looking man . . . which might explain how he was able to become, during the late 1980s and 1990s, one of the pre-eminent freelance celebrity photographers in America. His mildly pleasant good looks and almost entirely beige wardrobe allowed him to slip unnoticed past the bodyguards of Hollywood's biggest names, resulting in award-winning candid shots of such privacy-obsessed luminaries as Cher, Elizabeth Taylor, Sting, and the Artist Formerly Known as Prince. In many cases, the published photos have produced cries of surprise from their subjects, who don't even remember a photographer being present at the time.

"It's true," he says, running his hand through his thinning brown hair; "I'm not only not threatening, I'm not the sort of guy anyone ever looks twice at. And that's really helped me in my work." At the height of his career, Leyton commanded steep fees from any number of quality celebrity magazines (including this very publication). His most famous shot—of an exhausted, post-concert Madonna sitting in the backseat of a limousine, head bent back, applying Visine to her bloodshot eyes—actually earned him six figures. And that was *before* the singer responded, not with a lawsuit, but by purchasing the rights to the photograph to use as the cover to a CD single.

But that was yesterday; today, Leyton's career is in dire jeopardy. He is, in fact, unable to take a picture without extreme discomfort, and his vision has so badly deteriorated that he must confine himself to still subjects. "So I do occasional wedding parties and whatnot," he says with a grim laugh. "Class pictures, annual report photos. That sort of thing."

Such is the disastrous result of a run-in with the one celebrity who managed to catch Berry Leyton at his game: Viola Chute, the star of the UBN serial drama *Winds of Wyndhamville*.

"It's ironic," says Leyton with a sigh, as he sits on the deck of the ranch house he built for his family in a tony Dallas suburb—a house he is now in danger of losing. "I had no trouble at all getting shots of the biggest and the brightest, never a dodgy moment. And in the end it's some has-been TV actress who does me in."

In April, Leyton was hired by the tabloid *Weekly Inquisitor* to follow Chute to the Caribbean island of St. Lucia, where she was vacationing after her first half-season on *Wyndhamville*. He positioned himself outside the villa's gates, and waited day after day for his opportunity to arise.

Alas, while Leyton's nondescript appearance serves him well in crowds of other paparazzi, it affords him no camouflage against the verdant richness of the island's hilly terrain. "I got cocky," he says. "I was so used to getting my way, that I let down my guard." When Chute and a male companion emerged from the villa to pick mangoes from the trees on the grounds, Leyton started clicking . . . and Chute noticed him at once.

Instead of returning to the privacy of the house, as is the habit of most camera-shy celebrities in Leyton's experience, Chute, alarmingly, chose to accost Leyton physically, charging through the villa's gate "like some kind of enraged animal," he says. At first, he was thrilled by her reaction, and kept clicking away, never thinking that she might actually intend to harm him; "I just thought, wow, these great shots of Viola Chute going berserk," he says. "Then, she went berserk on *me*." In a swift, violent display of her rage, Chute allegedly took a swing that connected with Leyton's camera, driving it into his right eye.

After the attack, Chute reentered her villa, leaving Leyton literally blinded on the road outside. Unable to drive, he was forced to wait several hours for a native farmer to happen by on an oxcart and give him a lift to the town of Soufriere, where he was able to arrange intermediate medical care before flying back to the United States and checking himself into a Miami hospital.

In the months since, Leyton has suffered periodic bouts of blindness, palsy, and extreme, nearly crippling headaches. His career has all but evaporated, and the once globe-trotting journalist, now grounded at home, finds himself suffering from depression, as well. "But I've still got a family to support," he says, grimly determined; "and I'm going to support them. If I can't pay the bills anymore, I'll get somebody else to do it. That's why I'm suing Viola Chute. She's the one who *should* be paying. She's the one who did this to me."

Leyton's children—Rosie, 13, Michael, 10, and Anita, 9—gather round him and offer hugs of support as he explains that the amount of his suit—$10 million—is intended to provide for them throughout their lives, "since it isn't likely I'll ever be able to work full-time again." In order to pay his mounting legal bills, he is seeking representation among New York art dealers for a retrospective exhibit of his celebrity photographs; as yet, he has no takers. He is also considering selling limited-edition prints of his most famous pictures, but can't bring himself to do so without first clearing the idea with his subjects. "It's one thing if it's journalism," he says. "But if I'm selling these stars' pictures as *art*—well, that's making money off their image, and I just wouldn't do that without their approval. I have too much respect for them—well, most of them," he corrects himself with a laugh. "The real big ones, they know they're in the image business. They know that's their stock in trade. It's the small ones, ironically, who don't know it, who act like they're some kind of royalty. Well, I can't let myself be bitter. Bad for the soul." He kisses his daughter Anita on the forehead, as if drawing strength and calm from her.

This week, Leyton was shaken by the news that Viola Chute's attorneys are filing a countersuit, alleging invasion of privacy. According to Chute, Leyton climbed a tree outside the gate of the villa and crawled onto a limb that overhung the property before commencing to take his pictures. "That's absurd," he says heatedly; "a damned lie. This is a desperate measure. They must know they can't win."

This reporter asks Leyton why he doesn't use the shots of Viola Chute rampaging towards him to settle the matter; it would certainly prove that he wasn't in a tree when she accosted him. "I wish I could," he explains with a sigh. "But she knocked the camera out of my hands and broke it. The film was ruined." A poignant metaphor for a broken, ruined man. But Berry Leyton rejects the comparison: "I can't afford to be a broken man," he says. "I've got a family. And I've still got the fruits of my career, my pictures, which I hope can still be put to work for me. And, God help me, one day I hope I'll have justice, too."

FAX MEMO TO: Viola
FROM: Peter
SUBJECT: Urgent advice
DATE: 7/22/97

This Dallas photographer business is critical massing; I thought
you said he was no threat. Word to the wise: settle. Between the
Wyndhamville cocktease and the camera smashing, your rep's
tanking in town. Cash-splash the shutterbug and resolve Wylie-
Wyndhamville or by this time next year you'll be trading
blowjobs for infomercials.

Con amore furioso—
P.

P.S. Forget the million per. Kreiss peed laughing.

10 December 1986

My dear Helena—
May this card find you in good health and holiday
cheer—Much change here this year—Part of the estate
sold to a golf course and our duties reduced—Some let
go—General sadness as you can imagine—Other news
Bobby the part-time driver had his eye put out by
something called a fan belt—Otherwise all here is as
you remember—Rest assured you are well missed—

Fondest regards—
Beva

. . . Yes, angel, Milan was a *circus*. Poor Donatella! But these Italian women, you know—it's like tragedy completes them. The wonderful way they rise to the occasion . . . like iron, really. You should have seen her. And the service . . . beautiful! Renews your faith in the old rituals. It really helped me *transcend* my grief and reach a kind of deep, spiritual exaltation . . . oh, and I sat next to Jon Bon Jovi!

Did you hear that Princess Diana was there? My countrywoman. She actually sought me out, such an overwhelming thing to do—no wonder people adore her. Pressed my hand and told me she'd heard about my photographer troubles! I thanked her and said, I shall prevail; she said she hopes I do, she'd enjoy it vicariously. Before she could finish she was pulled away by some ghastly woman with a complexion the exact color of margarine. What a curse to be the most famous woman in the world! I'll settle for being the most infamous. A*haaa*-ha!

Anyway, I'm back, after a *hellish* flight. I couldn't smoke, of course, and I couldn't sleep, either . . . Yes, angel, I *tried* taking melatonin—too many admirers kept coming up to pay their respects. One of the flight attendants even had the cheek to ask if I die before next season. Meaning Grand Duchess Samantha, luv. No, let's not go *there*. Things will work out, you'll see.

Anyway, all the attention was sweet, but it's very awkward to have someone gush praise at you, then plop down in a seat just behind you. You know damned well they'll be watching every move you make for the rest of the flight. I was afraid of nodding off lest I drool on my shoulder or some such. Not even realize it till later when a snapshot turns up on the front page of a tabloid: VIOLA CHUTE'S DRUNKEN AIRPLANE BINGE. I thought it best to stay awake and keep busy. Spent a lot of time shopping from the in-flight catalogs. I bought you something, luv. Hasn't quite arrived yet. I hope I guessed your size right. And that you like plaid.

Anyway, I'm back, and I take it I haven't missed much . . . Hm? . . . Yes, angel, I know—my agent's been calling six times a day. I'll speak with him tonight. Things are *fine*. Just let me worry about that, all right? You do *your* job.

Speaking of which, where were we? . . . I think we left off with *The Bell Jar*, didn't we? God, I do miss *mio caro* Gianni, but how lovely to have his funeral interrupt *that* particular memory. Helps put it all in perspective. Yes, the show was the ruin of all involved, but at least I still had my health. I crawled away from the wreckage and spent some time nursing my wounds . . . What, luv? . . . Oh, no place special. The homes of a few friends. It's really not important, darling. Going underground in Los Angeles doesn't mean you *literally* go into hiding. You just stop working, and you immediately turn invisible. No one notices you, no one asks about you.

Of course, eventually I made it through my disappointment . . . and my checking account a*haaa*-ha . . . so I started sniffing out work again. Excuse me, Harry, *what*? . . . I don't *remember* when. My God, you're a regular Marcia Clark today, aren't you? I told you, it doesn't really matter. I'm not very good with dates anyway. Might've been six months, might've been a year. Anyway, I resurfaced, and got a job on that old game show, *Double Dutch*. Don't ask how . . . oh, never mind, I'll tell you. Very much *off* the record, angel. But I got it the same way I got all my big breaks: fucking the producer. A wonderful man named . . . oh, what was it? Lance, or Linc, something like that.

I don't know if you remember how the show worked. There were two contestants, both of whom had a celebrity partner. Each team was given the name of a movie, or a play, a song, or whatever, only with the syllables jumbled up. Then we were timed on how long it took us to unravel it. For instance, your name, E. Manfred Harry . . . that might come to us as, oh . . .

Freddy Ryman Hare. The first team to unscramble it correctly won the round, and after nine rounds, the winning player went to the jackpot round, where he had to invent double Dutch clues for his celebrity partner to decipher. It was all much more dependent on cleverness and quickness than any of the obtuse cattle roundups that pass for game shows today. I saw one recently where people ran into a room filled with floating money and got to keep whatever they could stuff into their clothes. A contest for people born without any sense of shame.

Anyway, back to my big break. One of the celebrities wasn't working out. Gloria Galen, do you remember her? Major Broadway star in the fifties, had her own talk show in the early sixties. A quick wit and a sharp mind. And she interviewed well, Linc said. Or Lance. But when they got to taping the shows, she fell apart. She just didn't seem to *get* it. The contestants who teamed up with her started complaining, and really, you couldn't blame them.

Finally, it got so bad—in fact, I remember the exact show. The category was song titles, and the clue was "Tis Ogrets Remiss." And Gloria sat and thought, and thought, and thought some more, and finally announced, "Alexander's Ragtime Band." The audience actually howled. Poor thing, it was actually a mercy that they took her off after that. But they needed a replacement, fast, and there I was, backstage and ready. See, I'd sat with Lance—Linc—no, wait! Luke, that was it! —I'd sat in the booth with Luke, time and time again, watching the show, and playing along—coming up with the answers before anyone on the set did. So he knew I could do it. He went to bat for me with the network, and the very next day, there I was, resurrected from oblivion, a "celebrity guest" on *Double Dutch*. And believe me, luv, it'd been so long since *anyone* called me a celebrity, I got a little thrill just hearing them say it. Of course, the other celebrity guest that week was Mickey Winkenbottom, whose only claim to fame was that dreadful Christmas novelty record, so I had to take it with a grain of . . . Hm? . . . Oh, you know the one. *Awful* thing. They dredge it up every December, even now. "Though the weather outside is beaut'ful

/ Let's stay in and do a snootful / And since we've no place to go / let's do blow, let's do blow, let's do blow." It *was* the Eighties, remember.

Anyway, I made quite a hit on *Double Dutch*. I had my patter down perfectly. Someone would give me a clue like, oh . . . Makla Oho. And I'd screw up my face and say, "Isn't she the one who married John Lennon?" And when the laughter died down, I'd pipe up with the answer. Which in this case I'm sure you've already guessed . . .

Oh, Harry, *really*. Oklahoma. It's not *that* hard.

I didn't stay with the show very long. Two months, three . . . I forget exactly. It had served its purpose, got me back in the spotlight, and I was eager to move on to bigger projects. It must have galled Luke a bit, because we'd more or less split up by then. Well, it was only to be expected . . . he was such a workaholic, wasn't he, and there I was, meeting male contestants who were just so *awed* at being near me. One of them actually told me he'd got his first erection watching me in *Passion on the Nile*. When someone tells you something like that, aren't you just *compelled* to sleep with him? Just for the satisfaction of making someone's dream come true? . . . Not *you*, Harry. The question was rhetorical. I've read your novel, remember. I know all about *you* and your hopelessly romantic sexual ethic. You didn't get laid the entire time I was in Milan, did you? . . . Don't bother answering, that was rhetorical, as well.

The irony is, even though I was a big success, I didn't stay with the show very much longer than Gloria Galen. Who, by the way, turned out to have a brain tumor. Died four weeks after her firing . . . Hm? . . . What's that, luv? . . . Oh, the clue she missed? "Tis Ogrets Remiss"? Angel, you *are* a dullard. Think about it . . . Don't just say "I give up," you haven't *thought*. *Think* . . . Harry, you can't *possibly* be so stupid. You're really making me doubt the wisdom of having hired you . . . You really *can't* figure it out? . . . Honestly, if you're any indication, it's no wonder they had to cancel the show. No one sharp enough left to play it.

All right, all right . . . It's the Cole Porter song "Miss Otis Regrets" . . . Yes, it does make sense once you know it. That's the point.

Sorry to be a bitch, luv . . . jet lag catching up with me. Be an angel and show yourself out . . . You *can* figure out how to work the door handle, I suppose . . . ?

DOUBLE DUTCH

A Lucas Schaff Production

October 1, 1982

Ms. Viola Chute
c/o Lionel West Talent, Inc.
9430 Sunset Blvd.
Los Angeles, CA

Dear Ms. Chute:
This letter serves to reiterate our discussion of two days ago, at which time I terminated your engagement with our show.

Our chief grievance is your conduct behind the scenes. We have received numerous complaints from the wives and families of male contestants whom you have apparently lured into compromising situations, as well as complaints from other male contestants regarding your attempts to force your attentions on them. Although these behaviors do not impinge on the actual content of the show, they have caused unsavory rumors to spread. Ours is a family program, and we cannot afford such notoriety.

An ancillary grievance is the increasing bawdiness of your on-air ad libs. We expect and even encourage our celebrity guests to ad lib, and occasional double entendres are not unwelcome. But there is a line that must not be crossed, and you have catapulted over it, time and time again—the most recent incident occurring on September 22, during the jackpot round. Your partner, Ms.

Angela Selvatichezza, was given the film title "Hard-Headed He-roes," which she innocently presented to you as the double Dutch clue, "Ed He Rose Head Hard." As you may recall, your ad lib—"I don't know why, but suddenly my mouth is watering" —so em-barrassed Ms. Selvatichezza that she could not continue play.

I regret that such indiscretions have forced us to take this meas-ure, and wish you luck in your future endeavors.

Sincerely,
Lucas Schaff
Producer

May 30, 1997

Dear Miss Chute,

I don't know if you remember me your fan in Illuggan! Yes
where you grew up! I wrote you a letter earlier this month but
I have not had a reply and I was wondering if it got to you! I
have been watching the mail every day because even though
you must get a lot of fan mail I am sure that a letter from
someone in your old home town would be very meaningful to
you, but I have not yet received a reply!

I have seen two more episodes of "The Winds of
Wyndhamville" and taped them for my collection as well just
because of you, you are brilliant in it! But I don't know if you
are even reading this I hope you are!

My invitation still stands that is the one to return to Illuggan,
you are our most famous daughter and it would be so brilliant!
I would make all the arrangements myself you wouldn't have
to do anything! And please do not think I am some kind of
freak you would not be embarrassed to be seen with me I am
an aspiring actor as I mentioned before and am considered
quite good-looking and have many friends! I am enclosing one
of my head shots just in case you don't believe me!

I have the utmost respect for you Miss Chute please respond
even if it is just to say no thank you!

Your number one admirer,
Andy Trebliss

THE GLENDA WORTH GALLERY
AND
IMPERIAL VODKA
CORDIALLY INVITE YOU TO
A PHOTOGRAPHY EXHIBIT
AND BENEFIT CONCERT
IN AID OF

THE BERRY LEYTON DEFENSE FUND

■

JULY 29, 1997
7:30 P.M.
THE GLENDA WORTH GALLERY
1001 N. HILLDALE
WEST HOLLYWOOD

SCHEDULED PERFORMERS INCLUDE
ANGELS ON TOAST
AUGIE BASTIAN
POWERS THAT B
ROADKILL
SHAWNA TATUM

ADMISSION $75 PER PERSON
CASH BAR AND HORS D'OEUVRES

7/26/97, 7:33 P.M.

You have reached the law offices of Gretchen Ojan. Our hours are Monday through Friday, eight-thirty a.m. to six-thirty p.m. After the tone, you may leave a message for Ms. Ojan or her assistant, Kevin Putnam. Thank you.

It's Viola, luv. Just wanted to say how much I wish I'd trusted my instincts instead of letting you talk me into a fucking countersuit. As long as that oleaginous little shitheel was suing me, I could reasonably claim to be the victim. Now that *I'm* suing *him,* he's milking it for all he's worth. I have in my hands an invitation to a *benefit* for the bloody little cretin. He's gone and set up a *defense* fund. And gotten *corporate sponsorship,* thank you very much. Not to mention a gallery to show, and presumably sell, his grainy little snapshots. Is this what you meant when you said a countersuit would scare him into going away? Just asking, luv. Because my idea of him going away is just a bit different, hm?

I want the countersuit dropped, *tomorrow.* I know the little bastard will claim it as a victory, and it'll look bad for me in the short term, but I think we've got to cut our losses. Sticking with it obviously won't do anything but help him get more and more publicity. And money.

And angel, remember, this entire mess simply *must* be cleared up by August eighteenth, when the show starts filming again. It's true I haven't re-signed for the season yet, but I mean to. And nothing's going to stop me going before the cameras. Certainly not some opportunistic little slug with a broken camera.

I'm still at the Pierre. *Call* me.

SUBJ: confusion reigns
DATE: 97-7-26 15:10 EST
FROM: emanfr@ysa.net
TO: nbcasem@bot.ubsm.edu

things have really got out of hand here. 1st of all i got absolutely
nowhere tracking chester viscount killwall. used every major search
engine—the only mentions of him were in lists of other nobles or
whatever he is in genealogical surveys. what a complete waste of
time. i even went retro—actually went to the goddamn library how
very 19th century i know. so i'm left wondering more than ever what
the hell he has to do with viola chute and whether it's anything to do
with her missing years.

she came home from italy yesterday btw acting like the queen of
fucking sheba after swanning around with so many celebs. however
we did get back to her dictation and she talked about making her 1st
comeback on the old game show double dutch which gave me an
idea. tracked down the producer luke schaff—he's in l.a. still in the
business only now producing infomercials. got him on the horn and
asked about viola and he said oh you mean eva peron. i said what do
you mean he said the bitch used me to get her mug on tv again then
dumped me like a sack of dirty laundry. said he ended up firing her
because she was such a slut she couldn't keep her hands off the contestants which is of course not quite the story i got from viola.

anyway i asked him what viola was doing just before he met her. said
he has no idea but she was living in an efficiency apartment with
clothes hanging all over and a smell of rotten eggs. pretty much abject poverty. he took pity on her and she was still beautiful and willing to do just about anything so what the hell they started screwing
and pretty soon they were an item. i asked whether she ever said
anything about how she got so low or what she'd been doing before

they met and he said no. she never talked about her past except the remote past when she was a b movie queen. also she never mentioned anyone named chester viscount killwall. he said maybe her agent would know some of this and i said peter grace and he said no he never heard of peter grace. he said lionel west that's who represented her at the time. so i tracked down lionel west but alas he's dead. i'm trying to find if he left behind someone who might know something. just on the off chance.

so all this detective work gave me the idea of contacting viola's daughter. patricia hume who was adopted by viola's 3rd husband corrigan hume and stayed with him after the divorce. i think corrigan hume is dead now but i put in a few calls to patricia and am waiting to hear back. don't know what her exact relationship with her mother is these days but i'll bet not so rosy. maybe she'll be willing to talk.

sorry to hear about your setback. who can ever predict what weird stuff nature has in store for us. in any case don't worry i'm sure your doctor's right the toenails will grow back.

smoochfest
harry

"FOR THE MAN WITH THE CAMERA"
performed by Powers That B
Glenda Worth Gallery benefit concert
7/29/97

You see 'em in the paper see 'em posin' for the pi'tches
The models and the 'hos and the million-dollar bitches
You lust without hope
You know it ain't dope
But to do without 'em do without 'em
Never gonna happen!

The man with the camera gonna keep 'em in your eye
That's the way they want it, gotta keep you satisfy
So yeah it ain't right
For bitches to fight
They made a deal made a deal
Now they gotta put out!

Queen shit of TV think she got it goin' on
Slam the man with the camera, whale on 'im good and gone
The lady gotta learn
Or else she gonna burn
She started it she started it
But she ain't gonna finish
Say she started it she started it
But bitch ain't gonna finish!

BERRY LEYTON'S REMARKS
Glenda Worth Gallery benefit concert
7/29/97

I'd just like to thank all of you so much for everything you've done for me tonight. I'd like to thank Glenda Worth for showing my stuff and for being such a great new friend and supporter. I'd like to thank Imperial Vodka for putting up the funds for this event, it's great to see a corporation with a social conscience, let's hear it for them. I'd like to thank the artists who performed tonight, Angels on Toast, Howie Bastian, Powers That B, Roadkill, Shawna Tatum. If you weren't all my favorites before, you are now . . . Hm? . . . What? . . . Oh hell, I'm sorry—*Augie* Bastian. What can I say, there's a reason I take their pictures instead of writing their copy.

Anyway, I'd also like to thank *AmeriScene* magazine for publishing my story and getting me all this attention in the first place. And I'd like to thank my lawyer, Powers Keenlyside, for everything he's done—which covers a lot of ground. Most of all I'd like to thank my kids, Rosie, Michael, and Anita, for standing by their old man at a difficult time.

The reason I'm thanking you all is not just because you've come out to help me tonight but because you've succeeded. I'm happy to report that just before tonight's event I got word that Viola Chute has dropped her countersuit against me. Which is a complete vindication and a victory and I hope you'll all give yourself a well-deserved round of applause.

If I can keep you just a moment longer, I'd like to say that I hope, in the end, that this isn't just about me. That maybe what we've done here tonight is show the world that fame and fortune don't put people above the law, or even above the common decencies that civilized people are compelled to show one another. Maybe what we've done tonight is taken a first strike against arrogance and hostility and inhumanity, and if that's the case, then we've all done our best to make the world a better place.

Thank you again, and God bless every one of you.

"The night is bitter, the stars have lost their glitter . . . and all because of the call that got awaaay . . ." Hi, this is E. Manfred Harry. Don't hang up and leave me wailing in despair. Leave your name and number after the tone and I'll get back to you.

Yes . . . Mr. Harry. This is Patricia Hume. I . . . I'm sorry, I really just hate cute answering machines. They set my teeth on edge.

Anyway, I'm calling in response to the numerous messages you've left on my own machine. I would've thought my ignoring the first several would have been an indication of my unwillingness to discuss my mother, with you or anyone, but apparently you're the persevering sort. So let me just lay it on the line for you: I am not on good terms with my mother. I do not approve of the way she's lived her life, or the way she's living it now. I cannot forgive her treatment of my father, or of me. As far as I'm concerned, she is a troubled woman more to be pitied than admired, but her capacity for harming the lives of those around her forces me to keep her at arm's length. I hope I am making myself perfectly clear, here.

However, I will answer *one* of your questions, in the hope that it will prove sufficient to keep you from calling me any further: I do not recall ever having heard my mother, or anyone connected with her, mention a Viscount Killwall, or a viscount of any other name. I hope this is enough to satisfy you, because I really have no intention of providing anything more.

Goodbye.

. . . And speaking of where-are-they-now?, your reporter has tracked down an old favorite of these pages and found her well into a long-run engagement in an exciting new part. Yes, *Viola Chute,* the vixenish star of such pop culture landmarks as *Passion on the Nile* and *The Private Life of Agrippina,* has found contentment in the role of loving wife and doting mother. Married these seven months to home-spa entrepreneur *Michael Winger,* vivacious Viola just gave birth to her first child (whoops! Either the bundle of joy was born prematurely, or *someone* was too eager to wait for the wedding night). Christened Patricia, the new addition to the Winger family has her parents utterly besotted. Daddy reportedly has put ASV SpaTonics on the block (don't bother counting your pocket change—he's asking $140 million), just so he can spend more time with his adorable new heir. As for the baby's camera-seasoned mother, rumor has it she's already thinking of a career for her bundle of joy—or rather, a dual career, as versatile Viola shops around for mother-daughter modeling opportunities. Not that she needs the money: "It's just that Patricia's so beautiful, she belongs in the public eye. And, well, I've kept myself in shape, so why not use my name and fame to help her to a good start?" Why not, indeed? Any takers, Madison Avenue? . . .

1406 Hayworth
West Hollywood, CA 90046

July 30, 1997

Dear Mr. Harry:

The executor of my father's estate forwarded me your
query regarding the career of Viola Chute. (My father
being Lionel West, by the way; you might need to be told
that because unlike Dad I use the real family name.)

Dad represented Viola from 1982 to 1987, as far as I can
tell, and he inherited a lot of her paperwork etc. from
before that. (Apparently she went through a lot of agents
in her time.) Since I am kind of an amateur sleuth I
searched my father's files for you since most of them are
still in storage where I put them when he died.

You mention you are looking for unknown materials that
might help fill in some blanks for your biography of
Viola. I don't know exactly what you are looking for but I
found a reel-to-reel tape in an envelope that Dad had
marked "Viola Chute—copy not to be made public." And
underneath that he wrote in big letters: "INSURANCE."
That was my Dad's code word for anything he had that
could ruin one of his clients' careers—it meant it was his
"insurance" that they didn't dare screw him in their
business dealings. I don't know what this tape contains—
I don't have a reel-to-reel player—but if it's marked

"INSURANCE" it is absolutely something Viola Chute
would never want made public.

If you would like to arrange to purchase this tape please
give me a call at (213) 555-1126. I would be glad to
discuss it.

Sincerely,
Neal Westheimer

NEW YORK
7/31/97, 9:40 A.M.

—idn't know you'd be here quite so *horrifically* early, angel.
You might have called first . . . No, no, you're here now, let's
just get on with it. Although I really must say—not that I owe
you any explanation, luv, but just so you don't go getting the
wrong idea—Mr. . . . uh, Mr. Duncan and I are *not* involved in
any kind of romantic . . . oh, don't look at me that way. He's
got to be a hundred years old. He's an old family friend, he
asked if he could come by to say hello. He just turned up even
earlier than you, that's all. In fact, I've changed my mind, I'm
glad you came by and scared him off. He's an old dear, but a
bigger bore was never born. . . .

Anyway, where are we? I can scarcely . . . No, I'm all right,
angel . . . Pale! . . . Well, it's been . . . I mean, I only just returned from Italy a few days ago, and . . . you know, I still
haven't really gotten over *caro* Gianni's murder. Awful shock . . .
All right, yes, now that you mention it, I am under a bit of
stress, too. You know I haven't yet signed for next season,
and . . . actually, Harry, I'd love it if I had just *someone* I could
unburden myself to. You're sure you don't mind? . . . Only I'm
at wit's end, and in my position, there are so few people one
can trust . . . Yes, angel, I know, I know I can trust you.
Haven't I already? All the juicy details of my infamous life and
times? . . .

The problem is, I haven't signed yet, and it's just over three
weeks till shooting begins. That means even now, scripts are
being written. Now, I can *hope* that they're being written with
Grand Duchess Samantha in them, but I can hardly ask, can I?
I mean, I don't want to show that I'm interested. For all the
producers know, I'm this close to getting my own series . . .
Yes, *The Sultans of South Beach,* clever of you to recall . . . Ex-

cuse me, angel . . . Oh, no, I don't really want to *take* the offer. I'm already in a hit series, why would I give that up for the risk of starting a new one? Especially since, as the star—well, if it failed, guess who'd be blamed. No, I'm just using *South Beach* as a bluff to improve my *Wyndhamville* contract, and it's got down to this excruciating waiting game, seeing who's going to give first. I'm good at many, many things, angel, but waiting ain't one of 'em. A*haaa*-ha.

So really, Harry, do excuse me if I'm a little distracted these days . . . I mean, all of that worry, on top of being away from my home, and my Mina and Sedgwick . . . oh, I *miss* my girls, Harry, I worry constantly about whether they're eating and getting enough exercise, and . . . Hm? . . . Oh, Harry. No. No, no, no. I am *not* also worried about that ridiculous photographer and his crybaby lawsuit. Naturally, it's irksome, but only the way a . . . a *mosquito* is irksome. Or a housefly. Any insect, you fill in the blank.

Angel, you're a true friend to let me spew all this into your lap. It's true, you know, I feel worlds better now, just getting it off my chest. Thank you so much. If there's anything I can ever do for you . . . Oh, Harry, stop. I haven't done a *thing* for you . . . Nonsense, I didn't *give* you this opportunity, you earned it. Now, stop, I mean it. You're embarrassing me.

Shouldn't we get down to business? . . . Help yourself to coffee, there's plenty left. Ches— Mr. Duncan never even touched his. Where were we, anyway? . . . *Double Dutch,* wasn't it? I think I've said all there is to say on *that* particular episode. And afterwards . . . hm, I think that's when I began experimenting with serial monogamy. Don't put it like that in the book, luv. But I sort of walked into marriage with Michael and then with Corgie . . . and after them there was Dennis Lawley . . .

Sorry, I'm rushing through all of this. But honestly, I have to say, the memories . . . they just aren't *there,* the way they are for the career bits. Maybe you can just make up some details. You're a novelist, use your imagination . . . Oh, don't worry about it. No one'll know. Michael's dead, Corgie's dead . . .

and God knows, Dennis is a nobody these days . . . I don't even know where he is, actually. If I'd only married him, I'd at least have the return address on his alimony checks. A*haaa*-ha!

The truth is, angel . . . and I'm confiding in you again, here . . . the only reason I ever bothered getting married again, after my initial fiasco with Regnal Chute, was that my career was over. There was nothing else I *could* do. *Double Dutch* had been a first step back into the business, but I overestimated what it could do for me. Try as I might, I wasn't able to translate my exposure there into any bigger projects. And, worse, I couldn't count on any similar breaks coming anytime soon, could I? . . .

So it was really a survival thing. I had no career, no prospects, no money . . . and along came this fabulously wealthy businessman who wanted to marry me and take care of me, so of course I said yes. The alternative being, well . . . I couldn't imagine. I literally couldn't envision any life for myself outside of the industry. Michael obviously could. So I found myself living in his house and sitting on his furniture and sleeping in his bed and bearing his daughter and it all felt like a dream. And then he died, and *another* fabulously wealthy businessman came along, and he wanted to marry me and take care of me, too. So again I said yes. Why, I'm still not sure; I had quite a bit of money by then, thanks to darling Michael's will . . . I suppose, by that point, I'd just lost so much confidence that I didn't know how to live my life anymore. I was just paralyzed; the future seemed an unfathomable blur. Also, I had this child hanging off my hip, and I sure as *hell* didn't know what to do with *her*. So Corgie proposed, and I said yes. And the dream continued for a little while . . .

I mean, there were times, during both marriages, when I tried to find my way back into the public eye, but for all my thrashing it never worked, and I just sunk down again into all that domestic torpor. It was . . . it was like it all happened to someone else . . . Give me a moment, luv. I'm trying to piece it all back together. I haven't lived the most examined life, you know—always too busy moving ahead to look back—and some of these events I haven't thought about in *years* . . .

I suppose, if I'm honest . . . none of this is for the book, re-member, angel; you're *making up* details for the book—and don't give me that look; I'm the one who's paying. But just be-tween us—just so you know . . . my God, you've really caught me in a chattering mood, today, luv! . . . the thing that brought me out of my funk and really propelled me back into the world—and by that I mean the business, the industry—*Holly-wood*, angel—was my daughter, Patricia. She grew up, you see. And she turned into such a . . . oh, Harry, she's my child. I don't want to say these things about her. But she turned into such a . . . bitter, judgmental . . . joyless . . .

No, I'm all right. Thank you; so sweet. I've got my own handkerchief. And besides, I don't cry . . . but do you under-stand what I'm saying, here? Patricia became, in a way, my ri-val. Corgie was really the only father she'd ever known—she was just a baby when Michael died—and she . . . well, she *stole* him from me. She turned that withering, damning gaze on me, and somehow she got Corgie to see me that way, too . . . and I couldn't help it, the two of them looking at me with such contempt and . . . and condescension, it just drove me to continue doing whatever it was that I'd . . . that I'd . . .

Oh, this is silly, dredging all this up, I'm not going on with it! Making a mess of my face and everything; I must look a fright! . . . Of course I do, angel, but thank you anyway for saying so . . . And it's all irrelevant, anyway—what mother *doesn't* have tensions with her daughter? And it's not like we never made it up . . . Yes, luv, of *course* we did. I wouldn't lie about something so close to my heart, would I? It was at Corgie's funeral. He died just two years ago, you know . . . Well, seeing him lying there in the casket, Patricia and I sud-denly realized we had nothing to fight about anymore, and how much time we'd lost . . . and we just hugged and cried. And she said, Mother, darling, do you think we can start over? And I of course said, My sweet pet, I think we already have . . .

And it's been that way with us ever since. We're just as close as
. . . well, mother and daughter. Although I don't get to see
much of her, now that she's away at school . . . But I'm *wildly*
proud of her . . .

Still, angel, *would* you mind if we stopped now? . . . I really
hadn't counted on delving so deep. I think I actually upset myself there, for a moment . . . Oh, thank you, Harry. So good
and true. I mean it, you really are. You're my rock . . . Here,
take my AmEx. I insist. It's not even lunchtime, the whole of
Manhattan is out there waiting. You go and have a good time
on poor vulnerable Viola. I'm just going to shutter up here for
a while and finish pulling myself together. *Quelle* drama
queen, hm? Isn't that what you're thinking? . . . Oh, Harry,
you *are* a scoundrel. *Go* . . .

VIOLA'S REMARKS AT CORRIGAN HUME'S FUNERAL
December 3, 1995

Good afternoon, ladies and gentlemen. I wasn't scheduled to speak today, but I . . . and I know some of you must be very surprised to see me here, considering that Corgie was very much my *ex*-husband. But I couldn't stay away when I heard of his passing, and now that I'm here, I'm moved by the show of love and affection by so many of our old friends. And it brings back to me what I've always known and simply allowed myself to forget: Corrigan Hume was a *good* man. He was a friend to me when I needed one, he took care of me . . . he took care of my darling baby daughter, Patricia, who was only . . . I forget how old. Not quite an infant . . . Darling, don't look at me that way, it's *true*. I was still breast-feeding you . . . What? . . . *Four?* You couldn't have been that old, could you? . . . Well, never mind. Whatever age you were, Corrigan Hume was our rescuer, our knight in shining armor, and it's in tribute to him that I . . . that I . . . Angel, please, I'm sure I'm not embarrassing anyone. These are all old friends of your father and me. If you'll just let me finish . . . I didn't *need* to be invited, your father and I were marr— Darling, just sit *down* . . . Ladies and gentlemen, Corrigan Hume and I were man and wife for almo— All right, young lady, that's quite enough. I haven't had a *thing* to drink. How dare you make such an accu— No, I think if anyone's causing embarrassment here, it's y— Patricia! Patricia, come back here! I mean it! . . . Oh, yes, hit and run, that's *so* like her! Fine, then, fine! I've got nothing else to say. Everyone can stop averting their eyes now, the family row is over, the gorgon is leaving. Carry on, Reverend . . .

. . . I said *carry* ON!

13 December 1987

My dear Helena—
May this card find you in the best of health and
happiness—The past year not so happy for me—
shingles—at my age no laughing matter—also not much
reason to recover what with the reduction in the estate—
also the master away so often and you know how it is
then—"when the cat's away"—Mustn't complain, healthy
now and given lesser duties mainly sewing—I know
you're saying what with her arthritis—but I'm allowed to
work at my own pace so never mind—What a lot of
moaning shame on me—Do you remember Penny the
chambermaid who was always so popular with the village
boys—Well she married a Moslem so she can never get
divorced—Never too old to enjoy life's ironies—There I
ended on a happy note—

Fondest wishes—
Beva

NEW CAST MEMBER FOR *WYNDHAMVILLE*
The Week in Entertainment
August 2, 1997

Angie Ashe-Tippett has signed on for twelve episodes of UBN's successful prime-time serial *The Winds of Wyndhamville,* starting with the season premiere, which begins shooting August 18. Ashe-Tippett scored a hit during the show's previous season as Sieglinde the She-Wolf, a neo-Nazi villainess, but it's unclear whether this will be the role in which she returns to the series.

"Angie is a hugely talented actress," says executive producer Franco Kreiss, "so we're examining some options. If she does come back as Sieglinde, we'll have to reconfigure the character"—no doubt to erase the neo-Nazi affiliation.

Kreiss refused to confirm a report that one of the alternate roles being considered for Ashe-Tippett is Grand Duchess Samantha, another character introduced last season. The role proved a comeback vehicle for former B-movie queen Viola Chute, who will not be returning to the series due to a contract dispute (the actress had demanded $1 million per episode). The producers are reluctant, however, to drop the popular Samantha character altogether, and although Ashe-Tippett is more than two decades younger than Chute, there is apparently talk of her taking over the part.

Ashe-Tippett's previous credits include a recurring role on the daytime drama *Hearts Crossing,* as well as featured appearances on *Breadside Manor, Popsy Dibble, Whatsamatta U.* and *Flyguyz.* Her film credits include *Ragin' Cajun, Elsewhen* and *Silver Bells and Cockle Shells.* By coincidence, her debut in 1988 was as the adolescent daughter of *Wyndhamville* star Georgia Kirkby in the People's Choice Award–winning drama, *Sea Change*. Kirkby is delighted to be working with Ashe-Tippett again: "She was bright and filled with promise when I first met her, and now, as an adult, she has realized so much of that promise. Her beauty, professionalism, and marvelous talent are going to serve our show remarkably well."

FAX MEMO TO: Viola
FROM: Peter
SUBJECT: Ashe-Tippett
DATE: 8/2/97

Bad luck about the bimbo. If Wylie's a bluff, Kreiss and Asher have called it. This ain't no party, this ain't no disco: swallow the 650 Gs they left on the table or ink a deal for *South Beach,* but do one or the other and do it last week. Any more ass-dragging and by the end of the millennium your marquee value will be confined to Trivial Pursuit cards. Also: I am your agent. It's customary to advise your agent as to the state of your affairs. One hates to roadblock the conga line that is Viola but would you kindly the fuck reach out and touch-tone.

Con amore furioso—
P.

...BUT A FREE MAN FIRST
My Journey Through American Government
by Dennis Lawley

CHAPTER 23

After the smoking ruin of the '92 elections, I experienced what I can only call an existential crisis. I had cut my cloth to suit the fashion of my party, and I had done so solely to get re-elected. I had, in the vulgar parlance of the day, "sold out." And I had nothing to show for it. Having suffered a landslide defeat against an opponent I had relentlessly smeared as a "tax-and-spend liberal," I was left with neither the office I had sought so desperately, nor the integrity I had sacrificed to get it. I was forced to reexamine not only my association with the Republican Party, but the very fabric of my own political consciousness.

I decided that there were two factors to my defeat: one political, one personal. The political was, of course, my adherence to platform politics. The 1992 Republican convention had disgusted the nation with its harshness, its shrillness, and its indemnification of the unfortunate.

Yet equally ruinous was my second, personal weakness. Although this weakness was also my greatest strength.

When I first met Viola Chute, I had no idea who she was; as the son of Calvinist parents, I did not frequent movie houses when I was young. Nor, as someone without interest in gossip columns, was I aware of the more sensational episodes in Viola's past. But I like to think that if I had known of them, I would still have been man enough to fall in love with her, propose marriage to her, and present her to the people of Minnesota as the woman I would take back with me to Washington. Viola herself, while not possessing a single political bone in her body, believed in me utterly, and not only adhered to every ridiculous, condescending and insulting dictate of my campaign staff (which involved wholesale changes to her hair, makeup and wardrobe, and at one point subjected her to the indignity of making pancakes for a church group), she supported me financially, as well. I would not have been able to continue my run for reelection to its admittedly disappointing conclusion had it not been for the continuing and unquestioning generosity of Viola Chute, my greatest supporter and friend.

In return, she was maligned by the media at every turn, and made to seem a virtual dragon lady whose very presence undermined my campaign. This was extremely painful to me. Likewise, after the election, when I suffered my aforementioned existential crisis, and began the long, painful, and necessarily inward-directed transformation from disaffected Republican to born-again Libertarian, I had no energy left for this wonderful, loving, all-giving woman; and so she left me. Again, she was portrayed in the press as a publicity-seeker who, denied the role of Senator's wife, abandoned the luckless candidate whom she'd chosen to provide it. Nothing could be further from the truth. And no casualty of my disastrous run for Congress in 1992 is more painful to me than my relationship with Viola Chute. She has recently gone on to great successes of her own. Let the record be set straight: she deserves them.

INTERVIEW WITH VIOLA CHUTE

by E. Manfred Harry

(Excerpt)

Homophile, July 1993

HOMOPHILE: In re-watching so many of your films in preparation for this interview, one thing I found interesting was that while you usually appear in some degree of undress, you never, to my knowledge, actually appear nude.

VIOLA: No, angel, I never did that.

HOMOPHILE: Is there a reason?

VIOLA: Oh, I know I'm supposed to have some wildly interesting answer, like . . . oh, my integrity as an actress, or a really big mole somewhere inconvenient. But the truth of it is more prosaic: I just didn't want to.

HOMOPHILE: Would it be fair to say that you were willing to give a lot to your audience, but not everything?

VIOLA: I suppose you could put it that way. It just seemed to me—still does, actually—that partial nudity is more interesting. It sort of entices you, in a way that complete nudity doesn't. I mean, think about it: you see a naked woman seated on a stool. That's all she is, a naked woman on a stool. But think of a woman on a stool wearing nothing but a skirt and high heels. Now, you've got the makings of a story . . . a fantasy. Do you see what I mean?

HOMOPHILE: I think so. You see her in the skirt and heels and you think, Why just that? . . . Have we caught her dressing, or undressing? . . . What's she like under that skirt? . . .

VIOLA: Exactly, angel. Bravo.

HOMOPHILE: I suppose that's why so many fashion designers are gay men. It's one of the only ways we *can* find women enticing. By taking them naked and dressing them.

VIOLA: Interesting. I hadn't thought about that.

HOMOPHILE: So you've never posed in the nude, even for photographs?

VIOLA: No, no. I made a point of it. And if you think I'm lying, think of this: when I was Senator Lawley's fiancee, his opponent dug up everything he could to use against him, including all sorts of wicked pickies of me—topless and bare-ass and what have you. Surely if he'd found any actual nudes, he'd have used them.

HOMOPHILE: I only ask the question because it surprises me. You're commonly held to be one of the great screen sex symbols, so it seems odd you've never done nude scenes.

VIOLA: Well, thank you for that rather inflated compliment, which I graciously accept. *(laughs)* But I think it may be the reason *why* I'm still thought to be a sex symbol at my advanced age. I mean, it's all about teasing, isn't it? . . . A woman drops her knickers and shows you the whole kit and caboodle, well—you've seen her, haven't you? She can't ever again give you the thrill of that first illicit gander. But a woman who runs around in a sheer teddy and lace panties can keep you interested for twenty-five years. I know, angel. I've done it. And I'm still doing it. Believe me, if I were to go nude tomorrow, the shoe would drop. My career would be over like that. I'd have ended the tease, you see. And the tease is all I've got.

P.O. Box 339398
Beverly Hills, CA 90212
August 3, 1997

Mr. E. Manfred Harry
c/o The Pierre Hotel
New York, New York

Dear Mr. Harry:

I have learned through a friend that you are researching a
biography of the actress Viola Chute. I have in my possession
a series of nude photographs of Ms. Chute that I would like to
sell. I prefer to remain anonymous and do not wish to explain
how I came into possession of these photographs. But given
Ms. Chute's recent notoriety I wonder if you might help me
find a buyer. I am asking five thousand dollars. Believe me Mr.
Harry they are WORTH IT!!

You may contact me via my post office box listed above.

Sincerely,
A Collector

SUBJ: ai yi yi
DATE: 97-8-5 07:01:03 EST
FROM: emanfr@ysa.net
TO: nbcasem@bot.ubsm.edu

so much to tell. things really heating up!!

1st i actually caught viola out at something. last week i had a morning appt with her to go over some notes but i deliberately showed up
40 minutes early. take a wild guess what i found. she was entertaining
chester viscount killwall!! yes yes yes!! she must've thought i was room
service or something because she just opened the door without
even asking who is it and when she saw me her face went completely
ashen. because killwall was right behind her and even though he's a
wee little gnome it's not as though i couldn't see him there. plus she
was just finishing a sentence when she opened the door and though
i didn't catch what she was saying she doesn't know that. i turned on
my tape recorder as soon as i could but it was too late. next time i
go to her suite you better believe i'll have it running from the get go.
anyway viola got all nervous and hustled him out and pretended to
me that he was just an old family friend who'd stopped by to see her.
called him mr duncan which is a name right out of macbeth—does
she think i'm stupid or what. anyway i got a look at the little weasel's
face as he was leaving and it was one of pure malevolence. this is her
blackmailer i'm sure sure sure of it.

the next thing that happened was that viola tried desperately to dis-
tract me from thinking about him. and since she is one of the great
liars ever to walk the face of the earth the only thing she could turn
to to accomplish this was—drumroll please—the truth. so she started
telling me about her married life with corrigan hume and her difficulties with her daughter and she actually wound up really upsetting her-

self. i especially liked the way she said she never cried while tears were running down her face. as soon as she realized how far she'd gone she started backpedalling—spewing all this bullshit about how gooey the mother-daughter duo is today. despite this i did get a momentary glimpse at the genuine viola and i'm sure she's regretting letting me have it—because it doesn't quite fit the hard-as-nails party-girl image she likes to convey. instead she comes across as someone very vulnerable with almost no inner life at all who sort of wilts when a spotlight isn't on her. kind of pathetic and sympathetic at the same time.

speaking of the daughter we've been exchanging voice mails—which is how i knew viola's sappy story was pure bullshit. this kid just downright loathes her mother. still i have to tell you i gotta side with viola on this one. i know the kid's just a student and you know how some adolescent girls are—little humorless militant the-world-is-a-terrible-place types. well maybe she'll grow out of it but in the meantime sheesh what a bitch. and there's no excuse for a kid that age to use this lofty tone like she's madeline albright or something. anyway she refused to help me so screw her.

i also talked to viola's old fiance dennis lawley the minnesota senator she met just before he ran for reelection. i thought he'd be a nutcase because he's connected to some anti-government think tank in florida that does things like issue press releases about how there should be no speed limits. but he was really a great guy bright funny and he spoke about viola with more tenderness than you'd ever imagine. really still carries a torch. he talks about her in the most glowing terms and takes total blame for their breakup. i'm wondering now whether this was the big one the love of viola's life that she'll never get over. probably not—probably they all started like this then went downhill fast and this one just never got a chance to run its course. but the fact is it sounds like she sacrificed a lot for this guy and i have to wonder about that. it'll be interesting to hear her version of events which should be the next thing we cover in our taping sessions because that's exactly where we are chronologically.

but it's getting harder and harder to get viola to actually sit down for a session what with her whole life apparently falling apart. she dropped her countersuit against that photographer so right now she's looking very much the loser in that arena. lots of jokes in the press and on tv at her expense which she can't stand at all—sends her into screaming rages. plus the photog's pressing ahead with his suit against her and it's going to interfere with the wyndhamville shooting schedule. i don't know why she keeps raving about that because for all practical purposes the show has dropped her. they got some actress about 25 years younger to take her place and maybe even play her role. you don't even wanna know what she was like the day she heard about that. i think she could have exploded half of manhattan with her brain waves if she focused hard enough. even her agent is telling her to give it up and instead take on the new series about miami but viola keeps insisting she can work things out with wyndhamville—even though she's still asking a cool mill per episode and they won't even consider it.

plus there's a few new wrinkles viola doesn't even know about yet. 1st i got in touch with the son of her old agent who has a tape recording of viola that apparently contains something very shocking that viola wanted suppressed. i can't imagine what it could be but i'm willing to bet it's got something to do with the blackmail business. unfortunately the guy wants 500 bucks for it and i just don't have that kind of money. boy did he see me coming. i gotta remember not to come off so eager in my initial approaches to these people.

which incidentally is how i'm playing it with another guy who wrote me peddling nude pictures of her. i don't know when they were taken or by whom or how graphic they are. but he heard i was doing her bio—obviously he doesn't realize i'm just her ghostwriter—and is offering me a chance to buy them. ridiculous amount of money—5000 bucks. still my god i'm curious. i keep wondering if maybe this guy is secretly killwall and these pictures are what he's been using to blackmail her—after all she's always insisted on never doing nude scenes. but if so why is he offering them up now when i know for a fact he's still negotiating with her? questions questions questions. maybe it's not killwall after all. but if not then who told this guy about me anyway. patricia hume? dennis lawley? both unlikely. must be someone i've talked to along the way though.

i get the feeling i'm not the only one this guy contacted either. the only comfort here is that even if he finds a buyer tomorrow it will be months before the photos see print because of magazines' long lead time. the one thing viola does not need right now is the extra dose of bad news added into the rest. she's already acting about as crazy as a rat in a coffee tin—bursts into incredible rants at the drop of a hat even in public. i told her if she doesn't get a grip she's going to queer the miami beach deal. you don't even wanna know what she said to me in reply.

at least no one but me knows about the tape recording. got to figure a way of getting hold of that.

anyway glad you're getting better. i never would've guessed that toenails growing back would cause such itching. resist resist resist!

smooch upon smooch
harry

...Kudos to celeb photog **Berry Leyton** on snapping up a primo comeback op! The injured shutterbug, currently suing *Winds of Wyndhamville* star **Viola Chute** to the tune of ten million, was just hired by startlin' starlet **Angie Ashe-Tippett** for a series of tasteful nude studies to be featured in the pages of upwardly mobile men's mag *Burnish*. "Angie's a real lady," sez Leyton. "She's helped me out tremendously by hiring me. My legal expenses are, as you can imagine, out of this world." Ms. A-T is apparently willing to endure the longer-than-usual sessions necessitated by the impaired vision Leyton has suffered since Chute's alleged assault. "I honestly don't mind," the serene blonde beauty says, smiling; "Berry makes me feel very relaxed. He can take as long as he wants." Leyton professes no performance anxiety: "These are essentially still lifes. I have way more control than I'm used to" —a reference to his late career as a frenetic, on-the-run paparazzo. As for the fact that Ashe-Tippett is replacing Viola Chute in *Wyndhamville* this season—Leyton calls that "a mere coincidence, but not an unhappy one." Look for the cheesecake shots in the October *Burnish* ...

EMMY-WINNING PRODUCER DIES

Los Angeles Times
August 8, 1997

Television producer Alex Wylie, 61, died late Thursday in New York City of what appears to be a massive heart attack.

Wylie, a four-time Emmy Award winner for such series as *Dixie & Dorrie, Las Vegas Legionnaires,*and *Jillian for Julian,* was reportedly in Manhattan to sign the actress Viola Chute to a new project he was developing for the independent Eureka network. Wylie and Chute were seen dining at Le Cirque 2000 earlier Thursday evening, and it was Chute's emergency phone call that brought an ambulance to the Paramount Hotel, where Wylie had been staying, at 2:30 A.M. He was pronounced dead on arrival at Mount Sinai Hospital thirty minutes later.

At press time, Chute was unavailable for comment.

Wylie is survived by his wife, Jerri, and three children, Ramona, 25, Alex Jr., 23, and Cheryl, 7.

8/11/97, 1:48 P.M.

You have reached the office of Peter Grace. No one is available to take your call. After the tone, please leave your name, the time of day, a number where you can be reached, and a detailed message. Thank you.

Well, of course, it's just Viola again, leaving her one thousandth message since this morning. Angel, I've been trying to reach you for two days now. Things an absolute shambles—you can't not know of it. Alex dead . . . I'm still in shock. One moment he was fine, laughing; the next . . .

Peter, luv, I'm in *desperate* need of your cool head. I don't dare leave my hotel room, the press are like wolves at the door. I'm frightened and I need your sage advice. Please, please, *please* ring me back.

I hope you're satisfied. There aren't many men in the world who can say they've reduced Viola Chute to begging. Usually it's the other way around.

I'm still at the Pierre. But then you know tha—

You have reached the office of Peter Grace. No one is available to take your call. After the tone, please leave your name, the time of day, a number where you can be reached, and a detailed message. Thank you.

Damn it, I thought you'd had the bloody machine mended! . . . everything's going to hell out here, angel! *Save* me!

From
THE WINDS OF WYNDHAMVILLE
EP 30048 A—"Remains to Be Seen"

EXT—WYNDHAM CANYON—TWILIGHT
*Establishing long shot of the suspension bridge over
the river, from last season's cliffhanger. Two tiny figures representing Grand Duchess Samantha and
Summers St. Simon are struggling near the railing.*

ANGLE ON ST. SIMON—He's leaning backwards over
the railing as two female hands extend from below
screen and push him.

               ST. SIMON
Darling . . . what's got into you . . . *noooo* . . .

ANGLE ON BRIDGE—*St. Simon tumbles over the
railing and begins a long plummet towards the river.
His scream continues as he falls.*

POV ST. SIMON—*He sees the bright, shallow water
of the river rushing up at him.*

ANGLE ON ST. SIMON—*He closes his eyes and pre-
pares for his death. Suddenly, a pair of powerful
arms grab him and whisk him off-camera.*

               CUT TO:
*The underside of the bridge. St. Simon is now clinging
to the waist of a lithe, blond woman who is pulling
herself up to safety by means of a cable she has
wrapped around her hands. We do not see her face.*

ST. SIMON
Who . . . who are you . . . ?

WOMAN
. . . Can't talk . . . Need to focus . . .

*She reaches the top of the bridge and with great dif-
ficulty pulls herself to safety. St. Simon now releases
his hold on her and the pair lie on the bridge gasp-
ing for breath.*
ST. SIMON
(beat)
. . . Thank you . . .

POV ST. SIMON—*The woman turns to him and
smiles. We now see that it is Sieglinde.*

ANGLE ON ST. SIMON AND SIEGLINDE—*He backs
away from her, astonished.*

ST. SIMON *(cont.)*
Sieglinde the She-Wolf!

SIEGLINDE
(serenely)
I see my fame precedes me.

ST. SIMON
You're that neo-Nazi villainess from Boravia!

SIEGLINDE
If your recent chat with your girlfriend taught you
anything, it should be that people aren't always
what you think they are.

ST. SIMON
Samantha! . . . Where is she?

SIEGLINDE
You still care for her? After she tried to kill you?

ST. SIMON
That wasn't her intention—I'll never believe it! And
I won't rest till I've learned what awful force pos-
sessed her to attack me.

SIEGLINDE
You will never learn it. At least, not from her lips.

ST. SIMON
What do you mean?

SIEGLINDE
As I swung out to rescue you, I saw another figure
topple from the bridge.

ST. SIMON
Samantha . . . ?

SIEGLINDE
(nods)
I'm truly sorry.

He gets to his feet and looks over the railing.

POV ST. SIMON—*The waters rush beneath him.
There is no sign of Samantha's body.*

ST. SIMON
Samantha! . . . Samantha! . . .

ANGLE ON ST. SIMON AND SIEGLINDE—*She approaches from behind and stands at his side.*

                    ST. SIMON *(cont.)*
Do you really think she's . . .

                    SIEGLINDE
No one could survive that fall.

                    ST. SIMON
At the last second, she must have realized what
she'd done, and hurled herself after me.
                    (beat; then, grieving)
You should have rescued her, not me.

                    SIEGLINDE
I didn't know she was going to need to be rescued.
And besides, my instructions were to save you.

                    ST. SIMON
                    (suspiciously)
Instructions? . . . From whom? . . . You're not working for Jocasta Wyndham, are you?

                    SIEGLINDE
                    (shakes her head)
No. She doesn't even realize you're her secret ally in
the Wyndham Industries hostile takeover.

                    ST. SIMON
Then . . . Drake, you work for Drake . . .

                    SIEGLINDE
If I did, would I have saved you? You're all that
stands between him and the expansion to his resort

community. Not to mention ... between him and Samantha.

                    ST. SIMON
Samantha ...

He looks desolately into the river again.

                    ST. SIMON *(cont.)*
Goodbye, my one true love ...

                    SIEGLINDE
Grieve, Summers St. Simon. Grieve for your beloved, and in time you will forget her.
                    (meaningfully)
And perhaps ... there will be others.

                    ST. SIMON
No. Never.

                    SIEGLINDE
Time is a great healer. As is ... love.

                    ST. SIMON
Who are you, warrior woman? ... You know so many of our secrets, yet reveal none of your own. What fantastic chance brought you into my life, Sieglinde from across the seas?

                    SIEGLINDE
When the time is right, you shall know.
                    (beat)
Are you able to walk?

                    ST. SIMON
I'm fine.

He moves away from the railing. His legs wobble and he falls.

SIEGLINDE

You're still suffering from trauma. Let me just . . .

She picks him up and carries him, with great gentleness, away from the camera and off the bridge, into the setting sun.

You have reached the law offices of Gretchen Ojan. Our hours are Monday through Friday, eight-thirty a.m. to six-thirty p.m. After the tone, you may leave a message for Ms. Ojan or her assistant, Kevin Putnam. Thank you.

Gretchen, it's Viola, and it's an emergency. I've just been handed a shooting script for the season opener of *Wyndhamville,* and I've been written out! My character killed! There's no way in *hell* I'm going to allow them to get away with this. I have to fight it . . . but in order to do that, I have to be *certain* I'll be free for the whole season's production schedule, and that means I *cannot* have this absurd September fourth court case hanging over my head *any longer*! Have you, or have you not, got rid of it yet? . . . Angel, I don't think you realize the gravity of my situation. I hired you to take care of this and it's high time you did so, because this is *one* client who is just about well and truly *fucked.* Will you do me the *enormous* favor of ringing me back and telling me what I want to hear? . . . And while you're at it, will you explain to me why, exactly, I am suddenly having to *beg* my people to return my calls? Hm? Have you all forgotten whom you work for? . . .

I'm in my suite, angel. Awaiting your call. *Anxiously.*

FAX MEMO TO: Viola
FROM: Peter
SUBJECT: Termination
DATE: 8/13/97

Later today you will receive by registered mail a letter from my firm telling you, in the required legal language, that I am resigning as your agent. But I felt it incumbent on me to provide you a more personal explanation of the reasons for this decision, to mute any shock or anger you might feel receiving that letter.

Viola, since you arrived in New York, you have acted on your own recognizance. You have not consulted me regarding any of your dealings with Alex Wylie. You have hampered my ability to negotiate on your behalf with Franco Kreiss and Sandy Asher, by setting unrealistic terms and then refusing to take my professional advice to moderate them. You have been uncommunicative and foolhardy, and the result has been a career implosion that I was unable to prevent because I was oblivious to its extent.

I cannot continue to represent a client who has such apparent disdain for my services. This would be doing neither one of us any favor.

I wish you the best of luck in seeking new representation. Please take my advice, in this if in nothing else: hire someone whom you are willing to let *guide* your career.

Con amore furioso—
P.

P.O. Box 339398
Beverly Hills, CA 90212
August 11, 1997

Mr. E. Manfred Harry
c/o The Pierre Hotel
New York, New York

Dear Mr. Harry:

Thank you for responding to my letter regarding the nude
photos of Viola Chute.

I would like to respond in detail to your questions regarding
the number of photos and the degree of explicitness of them,
but to be perfectly honest Mr. Harry this is all now academic. I
have reached a very satisfactory settlement with an individual
who has agreed to purchase the photos for an amount well
beyond my asking price. His intention is to distribute the
photos via the Internet so who knows by the time you read
this they may already be available for viewing! I suggest you
go to your favorite search engine and type in "Viola Chute
nude" and see what happens.

Thank you again for your interest in the photos and should I
come across anything similar I will be sure to let you know!

Sincerely,
A Collector

. . . *Darling* Harry, come in, come in. Doesn't it seem like *ages* since we've had a session! Life in Manhattan is so filled with incident, you lose track of time, you really do. Let me take your jacket . . . *Nonsense,* just slip it off . . . Brilliant. What would you like to drink? Hm? I've got champagne, sauvignon blanc, a lovely pinot noir, plus . . . let's see . . . iced tea . . . Coca-Cola . . . Yoo-hoo, whatever the hell that is . . . Harry, you have to have *something,* it's a *beastly* day and you look overheated . . . Well, fine, so you only came from the seventh floor. The air conditioning in this place isn't all it could be . . . A spring water, then? Consider it done . . . No, no, I'll get it for you, I'm just *loaded* with energy today . . . Isn't it wonderful to be *alive,* angel? . . . Alive and healthy and . . . I'm sorry? . . . I . . . I *what?* . . . You think so, do you? . . . I see . . . Harry, would you allow me to offer just a *hint* of constructive criticism? Hm? Now, I know you haven't had much experience with women . . . Oh, don't get all huffy, you *haven't.* Go on and tell me otherwise . . . Well, then. You haven't learned . . . learned the *hard* way, a*haaa*-ha . . . that one of the things you must never, ever say to a woman—*any* woman, any*where*—is "You look terrible." Even if she does, angel . . . in fact, *especially* if she does. And *doubly* especially if she's your employer and she happens to be feeling rather grand in spite of . . . well, in spite of several things which really *should* be depressing the high holy fuck out of her . . . Yes, luv, I *know* the *Wyndhamville* cameras start rolling in three days, and no, before you ask, I *won't* be there. My character's been killed off, hadn't you heard? . . . Yes, well, *que sera sera,* as Doris Day used to say. As if *she'd* know . . . What? . . . Oh, Harry. Don't be naive. There's not going to *be* any *Sultans of South Beach.* When darling Alex up and died on me, he took the project with him. It was really his baby, you see. He was the only one with the vision to see it through . . .

What am I going to *do*? . . . Oh, Harry, you are a character. I'm going to continue working on the only project I've got left . . . *This* one, you silly git. My *memoirs*. Why do you think you're here again, after all this time? You see, Harry, I really think I might've had too much on my plate. *Wyndhamville,* the negotiations with Alex, this book . . . well, now my plate's been cleared for me, hasn't it? And how lovely that I can now focus my attentions on . . . I'm sorry? . . . Well, of *course* we can still find a publisher. My God, Harry, what a pernicious little doomsayer you are. What are you worried about? Are you concerned about getting paid? Hm? Is that it? Here, let me write you a check right now . . . No, no, it's no trouble. My checkbook's in my purse . . . which is . . . where exactly? Where did I put my purse? . . . I had it right . . . I came in last night, and I put it right here . . . Harry, *please* be quiet, I'm trying to reconstruct what I . . . I came in last night, I took the freight elevator to avoid the fucking photographers, and . . . I came in and had my keys in my hand . . . for God's sake, Harry, shut *up,* you're getting your goddamn check and there's an *end* to it . . . And I know, I know for a *fact,* that I put the bloody purse *right here.* I *always* put it right here. When was the last . . . was there maid service this morning? . . . Harry, let me *think* . . . I had breakfast sent up . . . I took a shower . . . That's it! I took a shower and when I came out the breakfast things had been cleared away. Don't you see, the goddamn *maid* moved my purse . . . or did she just *take* it? . . . Because I don't see it anywhere, do you, luv? Hm? . . . Well, for God's sake, help me *look* . . . I swear to God, Harry, this is *all* I need. Bad enough the entire fucking *world* is caving in on me, bad enough my career is gone to shit and I'm being sued for assault and I've got Alex's fucking *death* on my conscience . . . Oh, don't look so shocked, what do you *think* killed him, you bloody imbecile? Hm? . . . What do you *suppose* we were doing in his hotel room when he had his seizure? Watching

CNN? You know better than *any*body that the only way I've *ever* been able to get a job in this business is by screwing the brains out of whoever was in cha— Oh. My purse. Harry, here's my purse . . . Who the hell put it here? I *never* put it here. Harry, did you put . . . you wouldn't have moved my purse, would you? . . . I swear to God, there's no way in *hell* I would've put my purse here . . . it doesn't even make sense. Even the *maid* wouldn't do that. It's like putting the wash-cloths in the minibar . . . Hold on, I'm checking to see if any-thing's missing . . . Hold on, it's . . . No, it's all here . . . It all seems to be h . . . here . . . I . . . Oh, Harry. Harry, I can't take it . . . I'm sorry . . . No, I'm all right . . . Actually I'm not . . . Look, just go, will you? . . . Go, *now* . . . Please . . . The truth is, I *can't* afford to pay you . . . I was bluffing. I'm sorry . . . I can't pay you, I can't pay anyone . . . It's all over. I'm sorry. I'll send you a kill fee as soon as I'm able, but right now I've got nothing left, luv . . . I should be getting some money soon from my perfume deal, if you can hold out till then . . . You won't say anything to the hotel, will you, Harry? They'd boot my sorry ass right out the . . . What? . . . Well, how am *I* supposed to know how you're going to get home? My entire life is evap-orating around me, Harry, excuse me to *hell* if I don't make my first priority getting you a fucking plane ticket . . . *Heartless,* am I? . . . Fine, if I'm heartless, then I can just send you pack-ing right now and not spare a *thought* about it afterwa— Harry, is that thing running? . . . Answer me! *Is that fucking tape recorder runn—*

10 December 1988

My dear Helena—
May this card find you in good health and high spirits—
So much change here—Where to start—Most of the staff
let go now—Many faces you might remember from your
time no longer here—Not me tho, still hanging about—
Seeing as that I'm what they call "frail" and haven't
anyplace else to go—My social worker verna says I can't be
made to go if I don't want to and much as I'm fond of his
lordship I've decided to stay put even tho it's certain he'd
prefer I clear off—Hard times for him apparently tho you'd
never know what with all the lovely things he still keeps hold
of—No he hasn't changed in that regard I'm sure you're
not surprised to hear—Anyway the house so big and empty
now, only Philip left upstairs and below just Fatima and
vicki who you don't know—It's Fatima who looks after me—
Your days here something of a golden age by comparison,
Imagine! —Don't want to be so melancholy so I'll draw a veil
over it now—You are well missed here if by none but me—

Fondest regards—
Beva

"The night is bitter, the stars have lost their glitter . . . and all because of the call that got awaaay . . ." Hi, this is E. Manfred Harry. Don't hang up and leave me wailing in despair. Leave your name and number after the tone and I'll get back to you.

This is . . . I have to confess I'd forgotten your message, Mr. Harry. An unpleasant surprise all over again.

This is Patricia Hume. I'm sorry to be bothering you when I said I wouldn't welcome any further contact with you, but I've been thinking that I may have been too hasty.

I don't know if it would be of any help to you but I . . . I am in possession of some letters my mother received. Cards, really. Christmas cards. I've had them for some years because she . . . she . . . Oh, this is silly. Despite my evasions I'm sure you're able to surmise that I stole them from her, Mr. Harry, so I'll just come out and say it. I was quite a bit younger and very angry with her, and before I left for school one year I took a box of correspondence from her closet. It made me feel very wicked and very powerful. Of course it was a petty thing to do, but I've never had the inclination to undo it. Judge me if you dare.

Anyway, most of the contents are either banal or disgusting, but these cards are different. They seem to be from the same person, covering a span of years. Most intriguingly, they are all addressed to one "Helena." I do not know who this person is, nor what her relationship to my mother might be. But you mentioned detecting another mystery in my mother's past, and I'm guessing this is related.

I'm willing to send you the cards if you'd like to have a look at them. Just provide me with a mailing address. And keep in mind that I *will* need them back, Mr. Harry. They aren't mine to give, or to sell.

You know how to reach me. Till then, goodbye.

1406 Hayworth
West Hollywood, CA 90046
August 16, 1997

Dear Mr. Harry:

Haven't heard from you so I am wondering if you are still
interested in my tape of Viola Chute. If you are please let me
know by the end of next week. Otherwise I am thinking that
perhaps it would be a good idea to find another buyer. I have
had the tape transferred to cassette by a professional outfit so
I have heard it now and believe me when I tell you it is a
shocker. I am certain that there would be media interest in
this but I will honor my first commitment to you if you are
still interested in buying. But oh yes—my price is now $750.
Because I have heard the tape and it is such a sizzler.

As usual you can reach me at (213) 555-1126. I am sorry for
not phoning you myself but I really prefer not to pay toll
charges to New York.

Sincerely,
Neal Westheimer

SUBJ: slight change of plan
DATE: 97-8-18 01:11:08 EST
FROM: emanfr@ysa.net
TO: nbcasem@bot.ubsm.edu

thanks for your last two emails. no i'm not avoiding you but there's been a shakeup here and i really haven't had time to think much less put 2 words together. here's the thing. viola fired me. yes that's right sacked me canned me let me go. what's worse i'm still in nyc and have no way to get home. just a couple dollars in my wallet and none in the bank. fortunately i have this old acquaintance here from many years ago—very well if you must know someone i once slept with—who's agreed to put me up though not for free. i have to sort of serve as his houseboy clean up after him do dishes whatever. not dig-nified but it's better than starving. and really he is a friend in need. i just wish he'd pick up his own goddamn socks.

anyway there's a lot that's led up to this current situation as you can imagine. the main thing is viola's career took a dive right into the crap-per. the new season of wyndhamville started shooting without her in fact they killed off her character—yikes did she go ballistic over that. but she also managed to screw up the south beach series by as far as i can tell fucking the producer to death. so she's now a gal with no job no prospects and from what she claims no money. and a big tab at the pierre hotel too not just for her suite but for mine which i qui-etly departed as soon as she fired me. screw her i'm not getting stuck with the bill after all i was here as her employee. anyway all this plus that photographer who's still suing her for assault. case comes up be-ginning of next month which has to have her shaking in her boots. it doesn't look at all good for her. guy's been peddling his story all over the media and they've been lapping it up making viola look like some kind of cross between marie antoinette and lizzie borden. plus oh yeah her agent resigned so she is literally on her own. and one more thing those nude photos of her i told you about have landed on the internet. she doesn't even know about them yet. i'd send her an email with the link but she doesn't have an address in fact i'm pretty sure she doesn't even own a computer. i had a look at the photos myself and they are pretty raunchy. doesn't look like they were shot too terribly long ago either early 90s maybe which is long after she resurfaced from obscurity. anyway her famous claim to have never posed nude is like everything else a big hairy lie.

anyway when viola does hear about these pictures i think it may be the final straw. she'll snap and do something desperate. i don't know what maybe take a rifle to the rooftop and start sniping. actually she'd never be able to fire a gun with those fingernails—maybe she'll just lob bottles from the minibar.

so thus ends another chapter in my brilliant career and i must say this one makes the crash and burn of my novel look like no big deal. i've been trying to figure out what i can do to top it. so far all i've come up with is a user's guide to self-immolation.

actually if you can promise to keep a secret i think i may not be entirely finished with the celebrated miss chute yet. a couple of things have occurred to me that i'm considering. 1st of all her daughter remember the one who at first wouldn't help me—well she called back this week and offered me some letters she'd stolen from her mother. xmas cards actually addressed to a certain helena. who is this woman you ask. well that's what i'd like to find out. it occurs to me i might continue my work on viola's life not as a ghostwriter of memoirs but as the author of an unauthorized bio. i've got more than enough material for the bulk of it all i need is the big revelation the shocker though i still don't know what that is. who is helena and what could she possibly have to do with viola that she would want to hide it. did she murder her. and if she did was it all tape recorded—that's another big scoop. viola's old agent's son finally listened to that tape he has and he tells me it's a sizzler his exact words. what is viola doing on it that could be so terrible her agent would keep it under lock and

key as insurance against her. one thing's for certain if i'm going to find
out i need money.

that's where my 2nd little brainstorm comes in. you remember when
i told you about the party for sir david cole the one where viola and
georgia kirkby ran into each other. at the time i wondered what gk
was doing in new york well it turns out she's been here all summer
doing a series of plays for an experimental theatre. so i got to wondering if maybe she'd be willing to finance my investigation into viola's
past. i know she has nothing left to fear from viola now that she's off
the show but if everything i've heard about gk is true she's a woman
who can hold a serious grudge and after viola pretty much stole her
show away from her she's got to have a grudge the size of arkansas.
i've already put in a call asking to meet her. keep your fingers crossed
she bites.

meantime do keep your spirits up. i'm sorry to hear about the smell
but you yourself said that's what necrotic flesh does. i still don't understand why your doctor can't just cut it away.

hugest of smooches
harry

STAR SETS ON OFF-BROADWAY SENSATION
Georgia Kirkby departs experimental revue to return to TV
New York Arts in Action
August 11–17, 1997

Seldom is one afforded the pleasure of seeing an actress of Georgia Kirkby's stature in a setting as intimate—or in material as challenging—as the Exquisite Corpse Theatre's ongoing revue, *The World Owes Me a Big Delicious.* Usually comprised of three separate 20-minute plays, the show has long been a cult hit among off-Broadway cognoscenti. But during its seven-year run, it has seldom taken in enough box-office to qualify as even a modest hit, and there was a strong possibility that this season would have been its last, had not Ms. Kirkby agreed to join the company for the summer. As a marketing move, this was as odd as any Exquisite Corpse fan could've hoped for . . . akin to recruiting Robert Duvall for a drag revue. But Exquisite Corpse had an "in" with Ms. Kirkby: its artistic director, Gervase Bellow, is the actress's son-in-law.

"I could scarcely say no when Gervy approached me," the Oscar-winner said last week. "To be honest, I was flattered. And I *had* been missing the stage." And so she pulled up stakes and moved to New York, joining the company for the months she was on hiatus from her UBN-TV show, *The Winds of Wyndhamville.*

Theatergoers responded as Exquisite Corpse had hoped, flocking to witness the oddly moving spectacle of one of the greatest exponents of Shakespeare and Shaw cavorting with actors something less than half her age in dadaesque skits that skirted and subverted the established repertoire (in honor of Ms. Kirkby, the show's material has skewed more classical than is their norm). Typical was the July offering, a staging of Act I of *The School for Scandal* in which every third line of Sheridan's great farce is replaced by one plucked at random from a current lifestyle magazine. At first the device is jarring, but by the end of the act there is a strangely illuminating rightness to Kirkby's Lady Sneerwell intermittently weaving into the action aphoristic non sequiturs from *Metropolitan Home* and *Martha Stewart Living*.

Now, however, the fall television season looms on the horizon, and the star must return to that less outre but more profitable arena. Indeed, *The Winds of Wyndhamville* has already resumed filming, but its producers graciously agreed to spare Ms. Kirkby for an extra two weeks so that she might fulfill her commitment to Exquisite Corpse. At the end of the month, she will move back to Los Angeles and once again take up the role of the beleaguered matriarch Jocasta Wyndham.

But she will leave in her wake a theatre company invigorated and restored by its most successful summer ever. Mr. Bellow now vows to "heap mighty scorn" on anyone who dares tell a mother-in-law joke in his presence, because, "Where would I be without mine?"

The last two weeks of Ms. Kirkby's participation in *The World Owes Me a Big Delicious* feature two new offerings: "Buzz Hamlet," in which she acts the soliloquy and other notable speeches from Shakespeare's masterpiece while speaking them into a kazoo ("After all," the star insists, "the words are so well known that the rhythm is all you need to convey the message"); and "An Urban Rail Conveyance Named Desire," in which selected scenes from Tennessee Williams's most famous play have been translated into Mandarin Chinese and then back again, by first-year English students in Taiwan. Ms. Kirkby allowed me a peek at the script, where I noted that Blanche Du Bois's immortal parting line—"Whoever you are, I have always depended on the kindness of strangers"—has been rendered as "What is your identity? Forever am I contingent upon the mysterious nice ones."

The evening will be rounded out by one play in which Ms. Kirkby does not perform: a revival of the company's popular "Kabuki Regis & Kathie Lee," a Nippofied reenactment of an actual episode of the daytime talk show. Tickets may be purchased by calling the Exquisite Corpse box office at (212) 555-1117.

From
"AN URBAN RAIL CONVEYANCE NAMED DESIRE"
Scene Three of
the Exquisite Corpse Production

STELLA: Stanley you are an intoxicated one! Intoxicated yes! *[She frolics about the table of play.]* Poker men! Now is the time to depart. Surely your clothes are flame retardant!

BLANCHE *[unchastely]*: Stella beware him! *[Stanley is pursuant to Stella.]*

MEN *[aged]*: Stanley this is done without difficulty. Now hear us.

STELLA: First you will grasp me I know! *[She takes a bow. He comes forth and vanishes. Heard now is a congested nose. Stella exclaims. Blanche cheers and speeds to the larder. Poker men converge to fondle and emit. An artifact is loudly undone.]*

BLANCHE *[whistling]*: My sister gestates!

MITCH: I lament this.

BLANCHE: Dementia, dementia!

MITCH: Fetch him hither, o men. *[Stanley is clipped on the bed by men whom he turns over. Immediately in their hands he grows flaccid. They vow their love for him as he strokes their epaulets.]*

STELLA *[singing]*: I long to travel.

MITCH: Poker men should refrain from entering a woman. *[Blanche sprints into bedchamber.]*

BLANCHE: I covet the garments of my sister. Let us find a woman above ourselves.

MITCH: Where are the garments gone?

BLANCHE [presenting storage]: These are mine!
   [She makes energy toward Stella.]
   Stella, Stella, exclusive one! Beloved tiny sibling, avoid such terror!
   [Enveloping Stella, Blanche navigates outdoors and ascends.]
STANLEY [stupidly]: What issue is at stake? What is our history?
MITCH: You discharged a hairpiece, Stanley.
PABLO: Now he is so pleasant!
STEVE: I am certain my offspring is so pleasant!
MITCH: Lay atop him and produce damp fabrics.
PABLO : I believe he is as precious as a planet, or coffee.
STANLEY [phonetically]: Make me wet.
   [The men murmur as they jerk him in the bath.]
   Copulate with me or begone, young pups!
   [Breathing is heard. The water goes down at an angle.]
STEVE: Let's all leave now!
   [They rush the poker table, tidy victoriously, depart.]
MITCH [unhappily yet orthodox]: Poker men should refrain from entering a woman.
   [The door entraps them and they fall silent. Moorish players behind a wall make blue scissor toys without speed. With some moment Stanley comes from bathing with water and patterns dancing in his shorts.]
STANLEY: Stella! [A hesitation is there.] Have I lost my wee plaything?
   [He fractures and tears, then goes to a dial and remains wiggling unhappily.]
   Eunice, I want to bear a child.
   [He contemplates, then suspends and measures once more.]
   Eunice! Persistently will I tinkle until an infant is in my mouth.
   [A piercing unknown voice appears. He vomits and the phone interrupts the floor. Unharmonic pianos swell the room as he transforms dim in the dark. At last he ventures half naked to the aperture. He shakes his head in time with a recessed canine and pulls his wife from his lungs.]

STANLEY: Stella!

EUNICE [telephoning from atop the quarter door]: No longer make lamentation and resume the supine!

STANLEY: I desire to have a child. Stella, Stella!

EUNICE: She remains rigid so cease or legalities will crush you!

STANLEY: Stella!

EUNICE: It is not permitted to pulsate a woman prior to recall! She will not come. She is being so fecund! You produce odors! You are the issue of Polish parents! May they transport you indoors and make other of you with rubber tubing!

STANLEY: Eunice, I desire a girl to go down on me.

EUNICE: Ahaha! [She collides with her door.]

STANLEY [With acrimony that bisects the sky]: STELLA! . . .

Washington—Sen. Hiram Withers, one of the chief proponents of the Internet Decency Bill currently before Congress, took to the Senate floor yesterday to deliver a thundering tirade against what he calls "the encroachment of online filth into the mainstream of American media"—using as his prime example a series of explicit nude photographs of Viola Chute, the star of UBN-TV's *The Winds of Wyndhamville*. The photographs first appeared on an Internet porn site last week, and have since become the subject of keen interest in industry circles and elsewhere.

Ms. Chute is no stranger to controversy—in fact she has openly courted it ever since her first husband, a British industrialist, was killed under suspicious circumstances. Only last week, she became the focus of prurient attention yet again, when a television producer, Alex Wylie, died of a heart attack during what appears to have been a late-night tryst with the actress. But with the release of the photos she has, in the opinion of Sen. Withers, gone well beyond the pale.

"*Winds of Wyndhamville* is a family show, and a favorite of many in my own family, including my wife and young daughters," the Minnesota Democrat explained. "And the people involved generally respect that; certainly Miss Georgia Kirkby is a sterling exponent of taste and decency. But when someone like Miss Chute, who has attracted a wide following, chooses to betray her audience by luring them into viewing such depraved material as these graphic and disgusting photographs, it is up to this body, as a guardian of the public welfare, to express its official dismay. And if, by passing the Internet Decency Bill into law, we can stem this rank and putrid flow of online corruption, we will have done our part to prevent further abuses of the public trust, and may sleep more soundly at night, having proven ourselves men and women of substance."

Ms. Chute herself was unavailable for comment. Sandy Asher, the producer of *The Winds of Wyndhamville* declined to say anything other than to note that "Viola Chute is no longer a member of the cast of this show."

The President is expected to sign the Internet Decency Bill should it be passed by Congress.

SUBJ: ladies and gentlemen miss georgia kirkby
DATE: 97-8-21 16:58:59 EST
FROM: emanfr@ysa.net
TO: nbcasem@bot.ubsm.edu

well you know what they say—when you get thrown from a horse you have to get right back on. so having been fired by one tv diva i got myself immediately hired by another. yes that's right i now work for gk though not as her ghostwriter in fact i'm still working on viola's bio it's just gk who's paying me now. if viola knew she'd have a seizure—that is if she hasn't had one already. she certainly has enough cause. her career's completely tanked she's stuck in a fancy new york hotel she can't afford she's under suspicion of manslaughter she's being sued for assault and lastly she's suddenly spreadeagled all over the web which has caused her to be denounced on the floor of the u.s. senate. i suppose all she needs right now is to hear that the biographer she fired has teamed with her worst enemy to finish the job. maybe i should drop her a line to let her know. no that'd be cruel. instead i'll just think about doing it and giggle a lot.

here's how it went down. i put out some feelers to gk's production co that i was no longer working for viola but was interested in pursuing the project as an unauthorized bio. wasn't two days before i got a call from a certain paul mumford to discuss this and when i got to his hotel room he turned out to be the little man who was on gk's arm when i saw her at that party for sir david cole. turns out mumford's her husband-slash-manager and for a pipsqueak he was pretty good at acting all haughty. why did you call this company to discuss a biography of viola chute this company has nothing to do with viola chute. i said well to be perfectly honest i heard that there was no love lost between viola and miss kirkby and i thought since i was on the verge of uncovering a scandalous secret about viola's past maybe your company would be interested in helping me out. mumford assured me that his wife slash client is not interested in pettiness of this kind so i went back to my friend's place and as i'm walking in the door i find him on the phone with this look on his face like he's at fatima having a vision of the virgin mary totally glassy eyed and grinning stupidly. he sees me and says oh hold on here he is then he hands me the phone and stage whispers GEORGIA KIRKBY.

yes it's the oscar winner herself she heard of my visit and would i agree to meet with her. i say of course what an honor what time. so next day i go back to the same hotel but a different suite much more lavish and I wonder if she and hubby have different quarters hm. anyway she ushers me in she's wearing this voluminous daishiki with her hair all up—obviously trying to dazzle but i confess she looked a bit ridiculous. a great big woman not at all trim and petite like viola so i can see that must've been one strike against viola from the get go. she opens her mouth to speak and it sounds like she's reciting shaw or wilde and i realize she probably doesn't have the ability to hold a normal conversation. everything she says sounds like a portentous declamation—even would you like something to drink—so i find myself inexplicably replying in kind—yes a glass of something cool would be most welcome. She says yes isn't it close I do find late summer an oppressive time and i say how true one feels more like one is swimming the streets than walking them and she laughs which i know is to flatter me because it's really not that funny. plus need i add it's not even really all that warm outside.

so down to business. she says she really must apologize for her husband calling me in for a meeting just to turn me down. it would've been so much more polite to do that over the phone there's nothing worse than making someone come to you for a rejection. i say well then isn't this just compounding the offense. she laughs again and says it could be seen that way but she really just wanted to make it up to me by giving me an opportunity to make my pitch to her personally. and i see this sudden glint in her eye that tells me that she is totally gung ho hundred percent behind this project and all i have to do is promise to deliver some dirt on viola chute and she will mortgage her ass to finance me.

187

so i spend almost forty minutes with her drinking pouilly fuisse and telling her about the mystery of viola's missing months and viscount killwall and the christmas cards and the mysterious tape recording and how viola fired me when she feared i was getting too close to discovering something which is of course a bit of a lie but i wanted to sweeten the story. gk eats it all up and by the end is interrupting me every 30 seconds with gasps and hisses and snarls and the occasional rude remark. i began to realize that there is a deep and long-standing acrimony between these two women that viola for all that she's the no talent b movie tart has the good sense to treat lightly. gk supposedly the more sophisticated and worldly of the two was making no secret of her complete antipathy. she doesn't exactly come out and say i hate viola chute but pretty close. calls her every horrible thing she can think of a whore a fortune hunter a liar and i'm shocked to realize that they're all pretty much true. suddenly i'm hating viola chute too. well not like i don't have cause.

by the time i leave the suite gk and i are actually hugging. my new best friend georgia kirkby. a real lady. why then does she scare the piss right out of my kidneys. anyway the upshot is i leave with gk's fondest wishes and her mastercard. my first order of business to get hold of that incriminating tape. meantime i hate to leave you in such dire straits but it's not like i could do anything anyway. how long have you been in the hospital now exactly. isn't there a specialist or someone you could call in. the way you describe the condition of that foot i can almost smell it from here and it ain't pretty.

hugest of smooches
harry

... Shakeups are the order of the day for the fragrance industry in general and Gotham-based **Lucerne Luxe Parfumerie** in particular. The designer-aroma giant, a subsidiary of Tyron-CPG Inc., is scrapping all but its three flagship scents—Distraction, Nonpareille and La Vie Lucerne—in favor of setting its sights on the youth market. Two new scents aimed at the 18–24 demographic—Wild Woman and Chi Chi—will debut in fall of 1998. The most significant casualty of this new direction is the company's planned line of celebrity scents, the first of which, based on TV actress Viola Chute, was announced only four weeks ago. According to a Lucerne Luxe spokesperson, the contracts with Chute had not even been signed, so abandoning the project incurs no financial repercussions. The company had been in a heated competition with rival **Bienvenu Perfumes** for Chute's name on a bottle, but Bienvenu will not be taking advantage of the collapse of Chute's deal with Lucerne Luxe, perhaps due to the actress's sudden departure from her popular role on *The Winds of Wyndhamville*—leaving the star with neither a scent nor a cent. Bienvenu is still interested in celebrity fragrances, however, and is currently in negotiations with Olympic gold medal figure skater Natasha Branda . . .

SCHEDULE CHANGE ANNOUNCEMENT
A&E Network
August 22, 1997

Please note that "Viola Chute," the episode of *Biography* previously scheduled for August 23, will not be aired. In its place A&E will present a repeat of a previous episode, "Saint Teresa of Avila." At this time, *Biography* has no firm plans to reschedule "Viola Chute."

SUBJ: uh oh
DATE: 97-8-23 15:11:01 EST
FROM: emanfr@ysa.net
TO: nbcasem@bot.ubsm.edu

well here i am after having spent 750 bucks of gk's money just to get that secret tape of viola and it turns out to be nothing more than voice rehearsals for the bell jar. granted they're utterly hilarious i mean viola sounds just like a sack of cats being drowned and there are gay men who would pay a mint for this kind of thing—build whole parties around it—but i don't think gk will be too thrilled when i tell her i spent a big gob of her cash just to get tapes of viola imitating primal scream therapy.

i wish i'd known neal westheimer was gay before negotiating with him. only a gay man would think this tape actually had media interest. what a disaster this has turned out to be.

maybe i'd better just skulk off overseas without reporting in to gk. that's where i'm headed now—britain to track down the mysterious helena. if she is still alive that is. god help me i'm actually hoping she's not because if i don't come back with a body gk will have my balls on a plate.

desperate hugs
harry

LETTER TO THE EDITOR

The World This Week
August 23, 1997

Dear Editor:

I am not yet without hope that the Fourth Estate will resume its prior role as a force for civil justice and a watchdog for government, but the lack of basic investigative reporting in your story on Sen. Hiram Withers and his attack on Viola Chute (National Affairs, 8/21) provides me little encouragement.

Surely it would not have taken too much digging for your writer, Mr. Klemm—or anyone else in the national media who covered this story, for that matter—to have turned up the interesting fact that Withers was elected to his Minnesota senate seat in 1992 after an exceptionally vicious campaign against the incumbent and especially, illogically, against the incumbent's fiancee. I know this firsthand, for I was that incumbent, and Ms. Chute was my fiancee.

This information would, at the very least, have established some doubt as to whether, in attacking Ms. Chute for having posed naked for the camera (and in implying that she herself was somehow profiting from the appearance of these photos over the Internet), the Senator was indeed acting as a guardian of national virtue, or simply, contemptibly, using his office to settle very old scores.

DENNIS LAWLEY
Jacksonville, Florida

June 21, 1997

Dear Miss Chute,

Well as you can see I am nothing if not persistent! I have
waited another several weeks but got no reply from my two
fan letters which were sent from your home town Illuggan
which apparently means nothing to you. I suppose fame and
fortune have that effect on some!

It is too bad but I am not downhearted because I am certain
that we are destined to meet and I thought that our hometown
connection was surely the way that it would happen but no!
How was I to know you feel nothing but scorn and disdain for
those you left behind! Well I won't say I blame you I will
probably feel the same myself someday. Then we can look back
on these letters and laugh together!

In the meantime I will await the workings of fate which I am
sure are bound to bring us together as I have said. I have a
"feeling" and I am never wrong! So do not think you have
escaped your number one admirer! I am in your future and
there is nothing you can do about it! I do not mean to scare
you just the opposite. As your greatest admirer and as an
actor myself you will find me good company and a faithful
friend.

Until then I will "see" you every Tuesday on "The Winds of
Wyndhamville" which is brilliant! And I will await the day
when fate provides the way for us to meet!

Your number one admirer,
Andy Trebliss

SUBJ: coming 2 u from jolly olde
DATE: 97-8-24 03:44:16 EST
FROM: emanfr@ysa.net
TO: nbcasem@bot.ubsm.edu

well here i am in cornwall the place viola chute actually grew up. parts
of it are kind of industrial but still pretty in an arid charlotte bronte
kind of way. scrubby brush over everything but spectacular cliffs brilliant wildflowers squeezing out from between sheets of rock. feel totally relaxed and happy here especially since the natives are a delight
and have made me feel so welcome. i told them i'm researching a life
of viola chute and though not many have personal memories of her
they're all bending over backwards to help in exchange for clues
about what happens next on wyndhamville. the show's just about 6
months behind so over here grand duchess samantha is just beginning to figure out that drake wyndham is a 1st class shit.

anyway landed at heathrow 2 days ago and spent the night in london
which was something. hadn't been there in 15 years and didn't even
recognize it. all bright glittering filled with happy people. mainly
tourists but still what a change from the 80s bleak land of the undead.
had a great dinner and took in a play a comedy with maggie smith i
was in 7th heaven. thank you georgia kirkby is all i've got to say. she
may not know it but she's bankrolling me in style.

rented a car next day and drove out here quite an adventure. i was a
nervous wreck about forgetting myself and ending up on the wrong
side of the road. had one near miss involving a van full of teenagers
who screamed obscenities at me. least i think they were obscenities
i couldn't tell because of the thick accents which is probably just as
well. if even one of them had yelled faggot i'd have had to turn around
and give chase well you know how i am and that would surely have
been the end of me. actually faggot means something else over here

i think probably they would've yelled poof or bum-boy or whatever neither of which sounds quite as threatening when yelled from a speeding car.

so here I am in this little town called illuggan staying in this quaint little hotel. more like a bed and breakfast except you'd have to be insane to eat the breakfast all fat grease blood. fortunately I filled my suitcase with granola bars before i left home. the proprietress—one miss carne—was very excited to hear why i'm here even stopped vacuuming to help me out. unfortunately she didn't turn off the vacuum just stood next to it smiling so we had to shout at each other to be heard over the motor which alerted several others in the lobby to my mission and it became quite a confab. old guy who said his name was tholly which I'm guessing is short for bartholomew said he used to be the mayor and he remembered viola from the pageant where she played britannia way back when regnal chute first noticed her. back when her name was still violet did i ever mention she changed it. anyway i asked who runs the pageant now. he said we don't have it anymore gave it up in the 60s after teenagers staged a sit-in 2 years in a row. fresh from my experience with the van i sympathized and we commiserated about dreadful teenagers for quite a while. then he told me the costumes from the pageant were in the town hall along with some scripts old programs etc. he knows this because they were taken out and put on display during the queen's jubilee in the late 70s when everyone was super patriotic. supposedly she's got another jubilee coming up in 2002 so tholly said i'd be doing them a favor if i could locate the costumes again. said i'd give it a try and why not it's as good a place as any to start. if i find a program from viola's year i can see who was in the pageant with her and maybe track them down. who knows maybe the mysterious helena was in the cast. so that's my agenda for tomorrow.

you'll never guess what else. i can't believe how this country has changed. i was walking around last night thinking how charming and wasn't it like i just stepped into a novel by thomas hardy or something when what do you suppose I saw but a bunch of suspicious looking men going into an unmarked pub. i followed them and yes a gay bar exists in this cornish backwater. had my first ever experience of being the most popular in the place because first of all i'm american and let's face it my teeth alone. second my proximity to viola chute which had the boys mad with excitement. i actually went home with someone. well not home back to the hotel which may have been a mistake because this morning miss carne did not stop vacuuming to greet me and gave me a look that had hellfire in it or maybe i'm just imagining.

so glad to hear the radical new treatment is working for you. so you might have to walk with a cane for a couple months who cares as long as you get to keep your foot. i know you'll probably go to wal-mart and get the first plastic 8.95 walking stick you come across but do yourself a favor get something that makes a statement. polished wood with an attractive handle. when robert mapplethorpe was dying he had a walking stick topped by a skull. maybe you can find one capped with a nice brass foot.

hugest of smooches
harry

What the coronation means to me is that there is going to be a new Elizabeathen age. The first Elizabeathen age was in the Sixteenth Century when the first Queen Elizabeath was on the throan. This was the age of the Goldin Age which was when there was the flowering of England's flower including William Shakespeere and Ben Johnson in poetry and drama, John Dowland in music, and many others. Plus the country getting rich from trade with Europe and also setteling in America.

The reason for all this was that Queen Elizabeath the first was very shrewed and knew to keep out of wars to save money that she could spend on trade. Also beating the Spanish Armadda. Everyone in England looks back on this time and remembers with pride because it is when England showed everybody else that we are the best. Then we got an empire and we could make everybody see it anytime we wanted.

But hard times came with the war and then there was a Mr. Gandhi who wore only a diaper who made us give the empire back by not eating. Frankly I think that was a mistake but I imagine when a man wearing just nappies showed up to see the king and queen they were so embbarrassed they did anything he said just to get him to leave. Anyway after that it seemed like the Goldin Age was a very, very, very, very, very long time ago.

Now it is 1953 and we have a new Queen Elizabeath the second who came to the throan very young just like the first queen only twenty-five. But unlike the first queen not a virgin but a mother with two children and also a wife. So it is not exactly the same but different. Also England today isn't just

England but great Britain with Wales, Scotland and northern Ierland. Plus many domminions across the sea.

But yet there are still many simillarities which is for instance today we have Nole Coward for drama, Benjamin Britain for classicle music and for regular music we have Gracie Fields. Also in Britain today we have the handsommest movie stars which the first Elizabeathans didn't even have any of since movies weren't invented. The handsommest of all in my opinion is Anthony Quayle whom I have seen every movie of. The Americans all think they have the handsommest but most of their big stars are not so handsome for instance Humphrey Bogart and Spencer Tracey. Clark Gable MAYBE but in my opinion Clark Gable is not in the same class as Anthony Quayle. To begin with Anthony Quayle does not have a silly mustache. If I was Clark Gable I would shave off my mustache and if I was the Queen I would have Anthony Quayle read something from the bible at my coronation just to show the Americans. Can you imagine Clark Gable reading something from the bible at the coronation? Out loud and all?

Also the Brittish have the most beautiful movie star so far and by that I mean Elizabeath Taylor. The Americans have stolen her and they act like she is one of them but that's all right because we all know she is Brittish. Plus her name is Elizabeath too, just like the new Queen. So maybe with two great Elizabeaths this is going to be an even more important age of flower for England than four hundred years ago.

So I am proud to be a Brittish girl! Long live the Queen!

From
"STYLE NOTES"
Los Angeles In Step
August 25, 1997

. . . Now let us consider the eyepatch. Ostensibly an article whose function dictates its form, it has nonetheless become an irresistible adornment whose regular reappearances in men's fashion seems inevitable, never mind the vagaries of economics, politics or cultural mores. The latest indicator that the patch is back: **Berry Leyton,** celebrity photojournalist *par excellence,* wore one last month to the opening of his exhibit, "The Unseen I" at the Glenda Worth Gallery in West Hollywood. Within days, patches could be spotted on Sunset, La Cienega and Wilshire, and today the city is virtually awash with one-eyed hunks. Local designer **Joel Meredith,** always on the crest of a wave, seized the moment, and is preparing to unveil an exclusive line of eyepatches in a wide range of colors, patterns and fabrics. "It's the new necktie," Meredith asserts. "Neither article serves any real purpose; they're just attractive accessories. The only difference is that you wear one around your neck and one over your eye." Leyton, who wears his patch due to a very real eye injury (inflicted by one of his more reluctant subjects—but then you're sure to have heard quite enough of *that* story), never imagined himself a trendsetter. "I've always been the guy no one noticed," he says with a laugh. "The one you wouldn't look twice at. That's how I made my living. I could get up Barbra Streisand's nose without her knowing I was there." Not to mention noses considerably less roomy!

But Leyton can't expect to remain unnoticed, not while he's squiring young bombshells around town. A reclusive widower since 1995, he has recently begun dating with a vengeance, juggling the Australian supermodel **Charysse** with *Winds of Wyndhamville* recruit **Angie Ashe-Tippett.** Ashe-Tippett, who met the photographer when he shot her *au naturel* for an up-coming issue of *Burnish,* says, "The eyepatch is definitely a turn-on. It gives Berry an air of mystery and intrigue he might not have otherwise. And that creates a nice dissonance with his sweetness and his old-fashioned integrity." Keep an eye on man-about-town Leyton for further fashion breakthroughs . . . and if you're following his lead already, one eye is all you'll have available for the task!

SUBJ: the brit brats
DATE: 97-8-26 02:08:16 EST
FROM: emanfr@ysa.net
TO: nbcasem@bot.ubsm.edu

back in london. basically ran out of steam in cornwall—found nothing there well nothing that pointed towards any mystery in viola's life. did find lots of stuff from her early life as violet though. photocopied some of it to use later when i start writing. illuggan town hall was just crammed full of old records from her school days including some school assignments she wrote with her own tender hand. what can i say except this is a girl who could turn even a patriotic essay into a rumination on hollywood. her future was certainly preordained.

anyway decided to come back to london and see if i could track down regnal chute's children. which proved to be easier than i thought be- cause chute's estate still manages several apartment and office build- ings in town and the kids are on the board. so apparently they weren't completely written out of the will like viola said—another lie what a surprise. so i have an interview with them this afternoon. they were originally not interested but once they heard i was doing a tell-all on their stepmother their people called me back and set up a time. amaz- ing the deep love and affection viola leaves everywhere in her wake. after that i went online and got some bios on the kids. there's the girl judith 41 years old and from her picture not a beauty severe hair and a scowl that could curdle motor oil. then there's the boy edward 39 who looks from his photo like he could be a bum-boy himself one of those prematurely balding men who mousses his remaining hair so that it's ever taller something i never saw any straight guy do. they quite the contrary specialize in the very attractive combover.

happy as i am about landing a meeting with the chute kids i must say i am not without some anxiety here. first off there's andy the lad that i met in cornwall and brought back to the hotel. now i remember why i don't date a lot. you end up getting one quick orgasmic splurt in exchange for taking on somebody else's decades of emotional baggage and in andy's case we're talking steamer trunks. turns out he is a complete showbiz junkie who lives breathes eats movies and supports himself in some sort of low-level government job while dreaming of a career for himself on the silver screen. i know what you're saying isn't that a description of half the gay men alive well no it's not but it is a definite type. where andy differs is that he lives in cornwall which may be the place on earth least like los angeles and therefore his dreams of stardom are—well let's just say he might as well dream of being an astronaut or the king of sweden. at least until now that is because after one night with me he is convinced i'm his ticket out of illuggan and onto a sony soundstage. i know it's ridiculous like i have any kind of connections or power hell i can barely keep myself fed but in andy's eyes i'm up there with david geffen. no wonder he went home with me so willingly that night. i mean i'm not the kind of guy who usually inspires instant lust. the only good thing about him is that he appears completely uninterested in viola. every time i mention her he just turns slowly away and drifts off somewhere.

the upshot is i have a stalker. when i told him i was going back to london he looked devastated for about three full seconds then he got this excited look on his face and said i'm coming too. i said what do you mean too—you can go to london or not it's your affair but you're not doing it with me. another devastated look. you can't stop me he said to which i replied i know i just said that but it's a big city and i've got things to do there and don't expect to see me. and you know what he says? YOU KNOW WHAT HE SAYS? oh i'll see you but maybe you won't see me. so yes totally totally a stalker. and stop laughing.

my other big anxiety is gk. she's suddenly getting a little tight with the purse strings and i think i know why. the complete overnight collapse of viola's career that's why. viola who just a few short weeks ago was the queen of tv is now fallen so low she can't get arrested. i mean that literally there have been no formal charges against her in the death of alex wylie which if there were she could at least fight them and prove them wrong. but how can she fight whispers and innuendo. the result is suddenly people are shunning her and wyndhamville is speeding along without her and she lost her perfume deal which incidentally was the money she was going to pay me from so yes once again i am oh so very fucked. anyway gk must be thinking that viola's career is falling to pieces quite nicely on its own so why does she need me traveling expensively around britain looking for something to torpedo her with. i had to practically beg her to wire me some money to get back into claridge's. she said why claridge's isn't there a youth hostel or something in town. i ask you A YOUTH HOSTEL what am i 17.

so i figure i better come up with some juicy horror story about viola molto pronto or gk will cut the cord and i'll be stranded again only this time across the atlantic instead of just across the country. remind me when this is over never ever to get involved with any middle aged movie queens ever again. not even to further andy's career. there i made a joke about him i can't really be so scared of him.

more later after i've met the delightful siblings chute. meantime write back and tell me how you're getting along with your cane. god damn it i knew you'd buy something plastic. how are you supposed to beat children with it if it doesn't weigh anything. plus the first hot day you go out walking it'll melt and then you'll be screwed won't you. no seriously i'm glad of your recovery you had me worried for a while there.

hugfest
harry

INTERVIEW WITH VIOLA CHUTE
by E. Manfred Harry
(Excerpt)
Homophile, July 1993

HOMOPHILE: Is there a dream role for Viola Chute that you haven't taken on yet?

VIOLA: Oh, angel! Bless you. I'm not accustomed to thinking in those terms. At my level of craft, you just worried about making enough money to eat, never mind what the goddamn role was. I'd have happily played Little Lulu if it came with a regular paycheck. That said, I did quite enjoy playing queens. Something in it appealed to me. (*laughs*)

HOMOPHILE: I just want to point out how hard I'm biting my tongue right now.

VIOLA: Good for you. There's not a joke you can make out of that that hasn't been made before. Believe me, I've heard them all.

HOMOPHILE: Well, then, what about your private life, as opposed to your professional? Any roles left to tackle there?

VIOLA: Well, of course, that's a different story . . . always trying to finagle myself a new, more attractive way of living. Although I'd be hard-pressed to come up with an actual role I haven't played. Daughter, fiancee, wife, divorcee, mother of three . . . I suppose the only role I haven't played is whore, and there are people in this town who'd argue that.

HOMOPHILE: I'm sorry, I thought you only had one child, not three.

VIOLA: Did I say three? . . . Sometimes I forget myself and include Regnal's brood in the counting. I was very young when I married him, you know, and I suppose I fancied myself the kind of dazzling, with-it young stepmother who would sweep the little darlings off their feet . . . didn't happen that way, of course. Terrifically loyal to their real mother, who was still very much alive and very much resentful of me. We had some excruciating family weekends together, Regnal and the children and I. I did give it my very best shot. And after Regnal's death, I financed their schooling, continued doling out their allowance . . . Regnal hadn't really provided for them in his will; I'm not certain why. He'd told me Augusta—that's the ex—had taken him to the cleaners in the divorce, and he begrudged her every penny of it. I suppose he figured any money he left the children would be appropriated by her.

HOMOPHILE: Are you in touch with the children today?

VIOLA: Not in any real sense. The last I actually saw of them was at the graduation of the girl, Judith, from Cambridge, sometime in the Seventies. Very posh do, of course, and I quite innocently dressed all wrong for it. A crimson Valentino skirt and jacket and a hat with a veil—Judith said I looked like I was in mourning for Anne Rice. She occasionally lapses into wit, does Judith, much as she might resist. Anyway, I'd footed the bill for her entire education and not even a thank you. In fact, I was rather shunned at the family party afterwards. A party, I might add, that I paid for. Now I don't want to make too much of it, but I scarcely think a crimson Valentino dress cancels out six years of university tuition. But there you are. Fortunately, I was spared the expense of an advanced degree for Edward, the boy . . . he didn't go on much past prep school. By which time I couldn't have afforded it, anyway. I did continue to hear from him for several years or so, whenever he needed money to bail himself out of some predicament or other. Strike that . . . shouldn't want him read that. Actually, go ahead and use it. As he sows, so shall he reap.

HOMOPHILE: Is their mother still alive?

VIOLA: Oh, I'm sure of it. Things that evil never die.

. . . may as well begin, Mr. Harry. I'm certain Edward has
forgotten he's to be here. Since our mother passed on last year,
he's gone quite wild. I'm sorry to say it, but there it is. He grew
up without his father on hand, didn't he; and a mother alone
can't rear a teenaged boy, I'm convinced of it. Especially a
mother like ours, who had to contend with an antagonistic stepmother . . . each time she'd try to discipline Edward, he'd write
complaining of his treatment, and Viola was always happy to
send him money. That gave him the freedom to go off and ignore everything our mother was trying to instill in him.

Oh, yes, Mr. Harry. That woman made our lives hell, and
she took both pride and pleasure in it. I suppose she told you
she paid us an allowance and put me through university, hm?
Well, never you believe it. My father *did* provide for us in his
will, but you see, it had been so long since he'd lived in the
world—and by that I mean, lived in it without the buffer of
staff—that he had no idea what anything cost. A bottle of
milk. A new dress. A Cambridge education. He was stuck in
1956. And so while he did provide for us, the provisions were
insufficient. Viola—who as you know was in the process of di-
vorcing my father when he died and yet brazenly took all his
money anyway—was only too happy to step in and pay the
balance needed for us to live our lives. Initially I thought she
was doing so in a bald attempt to purchase our affections. But
I came to understand that it was done for public consumption;
so that she, the Cornish Black Widow, could turn to her de-
tractors and say, Look here, see what a good woman I am, providing for my stepchildren in the absence of their father. She
said this *endlessly,* and, if your experience is any indication, is
still saying it.

Now my mother—well, she didn't know how to manage money. How could she? During the entirety of her marriage, my father never as much as let her sign a check. So despite doing quite well in her divorce settlement, she squandered so much on bad investments. And a lot of what was left was simply stolen by charlatans. She had a weakness for bad men with big schemes. Of course, I understand it wasn't long before Viola had let the bulk of my father's fortune dribble through *her* fingers, as well. One might think I'd be bitter: the daughter of a millionaire, reduced to working for a living. In fact, I thank God for it. I thank God my father provided for us not with a trust but with interest in certain of his real estate holdings—an interest I was able to broaden some years ago when Viola herself was in financial difficulties and offered the corporation her own share in those properties. I was delighted to be able to take them off her hands. Now I have a controlling interest in what's left of my father's original venture, and although it takes a great deal of management—as it did for him, during his lifetime—I find I have a talent for it, and while I may never be a millionaire, I am doing rather well.

I'm sorry, listen to the way I go on. You must think me unconscionably arrogant. Not at all; it's just that I'm quite overcome by anger when I think of that woman and the havoc she played with our lives. Did you know my parents weren't divorced when she met my father? It's true they were separated, but they were working out their differences and I had every hope of a reconciliation. It's a dreadful thing for a very young girl to watch the loving parents of her childhood become shrieking combatants. I lost years to self-loathing, convinced it was somehow my fault. But I've long since worked through all that and I'm rather proud of the life I've built. I shouldn't apologize, I know—you're an American, this is how you talk in America. But over here, it's just not done. One simply doesn't talk about one's trials. Just about the weather, or sporting events. Or dogs.

But really, it's only Viola Tregothan who loosens my tongue. The way she took my father's name and cheapened it with her career of coarse performances in filthy pictures. The way she continues to fictionalize her life and, by association, mine. Her disgusting obsession with money and the way it rules her, and how she forced us to be ruled by it too.

I'm sorry, am I frightening you? . . . It's just that you've been moving rather noticeably across the couch. It's all right to tell me. My therapist has taught me to take my cues from others. It's just I have trouble *reading* the cues sometimes. I really think I *was* frightening you, Mr. Harry, and I'm sorry. It's that *woman* . . . Here, let me freshen your tea.

. . . Oh, yes, thank you for reminding me. The "mystery" you mentioned. I'm sorry, when I heard you were researching a book on that woman's life, I got a bit excited—finally, a chance to tell my story! But I may have lured you here under false pretenses . . . There you are. Nice and fresh. Toast? . . . Scone? . . . No? . . . All right then.

Where was I? . . . Oh, yes. I never meant to imply that I knew anything of Viola's travels, or where she may have been at any given time. If there is a period for which her movements are unaccountable, my own theory would tend toward the sensational . . . I won't offend you with it. You know her history with men better than I do, anyway. But you seem to think she may have been in Britain during this period? . . . That's quite intriguing. I can assure you, I never once heard from her. And yes, I would remember. Every conversation I have ever had with that woman . . . and they are few enough . . . is seared into my memory.

I'm sorry Edward isn't here; he may have been able to help you. Having no shame, he spoke to her more frequently. But then, he's also a bit unreliable, my brother. Perhaps it's just as well you've missed him.

Hm? . . . Oh, must you go? . . . Why, yes, it has been an hour. I had no idea . . . goodbye then, Mr. Harry. Will you keep me apprised of your findings? . . .

HOTEL PIERRE

August 27, 1997

Dear Ms. Chute:

This is in the way of a reminder of our telephone conversation
of two days past, when we requested that you settle the bill
for the room previously occupied by your associate, Mr. Harry.

We would greatly appreciate your swift attention to this
matter. I have attached another copy of the invoice, for your
convenience.

Sincerely,
Georgette Klein
Manager

17 December 1989

My dear Helena—
So late with this card!—but all here is upheaval—
I am to leave at last—No one here who can do for me so I'm
to be sent away—a place in Edinburgh for the aged—I
shall have my own room this much is promised so perhaps
it won't be so bad—Certainly no sadness in leaving his
lordship who is never here for one and the house so drab
and quiet—Money problems I think but you didn't hear
that from me—I don't know when I shall write you next but
perhaps it will be on a happier note—I am not at all
displeased that my labours have now ended—not that I've
been working much but at least now I shan't feel guilty for
shirking—Sweetest Helena may this Christmas season
bring with it the fufilment of all your hopes and dreams—

Fondest regards—
your Beva

SUBJ: judy judy judy
DATE: 97-8-27 22:15:03 EST
FROM: emanfr@ysa.net
TO: nbcasem@bot.ubsm.edu

so my latest theory is that melodrama is a virus and i caught it from viola. because you wouldn't believe the shit happening to me. i'm headed for scotland now to track down—actually i'd better take this in chronological order.

went to see judith chute which was kind of a shocker because even though i knew intellectually she was older than me i kept thinking of her as a kid. then i met her and she looks REALLY old—older than viola even. all haggard with dry hair gray skin. they must've gone berserk with the airbrush on that press shot i saw of her. and she's a total fucking lunatic on top of it. crazy eyes a compulsion to tug at her shoulder pads every 2.5 seconds and a tongue that kept darting out like a gecko's. plus a habit of rubbing her kneecaps like she was trying to start a fire there. i've known people who had nervous tics before but this gal's got a whole nightclub act. why am i so sure that viola is responsible. maybe because judith was violently obsessed with her i mean you should hear the tape of our interview. she could barely speak viola's name she usually just said that woman. but whenever she did say viola there was the tiniest fracture on the o as if just saying the name was cracking her to pieces.

didn't get much from her—she clearly arranged the meeting just so she could vent her spleen. the brother wasn't there though and i got the impression she was sort of relieved about that so i thought hm. when i got back to the hotel i tried contacting him again. no go so i occupied myself as enjoyably as i could which since this is london was considerably enjoyably. over dinner—at a lovely place on the south bank called ransome's dock—great food super wine list and not at all pretentious so perfect for you—anyway over dinner i had another look at the wad of xmas cards lent me by patricia hume and this time I put them in chronological order and read them through. and suddenly they make more sense in fact a little story begins to gel. they're clearly written by an old serving class woman named Beva who over the years experiences a physical decline at around the same rate as the estate she works for and in the end she's sent to a nursing home in edinburgh. don't know why i didn't notice this before—probably because i wasn't really reading the cards just skimming them and since they were out of order nothing jumped out at me except the oddness of viola having them.

so then i start thinking maybe i'd better go to scotland and track down this beva woman if she's still alive. how many nursing homes can there be in edinburgh and even if a lot how many bevas can there be there. enough to check on in a few days certainly. and then i recall the viscount killwall you remember viola's blackmailer. i remember he's from scotland too and suddenly i'm so excited i can scarcely finish my monkfish. it's all coming together. it still doesn't make total sense but it's getting there and this beva must be the key. either she knows something or—my preferred theory—it's what she doesn't know that's crucial.

i can hear you asking what that's supposed to mean. well i might as well give you my pet theory which i've arrived at after much thought. i believe this helena person was killed—perhaps accidentally—by viola. the viscount finds out about it or maybe he's a witness anyway he helps viola out by arranging a cover story where helena just disappears without saying goodbye. but helena has a close friend on the staff this woman beva and beva says oh but i want to write to helena. wherever she's gone. so to keep her happy and quiet killwall gives her an address in los angeles; which of course belongs to viola but beva doesn't know that. so she goes on happily writing to her faraway friend not realizing that the friend is actually pushing up daisies right there on the estate.

a little gruesomely gothic perhaps but see how it all fits. and covering up an accidental slaying is one of the few things viola would definitely want to keep well hidden. plus in one of her later cards beva mentions the viscount having money problems so you see it's all just too nice and tidy—he comes running to viola to bankroll him with her tv money and if she doesn't pay up he'll squeal about helena's death. i know there are still questions for instance what was viola doing in scotland in the first place and who exactly was helena and how precisely did viola kill her. i'm hoping against hope i can get some clues from beva on that.

my mind is obviously mired in gory speculation so perhaps i'd better sign off now. more later. meantime how about you. tap-dancing yet or what.

harmless hugs
harry

NEW "SO WRONG" ANTHOLOGY
COLLECTS BAD BOOTLEGS

Sounds & Stylus, August 30, 1997

Hippo Records' first two *A Song So Wrong* collections, featuring excruciating versions of pop standards by unlikely artists, have surprisingly proved to be the tiny independent label's biggest hits. Accordingly, they have announced a third entry in the series, this one entitled *A Song So Wrong: The Bootlegs.* Unlike the previous discs, which included hideous studio recordings the producers had unearthed in their heroic search for the worst of the worst, the new disc will contain surreptitiously recorded live performances, such as Lawrence Army Dell's jaw-droppingly bad rendition of "And I Love Her So" from a press party honoring his wife's 50th birthday, and a version of "Don't It Make My Brown Eyes Blue" sung at a 1984 AIDS benefit by irrepressible septuagenarian Edith Packer, that is so horrifically phlegmy you may feel a need to towel down afterwards.

Also tentatively included at press time is a must-be-heard-to-be-believed version of "Love for Sale" sung by Viola Chute. The cut breaks the unwritten rule for the rest of the disc in that it was not recorded at a public event—it was taped during private vocal lessons the actress took in the early '80s, after she had signed to star in a stage musical. "We realize it's edging towards mean-spiritedness," admits producer Kevin Jayson; "all the other stars had performed in public, and so were fair game. But this cut is so appallingly bad we felt we just had to include it. There's scientific interest, really—the sounds she makes aren't quite human." Co-producer Ian Chang disagrees: "Actually, these are sounds any human being might make . . . if, say, they were undergoing surgery without anesthesia."

Chute reportedly has phoned the label to demand the return

of the tape; but there is some question as to who really owns it (the label purchased it from the son of the star's late agent). Barring any legal challenge—and Chute has not presented such—Hippo intends to go forward with the disc, which should be in stores by early September.

Harry you might want to check to see
what happened to your boyfriend!

I am afraid he had a little accident when
he left you oh dear!

Wouldn't it be terrible if what happened
to him happened to all your boyfriends!
Well wouldn't it!

But then you know who truly loves you so
you shouldn't be seeing them anyway!

Should You!

My advice is be a bit more careful next
time!

You-know-who
You-know-where

SUBJ: danger will robinson
DATE: 97-8-28 04:43:16 EST
FROM: emanfr@ysa.net
TO: nbcasem@bot.ubsm.edu

just a few hours after my last email and so much to report! really should wait till tomorrow to write but i want to get this down while it's still fresh plus i'm so wired anyway.

about two hours ago i get a call from the lobby there's a visitor to see me none other than edward chute. i go down to meet him and find he's 1 really drunk and 2 exactly what i figured gay gay gay i tell you. gay in that upperclass brit way of not really saying so but totally ravishing any nearby male with his eyes which as it happens includes me. which is fine because it gives me the upper hand. we talk for a while in the lobby. he says he was sorry to miss the meeting with judith but could we talk now and he suggests my room. we go back there and he has a cocktail which must be his one millionth of the night because he can now barely stand. then before i can even locate my tape recorder he starts into this long tirade about judith and what a bitch she is and how viola is the only one in the family who's ever been nice to him but he's had to betray her just to keep the peace and now that his mother's dead he wants to make amends and can i help him. i get a creepy feeling about this and tell him sorry i've pretty much burned my own bridges to viola and he starts crying no really bawling right there in my hotel room. this goes on a while and i mean what can you do. i kind of look hard at my fingernails waiting for it to subside and when it doesn't i figure what the hell and get a drink for myself.

eventually edward sobs himself out and apologizes sorry sorry no really unforgivable what must you think of me etc. i ask him please to tell me the story of him and viola and he says no story really she just was always nice to him. he was just a kid when she married his old man and so when judith and his mother were so hateful about her he couldn't understand why. the whole idea of divorce was beyond him all he could see was this beautiful kind lady being slandered and vilified by his sister and mother. it got worse after his father died of course when viola laid claim to the family fortune despite she and regnal being in the midst of a divorce. edward couldn't really understand that either—too young to comprehend finances all he knew was that his dad was dead and his mum and sis were more thermonuclear than ever on the subject of viola. so even though viola always helped him out whenever he asked he always felt it was his duty to side with his blood relatives and spurn her in whatever small ways he could. the end result is the guy's grown up just as obsessed with viola as his sister only for different reasons and in my opinion they're both about as crazy as a badger in a trap.

so then i ask edward when was the last time you spoke to viola and he gets this look of horror and says in a small voice oh years ago. seems when he got out of school and suddenly had to go and work for a living he found himself missing his father's money for the first time. so he made up for lost time by being even more indignant about viola than mom and sis and in fact took a final public swipe at her that severed their tie but good. he wouldn't say what it was but i get the feeling it was more humiliating for him than for viola because he's never gotten over it while she's never even bothered mentioning it. funny isn't it viola just shrugs about regnal's kids and says well what did i expect then goes on with her life not even thinking about them. while they spend every day of their adult lives immersed in viola viola viola. a really tragic irony.

anyway he makes like he's getting ready to leave and i realize if he goes i may never get a chance at him again certainly not this emotionally vulnerable. so i pour him another drink which of course works like a charm he sits down again. i press the point asking what was the terrible snub he gave viola. i've got to know because i have this feeling everything hinges on it he blushes bright red and says no no no i could never tell anyone but i turn on the charm and act sort of seductively—don't laugh i didn't say i was good at it he was just drunk enough for it to work. i finger the collar of his coat and say plleeeease. finally he breaks down and says all right big dramatic pause here it is. turns out the last time he spoke to viola was in the early 1980s when she showed up on his doorstep in london and irony of irony asked him for cash. he laughed in her face and told her she'd taken quite enough of his money when his father died and then slammed the door in her face.

early 80s early 80s this is plaguing me you know because viola's so-called lost years were 79 to 82. i press him for when this was exactly and he thinks really hard and says 82 or 83 because he remembers that's when he lived in that apartment. well i know it's not 83 because by that time viola was married to michael winger so it must be 82 but when when when in 82. if it was early in the year that would fit per-fectly because by april viola was back in l.a. doing double dutch. i ask edward what time of year it was and hip hooray he says winter. he re-members because the other reason he wanted to slam the door on her was that the cold air was coming in.

so in the first few months of 82 just before she returned to l.a. viola was in london begging for money. but was she in britain all along that's the question. i think i can find the answer by going north. beva has the answer i'm more and more sure of it.

ah but my story is not yet done. more harrowing complications can you stand it. seriously at this point it gets rather creepy so hold on. edward leaves my room and about an hour later someone slips a note under the door. i see it and get a chill because somehow i just know it's bad nastiness. i open it it's a scrawled message about some-thing bad happening to my quote boyfriend unquote. which I assume must mean edward because it's signed you know who and in fact i do know who—my stalker andy from cornwall who has apparently fol-lowed me to town and is now watching my every move and well ex-cuse me but brrr. and when he saw me bring edward to my room he made what for him must have been an obvious conclusion and acted accordingly.

i kind of freak out that i might have been indirectly responsible for edward being harmed so i call the front desk and ask if there's been any incident in the hotel involving my friend edward chute and i describe him. and the desk clerk says ah yes the gentleman in question fell down a flight of stairs and had to be taken to hospital. then he clears his throat and says something about edward being unsteady on his feet which is of course just a polite way of saying drunk. and of course that's true but i get the impression edward is the kind of guy who is drunk a lot of the time and has made sort of an accommodation for it so that he doesn't just tumble down staircases. no no no edward was pushed.

anyway i ask which hospital then i call and learn edward is okay in fact he's just being released. at first they thought he'd broken his jaw because his speech was so slurred but then they realized he was just smashed. apparently his face is badly bruised though and he fractured a wrist.

okay so seriously creepy but i figure it's all right i'm heading to scotland as soon as i can pack and get to victoria station and i'm pretty sure andy won't be able to track me there. but on the other hand. but on the other hand. look i wouldn't say this to anyone but you and that's only because you tell me everything even how you kind of liked the smell of your putrefying foot which btw is the kind of confidence you might want to spare me in the future. anyway the worst aspect of this whole situation is that part of me a very little part buried deep down likes the idea of having a stalker. let's face it when your romantic life has been the kind of blight mine has for going on what six years well hell even a sociopathic cornishman feels like an improvement. if you ever tell anyone else i said that i'll deny it. and then i'll come west and stamp really really hard on your foot. which while we're on the subject i'm glad to hear is nearly back to normal. are the toenails all still black if so you can always just paint them ha ha.

more from the moors.

smooches
harry

"The night is bitter, the stars have lost their glitter . . . and all because of the call that got awaaay . . ." Hi, this is E. Manfred Harry. Don't hang up and leave me wailing in despair. Leave your name and number after the tone and I'll get back to you.

Good God.

I'm sorry, but that's an *appalling* greeting, Mr. Harry.

This is Georgia Kirkby. You said you'd be checking your home voice mail while you're abroad, and I'm taking you at your word. I know you said it would be quicker to email you, but I don't know how to do that. Computer still in the box, if you must know; I dislike devices. Took me years to reach an uneasy truce with the telephone. I prefer letter writing above all, but time is of the essence here.

Mr. Harry, I've yet to hear anything substantive from you, but in checking my accounts I can't help notice the alacrity with which your bills are mounting. I'm aware that you need to live while you're conducting this investigation but perhaps you might consider using the credit card as if it were your own, and not bestowed on you by some faraway Lady Bountiful. My interest is in your investigation and ultimate discovery, not in the replenishment of your wardrobe or in room service at Claridge's. And is that a charge for theatre tickets I see? Are you a theatrical enthusiast, Mr. Harry? I didn't know that. You were in New York for weeks, but to the best of my knowledge never came to see *my* show.

If I haven't heard a suitable report from you in a day or two, I really think it may be best to call this whole venture to a halt and bring you home. I agreed to it in a moment of passion, and it definitely wasn't my best self at the helm. I won't say I'm regretting it, Mr. Harry; but I reserve that right for later.

8/29/97, 1:21 P.M.

You have reached the law offices of Gretchen Ojan. Our hours are Monday through Friday, eight-thirty a.m. to six-thirty p.m. After the tone, you may leave a message for Ms. Ojan or her assistant, Kevin Putnam. Thank you.

Gretchen, luv, it's Viola. Got your message—and well, what can I say. I'm terribly sorry the check bounced. Can't imagine how that happened. Though I confess I've been in something of a fiscal muddle lately; you know how I am with records-keeping and what with being in Manhattan for so long I just don't have access to my files back home and . . . I don't know, crossing all my t's and dotting my i's has never been my forte, and it all seems to have got away from me. I'm very embarrassed. But the thing is, I don't know when I'll be able to get home and straighten things out. The police have asked me not to leave town because the investigation into poor Alex's death isn't closed yet, although I can't imagine why, there's clearly nothing to investigate but a coronary.

In the meantime, considering how vital it is that we not lose even a day when we're so close to our court date, could I convince you, angel, to continue doing your typically splendid job on the promise of future payment? Hm? Which I can absolutely say without any hesitation will be as soon as I get back to town.

Thanks, luv. You're my hero, you know that.

Kisses to Kevin!

I DON'T KNOW WHERE YOU THINK YOU ARE
GOING!

FARTHER AND FARTHER AWAY DO YOU THINK
YOU ARE ESCAPING ME!

BECAUSE YOU ARE NOT!

I ALSO HOPE YOU FIND THIS EXCITING! WHEN
WE FINALLY MEET AGAIN IT SHOULD BE VERY
HOT! ARE YOU HOT RIGHT NOW?

I AM HOT RIGHT NOW!

I LIKE FOLLOWING YOU!

I FEEL LIKE I COULD DO IT FOREVER!

You-KNOW-WHO
You-DON'T-KNOW-WHERE

SUBJ: scotland the brave
DATE: 97-8-29 06:15:15 EST
FROM: emanfr@ysa.net
TO: nbcasem@bot.ubsm.edu

arrived in edinburgh a few hours ago. listen before we go any further there's something i need to say and remember this please it's important. if anything happens to me here meaning if i should get hurt or killed even if it looks accidental it's not. it's my stalker who is getting just a little too weird for comfort somehow he's managed to follow me here. i need you to remember this just in case I'm in no shape to tell anyone you have to be the one to blow the whistle on this guy.

dig this i was at victoria station buying a ticket for my train and when i turned around to pick up my suitcase there was a note on it from him he must have come right up behind me and slipped it under the handle. it's totally creepy i haven't even seen the guy since cornwall but he's been dogging my steps and just forget everything I said last time about kind of liking that i don't anymore. not. one. bit.

anyway when i got off the train in edinburgh i switched cabs about three times before getting to my hotel so maybe i gave him the slip we'll see. meantime i got here early enough i was able to do some smilin and dialin. and guess what i think i've found beva. i only had to call three rest homes before i found her at a place called the john de balliol. but now i have the problem of getting in to see her. see when i called I asked if they had any residents named beva i'm sorry i don't have a last name and the woman said why yes beva martin she's been here eight years. and i asked if i could come in tomorrow to speak with her and she immediately balked and said why would you want to see beva. i thought about telling the truth that i was researching a life of viola chute but if she asked why I'd want to talk to beva about viola chute i don't know what i'd say. i'm still not 100 percent sure there even is a direct connection between them it's just a hunch. so thinking quickly i said oh i'm a distant relation of beva's from america and i'm researching a family history. there was a long pause and then the woman said you mean beva is a relation of yours but you didn't know her last name. oops busted. i said oh but she's a distant relation and i didn't know if she had married or remarried or really anything about her other than that she used to be in the employ of one of the great houses up here. and that seemed to mollify the woman but she still didn't give her permission. she said beva was not quite all there anymore and it might confuse or upset her to have a visitor after all these years especially one asking questions. i have to go up tomorrow and make my case before the resident director.

boy this better pay off that's all i've got to say because i've come a very very long way for this—scotland for christ's sake—and i'm flat broke just surviving on the credit card of some quixotic movie star who's acting like she might revoke the privilege at any minute. and i mean it's one thing to be stranded in new york city but to be stranded in edinburgh yikes. there's no way i'd ever get home i'd have to just settle here. pretty town though in fact very very pretty i suppose if it came to it i could learn to like it here.

to make things worse i've been checking the american papers and the internet and it appears viola has just completely fallen off the radar screen so i have to wonder whether anyone will even give a shit about her by the time i have this story to peddle. my one hope is that she runs true to form does something so desperate and outrageous that it propels her back into the headlines again. but she's getting older maybe she isn't up to it. plus look at the whole alex wylie incident i mean she basically fucked a guy to death and even that's being treated like old news. so how much hope is there i wonder. the public just seems to be over her.

funny thing though i find i actually miss her. i look back on my life the past few years first working on the novel then trying to get my journalism career back on track—it's been a pretty lonely haul. and then viola came along and it was the first time anyone was ever really interested in me as a person. and no my stalker doesn't count. he's convinced himself he cares about me but all he really cares about is using me to get to hollywood.

sure sure i was just a sidekick to viola and no one will ever interest her as much as she interests herself but she was good to me she listened when i spoke she tried to convince me to get laid she even bought me things. she was a good friend and i don't have many of those. and don't get your nose out of joint you don't count because you're halfway across the country and besides your own plate has been full first with your divorce and then the infamous foot. naturally you are in a class by yourself but what i'm trying to say is so's viola.

so here i am trying to dig up something she doesn't want dug up just so i can add to the general shitload of misery she's suffering under right now. got a bad case of the guilts i guess.

but the hell with it i've come this far. let me discover the deep dark secret at least. i can always not use it.

remember what i told you. about if i end up dead.

hugs hugs and more hugs
harry

You have reached the law offices of Gretchen Ojan. Our hours are Monday through Friday, eight-thirty a.m. to six-thirty p.m. After the tone, you may leave a message for Ms. Ojan or her assistant, Kevin Putnam. Thank you.

Gretchen. It's Viola. I suppose I ought to be grateful that I've chosen an attorney who can be such a fucking hardass. Excuse me, however, if I don't feel entirely happy about it at the moment.

Regarding your threat—and yes, it was a threat, angel, however you might wish to frame it otherwise—that you'll no longer represent me unless you're promptly paid . . . well, luv, that would rather amount to cutting off your nose to spite your face, wouldn't it? Hm? I mean, you're entitled to the money, and you'll *get* the money, but drop me now and of course you'll never see a penny of it. So it really wouldn't make sense to go that route.

Also, you know what a high-profile case this is—I'm a television star, and that bastard of a photographer has turned himself into a one-man victim industry—so do you really think it's wise to give up the potential publicity? The TV appearances, angel, you with your hair newly styled, looking smashing in that ash-gray Armani of yours, microphones waving in your face while you spout a bunch of legalese that means nothing? Lawyers *kill* for that kind of exposure. Don't pretend you're not one of them.

That said, I can understand your anger. You've put a lot of work into this case and you deserve compensation. I want you to *have* compensation, luv. Alas, at this exact moment, I'm not able to provide it. At least not in the usual way. I was thinking, however, that we might come to a different understanding . . .

You know that choker of mine you're always admiring? The one with the emerald? Would you perhaps accept that as a kind of pawn, against the day I settle my account with you? . . . Or as yours forever, should that day never come?

Just let me know, angel. And yes, I'm still at the Pierre. Don't listen to what people are saying: they're just vicious gossips. I'm here and I'm not budging.

Kisses to Kevin.

—elieve I've ever spoken into one of these before. Makes one feel a proper pop star. Shirley Bassey! Here, shall I sing a lick of "Goldfinger," then? I know all the lyric, my pet. You think, she's an old woman, but I know a thing or three as would surprise you . . . Am I speaking the right way? Will it suffice? . . . you're a good-looking young man, you are. I fancied a young man once as look liked you. A proper cad he was, but that's not you, is it? . . . A gentleman through and through you are, I can tell, and never mind you're American . . . I had an American friend once, during the war, name of Dorothy but liked to be called Dot which I thought very comical . . . You don't perhaps know her? . . . Of course not, you being so young and Dot dead these many years . . . A burst kidney, did you ever? It doesn't bear thinking of . . . But the way that woman would carry on! Drinking and men at all hours. One doesn't wonder . . . How old are you, if you don't mind me asking? . . . Thirty-nine? You don't look at all thirty-nine. I'd have said twenty-five at the outside . . . Remind me why you're here, my pet. I'm an old woman, I forget things . . . My life in service? Oh, you do disappoint. I thought perhaps you'd come to hear about my many love affairs . . . Don't mind me, pet, I'm being silly. The sad fact is, I haven't had any . . . result of a life lived in service. And it was a full life in service, too, from the time I was a girl . . . Fourteen I was, sent to work the kitchen. Not cooking, mind you . . . Never one for the oven. I like to eat well enough, but . . . alas . . . Now, the one time I was ever out of service was the war. That was a grand time! Put to work driving a truck, wasn't I, off gathering up rubber for the war effort. I wore overalls and a fisherman's hat and oh it was glorious. And there was a young man who came to call on me then, so you mustn't think it was all . . . What was his name, then? . . . Don't tell me . . . I know it . . . How can I forget such a thing? . . . I want to say Donald, but no . . . he . . . don't tell me . . . he . . . he was the first over that . . . that why, why I once didn't make the feeling of having been up the time before—and that's, and that's the only one, not ever so pleased at making out that he wasn't at all what one looked fo— Hm? . . . Oh, dear, was I running away with myself? You must just give me a good squeeze when I do that, to bring me round . . . Matron says I speak nothing but nonsense and have no place here, she'd like to send me to a sanitarium . . . Have you met matron? Fierce woman, a look in her eyes that can stop you growing. And she doesn't half fancy herself grand! Coming round the wards in her bracelets and her earrings as though just off to tea with the lord mayor . . . if you see her, you mustn't mention me running away with myself, it wouldn't do at all . . . You will remember, won't you? . . . Thank you, my pet, you're a proper gentleman, and there's an end to it. And good looking as well! How old are you? . . . Thirty-nine? You're never thirty-nine! Twenty-five, I'd have said. I'd have wagered a quid on it . . . I'm sorry, my pet, what are we talking about? . . . My life in service? Is that all you want to know about me? . . . Don't you want to know about my many love affairs? . . . Never mind, I'm having you on. Verna down the other end, she got asked by a young man from the BBC about her love affairs . . . Gave her a proper teasing over that, we did . . . Helena? You want to know about Helena? . . . Yes, I remember her. Course I remember her. I'm just . . . Helena as worked for his lordship, then? . . . His lordship, my employer that was. Before I came here. Do you know him? . . . Killwall was his name. Chester, Viscount Killwall . . . Oh, you *do* know him! Now there's a thing! I hadn't thought you might. I've not heard from him, you know. Will you tell him? . . . Thirty-five years in his service. One doesn't expect a visit, but a nice card on one's birthday or . . . I know he's a busy man and very important, but . . . but he . . . well, one doesn't mean to presume but he . . . he ought to really have made a wonderment of why

it takes so long a spell for naught to come of it, ever, ever having expected such a way for it to have come abou— Heavens,
was I at it again? . . . Thank you for the squeeze, my pet . . . Are
we relations, then? . . . thought that might be why you've
come to see me. . . . No? . . . Not a relation, and not the BBC?
As that's the only reasons the young ones ever come here . . . Oh,
it's Helena, is it? Yes, I remember Helena as worked for his
lordship. Up at the house . . . She wasn't there long, you
know. No one ever expected that. From the moment she arrived, she had an air of caged animal . . . What did she *look*
like? Didn't you say you was her relation? I'm very confused . . . Well, she was a youngish sort . . . younger than me,
anyway. Not particularly pretty. Though she had possibili-
ties . . . we always told her, with a little effort, she could be almost handsome . . . Shame to see a young girl like that wasting
her youth attending his lordship . . . I shouldn't say, because
it's not the sort of thing one speaks of, but his lordship was
never one for the ladies . . . See, he'd had some gentlemen's
gentlemen before, hadn't he—valets as you'd call them in
America—and there'd been a lot of talk about that. That's all
I'll say, and draw a veil over it . . . But you can imagine, when
Helena arrived, we was all quite relieved, because she could
bring breakfast to his bedroom and dress him every morning
and undress him at night, and we all knew there was never a
worry in it . . . Funny thing, isn't it, just the opposite of what
you'd expect . . . But Helena hated it, she loathed his lordship,
and the awful thing is, she let it show . . . I used to tell her,
Helena, you've got to be more of an actress, you can't let it show
in your face so. And once, I remember, she said to me, Beva,
you don't understand, he *enjoys* my contempt. What ever do
you suppose she meant by that? . . . I often wonder . . . Anyway, the poor wee lass, I was her only friend, the others all
thought her too grand. And she was, in a way . . . You could
tell for dead cert she'd never been in service before. Didn't
know how to do *anything* . . . I had to teach her how to bleach
knickers and starch shirts and iron sleeves, it was comical . . .
She never did learn to his lordship's satisfaction. But then she

didn't stay long. You heard the way she left, I suppose? . . . What, not even that? . . . not even . . . not even . . . What . . . what is this thing? This thing in my face, I . . . I'm . . . I'm sorry, who are you? I don't recall as anyone asked me if I was up to seeing any . . . Where's the girl? Maggie! . . . *Maggie!* . . . What time is it? I need to get up, I've got things to do . . . Where's my *mending* kit? . . . What's this *thing* in my face? . . . I don't understand what's *happ*—

From
"DOWNTOWN BEAT"
New York Herald Tribune
August 30, 1997

... Rumor has it that a certain newly ex–television star has been asked by the management of the Hotel Pierre to vacate the premises for nonpayment of her bill. I guess it should come as some comfort to the has-been in question that even when you can't get arrested in this town, you *can* get *evicted* ...

HOMICIDE SUSPECTED IN PRODUCER'S DEATH
Los Angeles Times
August 30, 1997

LOS ANGELES—The Los Angeles County Coroner's Office yesterday released the results of an autopsy performed last week on television producer Alex Wylie that revealed traces of amyl nitrite in the deceased's blood. Wylie, 61, died in New York on August 7 of massive heart failure, and authorities are now looking into the possibility that abuse of the drug was at least partly responsible for the fatal attack. "In which case," says Detective Sgt. Mason Ellerbee of the New York Police Department "whoever provided him with the substance is potentially guilty of manslaughter."

At the time of Wylie's death, he was socializing with television star Viola Chute in his room at the Paramount Hotel. Police are expected to question Chute again about the events of that night, but as of this writing the actress is not officially a suspect.

Amyl nitrite is a chemical compound used chiefly as a resuscitator in cases of drowning and prolonged fainting. Under the street name "poppers," the inhalant is also popular in discos and gay nightclubs due to its powerful stimulation of the heart muscle.

INJURED PHOTOGRAPHER RECEIVES
LIFETIME ACHIEVEMENT AWARD

Los Angeles Times
August 30, 1997

LOS ANGELES—Dallas photojournalist Berry Leyton has been selected as this year's recipient of the prestigious Merrill B. Priest Award, given out each year by the Society for the Celluloid Arts in recognition of "a lifetime of achievement in the area of celebrity iconography."

The selection is controversial on two fronts. Firstly, it is the first time in the history of the award that it is being presented to a photographer outside the Los Angeles area. Although Leyton, a Dallas native, recently relocated to Burbank, his body of work predates this move. Indeed, Leyton's career is, by his own estimation, now over, due to an injury he sustained in an April confrontation with the actress Viola Chute, who objected to being photographed while on holiday in the British Virgin Islands. (Leyton is suing Chute for assault; the opening arguments in the case are being heard next week.)

The second controversy is over the nature of Leyton's work. "Merrill Priest was a studio photographer during the Golden Age," says the film historian Jonas Loman. "He specialized in crafting hyperreal, almost godlike identities for film stars by a brilliant commingling of gesture, makeup, and lighting. All the recipients of the award that bears his name have done likewise. This Leyton person is a paparazzo; he chases celebrities and snaps them on the fly. It's all grainy and candid—the antithesis of what Priest devoted his life to."

But Leyton has numerous defenders. "The whole idea of celebrity has changed," offers cultural critic Paola Molinara. "We're not interested in the false fronts anymore; we want to see the naked truth—the human being behind the eight-by-ten glossy. Freelance 'event' photographers like Leyton specialize in that—capturing the unguarded moment, the telling glance. He points the way toward a new era in celebrity portraits."

Loman sniffs at this. "The man's benefited from a sympathy vote, that's all," he says. "There's a tremendous amount of support for him in his case against Viola Chute, and people seem to want to compensate him for the loss of his career. But this is the wrong way to do it. Merrill Priest is rolling over in his grave."

Leyton is reserving any comments for the awards banquet, which is scheduled for October 15.

"The night is bitter, the stars have lost their glitter . . . and all because of the call that got awaaay . . ." Hi, this is E. Manfred Harry. Don't hang up and leave me wailing in despair. Leave your name and number after the tone and I'll get back to you.

Isn't there a way a caller can bypass that greeting? . . . Pressing the pound button, or something? I know people who have that option. You should look into it.

This is Georgia Kirkby, Mr. Harry. I got your message this afternoon. I'm very glad to have heard from you, but a bit confused. I understand that you're excited about this old woman you seem to have found in Edinburgh—Edinburgh, Mr. Harry!—but I still don't quite comprehend what she has to do with Viola Chute. You keep mentioning her insights into a certain "Helena" but I don't recall anyone of that name from our discussions . . . exactly whom are you investigating, Mr. Harry?

By all means, do speak to the old woman again, if you think it's absolutely necessary. But after that, I'd like you to put your notes in order and come back to the States. To Los Angeles, please; I'm headed there tomorrow to resume shooting my show. When you arrive you can show me what, if anything, you've found, and we can discuss whether it's of any use to me.

Oh . . . and I do advise you to purchase your plane tickets by the end of day tomorrow, because after that your credit card may no longer be of use to you.

Goodbye, then.

EDINBURGH
8/31/97, 11:14 A.M.

. . . ery nice indeed of you to come back after I made such a to-
do the last time. Imagine my going on so, as though I was half
daft! What you must think of me. Fagged, is all I was . . . It
doesn't half get wearying here, you see, as there's naught to do,
and that can drain a body, can't it? . . . And then, just when
I've got the rhythm of doing nothing, 'round comes nosy you
with all your questions, dredging up all those memories, well,
you can imagine it made me feel a mite rough . . . Not your
fault, my pet, how could you know . . . But then your friend
coming round later to do the same! I was all in . . . Why didn't
you let on as you was a fancy boy . . . Your friend told me . . . Oh
dear, I don't recall his name now. You must know who I mean.
Begins with an A . . . But didn't you let me go on and on about
his lordship, tiptoeing around the word, when all the time you
were sitting there saying piss all . . . Sorry, my pet, but now I
know the kind of man you are, I feel a mite freer with my
tongue . . . Andy, yes, that's right, that's the name . . . See,
there was more than a few poofters in his lordship's service,
and didn't they make it all a lark, everything a laugh and nothing sacred . . . Heavens, my pet, I don't recall *when* your Andy
came round, it was before my dinner, that's all I know . . . Bit
of a rascal, your Andy. You'd have blushed to see him flirt . . . Me,
though, I lapped it up like milk. At my age, that kind of attention is always welcome and never mind it's from a poofter
young enough to be my grandson . . . Cornish, isn't he? Not as
thick an accent as I'd have thought, but with telly today people
are sounding more and more alike, aren't they . . . You all
right, my pet? You look like you've had a proper turn . . . I've
some bicarbonate of soda and you're welcome to it, I won't
drink the bloody stuff. Hurts my tongue. But they will insist on

238

giving it me . . . Very well, then, but I've nothing more to offer . . . A Yank, aren't you? . . . How old? . . . Twenty-five?
You're never! I'd have guessed thirty-six, thirty-seven . . . But
at my age, what do I know? You all look like wee ones to
me . . . It's hell being old, my pet. Don't ever do it. You don't
want to end up like me at the end of the day, no way to fill all
the time . . . Very . . . very mis . . . dis . . . di . . . what I . . . I,
oh . . . all the hours, you see . . . the hours I spend, I spend, I
spend all my time and no time for a change, do him some good
for nothing is what he amounted to, little more than that, that
was before you say another word in your ear to the— Now,
pet, you mustn't tweak, it's not gentlemanly . . . What was I
going on about? . . . Helena? . . . Helena as worked for his
lordship, years agone? . . . Why on God's green earth was I
talking about Helena? Haven't mentioned her to anyone in
years . . . Well, yes, she was in service with me, and heaven
knows I tried to befriend that woman, but she would act like
cock of the walk, wouldn't she . . . Never a popular one with
the others, was Helena . . . Hm? . . . Oh, you didn't hear how
she left us? Great scandal, it was . . . She was his lordship's
personal atten— say, *haven't* I told you this before . . . You're
sure, then? . . . She was his lordship's personal attendant, his
gentleman's gentleman if you like, except of course for her being a woman . . . *That* wasn't the scandal, my pet, because no
woman had much to fear from his lordship, he was like you, a
great bloody pansy . . . Sorry . . . Well, his lordship is a collector, isn't he . . . Oh, everything, paintings and statues
mainly, also jewels and crystal and such, anything at all posh,
he'll buy it up just like that . . . And didn't we wake up one
morning and find Helena gone, and not just Helena, but a set
of silver candlesticks . . . Quite a shock, it was, because she'd
been with us for going on two years, so we all thought as we
knew her . . . When the theft was discovered—it was young
Jean who noticed the candlesticks gone, she got hysterical and
Mr. MacInerny had to give her a brandy to settle her, which
was the wrong thing to do because didn't she go on to be a regular old soak . . . Where was I? . . . Oh, yes, pet, thank you.

When the theft was discovered, his lordship had Tommy set the dogs after Helena, gave them a good scent of some of her old stockings as was in the laundry, and didn't they go tearing away, baying so's to put the fear of God into you and no mistake . . . Well, Helena got away, didn't she, so we all figured she'd had herself a good head start, probably during the wee hours. But then the candlesticks was found by Bob some weeks later, when he went out to do the tilling. And they wasn't that far out on the grounds, so we figured Helena must've heard the dogs coming after her and dropped them to give her more speed. So she can't have left all that early . . . The police was called, of course, but they did bugger all . . . Now, my pet, I'll tell you something, because I don't want to take any secrets to the grave, I don't believe in it—and well you're here, aren't you, and you're asking about Helena, and if I don't tell it now, when will I? So here it is, then: Helena wrote to me not six months after to say as she was well and happy, in America of all places, and that she thought of me oft, and it ill pleased her that I might think less than well of her after all my kindnesses, what with her running off like a thief and not even a proper goodbye . . . She said it was a terrible thing she did, or tried to do, but she was that unhappy, and one morning as she was starting her duties she just snapped, the poor lamb, grabbed the nearest thing of value and bolted . . . Well, she never was happy with his lordship, I knew that, quite miserable to be honest, so I guess I understood, so I wrote her back thanking her for thinking of me and for explaining it all. And no one else ever knew it, but we wrote each other for some time after . . . I still send her a card each Christmas, don't I . . . Course I have the address, you daft thing, how else would I send it? . . . What? . . . Why ever would you be wanting Helena's address? . . . Never mind, my pet, you can have it, it's in that drawer there . . . No, the next one down . . . See there, the book with the roses on the cover, that's my address book . . . Open it to T . . . Helena Tregothan being her name . . .

What's that? . . . Viola Chute? . . . The film star, you mean? . . . Did Helena ever *mention* her? . . . Now, it's a funny thing, you saying that. I'd quite forgot. . . . but didn't we used to tell Helena how much she looked like Viola Chute. If only she'd tart herself up a bit, we'd say, she'd be the very spit—

. . . Oh, you're not going so soon? . . . very well, then, my pet, you're a dear one to come and see poor old Beva, and look how much better I've behaved, not running off with myself even once . . . Mind, I've got a clearer head today than matron will ever credit, but that's because I've got someone to talk to . . . You'll come again? . . . Do try, my pet . . . Andy says he'll come again . . .

SUBJ: THE SECRET THE SECRET THE SECRET
DATE: 97-8-31 05:11:44 EST
FROM: emanfr@ysa.net
TO: nbcasem@bot.ubsm.edu

wow i guess i've really finally discovered something important here because for the first time i'm kinda scared to write to you i mean maybe someone will hack into this file and read it. i know i know like there are hackers everywhere dying to know the secrets of some middle-aged actress. all right then i'm throwing caution to the winds. here's what i've figured out.

i was way off base with my whole murder theory but the truth is even stranger. viola chute and the mysterious helena are one and the same. see helena's last name is tregothan and according to beva— who admittedly is mad—she was the spitting image of viola. at first i thought maybe viola had an estranged sister named helena who would naturally have her same last name and look something like her but then i remembered i've seen all of viola's family records no sister brother sibling of any kind. plus the dates helena worked for viscount killwall—oh wait i haven't even mentioned that part. get this helena and beva worked side by side for killwall the blackmailer—anyway the dates helena worked for him are exactly the dates viola is unac- counted for. plus when helena left killwall she tried to steal some sil- ver candlesticks but didn't get away with it and this is just before viola turns up on edward chute's doorstep in london begging for money. it all fits see.

plus the smoking gun beva gave me—the address she has for helena is a po box in viola's zip code. eureka baby!

so apparently after her career failed viola went to scotland to live on the estate of a faggot nobleman where she pretended to be a ser-

vant named helena for 17 months then got fed up and fled penniless
back to the states. i guess maybe i was premature in trumpeting that
i discovered the secret because there's still a big part of it missing the
rather urgent question of why. why the flying fuck would she do
something like this. was killwall blackmailing her even then was there
something he was holding over her head that made her do whatever
he wanted even posing as a chambermaid. i know i can get to the
bottom of this if i can only get to killwall and have a look around his
house so you guessed it i'm on my way north. according to beva the
mansion there is virtually empty no staff to speak of even killwall himself barely goes there anymore. perfect for snooping yes as in break-
ing and entering. cover me with derision if you must i don't care i'm
hot on the trail now and nothing will stop me.

plus i've got someone hot on the trail of ME which is the sort of
thing that gives you a different feeling about the rule of law. remember my stalker andy course you do. well he's in edinburgh apparently
no farther than a dozen yards from me at any given time because
god damn if he doesn't seem to know every tiny thing i do. after i
went to see beva so did he. also he somehow managed to get a key
to my hotel room—i smelled his cologne when i got in and the bed
wasn't made which it was when i'd left. plus forty pounds stolen from
my dresser. this guy is seriously sicko plus i mean you should see the
notes he's been leaving they don't even make sense anymore. the last
one said he could read the thoughts in my head and he knew i was
excited by this cat and mouse game and it was going to be totally hot
when i finally got caught. no i'm serious that's what it said this is apparently a turn-on for him and he's convinced for me too. which not
to protest too much but no no absolutely not period finito end of
story.

at the present time i'm sitting at a train station looking over my shoulder every ninety seconds in case he's here watching. that and the fact
that i'm typing on a laptop make me stick out like a sore thumb here
so if andy is anywhere in the vicinity he should have no trouble spot-
ting me. but really i think i may have given him the slip this time because i got up at about two a.m. and snuck out of the hotel. didn't

check out either so as not to alert andy—but also i'll be coming back
this way on my return trip and i'll need a place to stay. one thing wor-
ries me though i settled my bill before i left because gk is threatening
to pull the plug on me yeah i know the fucking pig bitch but what
could i do. i just don't want anything unusual making andy suspicious
and a closed account might do that.

oh here's my train

still waiting for you to reply from my last email. i know i scarcely gave
you time. i want you to know even though i'm involved in numerous
intrigues and escapades i still think of you a lot and am hoping for
your swift and permanent recovery.

got to board now remember what i said before about if i die. you'll
be the only one who knows.

hugs
harry

This is exciting!

I have always wanted to see the Scottish Highlands!

But I am intrigued I don't know why we are going there!

I like it that you are a man of mystery! It makes me HOT!

By the way you shouldn't leave food in your seat! If you didn't want to finish that sandwich you should have taken it from the train and tossed it!

Don't worry I took it and finished it off for you! Delicious!

You-know-who

P.S. I am running out of money so this will have to end soon! VERY soon!

. . . *Winds of Wyndhamville* fans who have been waiting for a knock-down drag-out between Jocasta Wyndham and Grand Duchess Samantha will be happy to hear the match has taken place—but alas, not on camera! Seems last night, former cast member **Viola Chute** crashed a party honoring **Georgia Kirkby** at Chef **Arnold Drake's** new Chelsea bistro, Clopant. The bash was a private affair thrown by the Exquisite Corpse theatre troupe to thank Kirkby for rescuing them from penury (the star famously spent the summer guest-starring in their off-Broadway revue). Chute, who didn't let herself be deterred by a little thing like not being invited, melted into the crowd and spent nearly an hour telling anyone who would listen that Kirkby had personally driven her from the show and ruined her career. When the guest of honor finally noticed her, heated words were exchanged; Kirkby then threw her drink in Chute's face, and Chute pushed Kirkby, derrière-première, into the layer cake the troupe had had made in her honor. Chute was then forcibly ejected by Clopant management. Seems the embattled actress just can't stay out of trouble. Last week she lost her job and was denounced in Congress for degeneracy; this week she faces eviction from the Hotel Pierre. And next week, she'll be on trial for assault in Los Angeles—that is, if the NYPD allow her to leave town, which isn't likely since she's under suspicion of reckless homicide in the death of producer Alex Wylie. Say, wasn't Samantha supposed to be the *good* girl? . . .

"The night is bitter, the stars have lost their glitter . . . and all because of the call that got awaaay . . ." Hi, this is E. Manfred Harry. Don't hang up and leave me wailing in despair. Leave your name and number after the tone and I'll get back to you.

Mr. Harry, this is Georgia Kirkby. I'm still in New York; I was forced to miss my flight to Los Angeles last night by . . . an outrageous . . . event that . . . that I . . . never mind, Mr. Harry. I am apparently too angry to speak coherently on the matter.

Mr. Harry, I want to see you as soon as possible. I want all the information you have collected on that dreadful woman. I'm flying out this morning, so if you left London last night it's possible we may arrive in Los Angeles at nearly the same time. Should you happen to retrieve this message while in the air, please take this opportunity to call Julia at my production office and give her your flight information. I would like, if possible, to meet your plane, or have you meet mine. In the event that this is impracticable, just make an appointment to see me. The earliest you can manage. Julia has my calendar.

Thank you. Goodbye.

From
THE SLACKER'S GUIDE TO GREAT BRITAIN
by Jo Mo Patterman
eXPress Ltd., 1995

. . . Going north toward Pitlochry on the A9 you'll pass through County Killwall and the estate of the Killwall clan, **Ballawinnie.** And yes that's its real name, and yes, every American under forty immediately rechristens it Ballsandweenie, so don't think you're so clever. Anyway you don't get a great view of the place from the road, you can see it better from the River Tummel if you're into canoeing or whatever. The house sits on about 500 acres of pristine Highlands property—or I should say sat, because a lot of the estate has been sold off to commercial interests by the latest Viscount Killwall, who is about a hundred years old with no kids so maybe he figures what the hell. One of the buyers was a sports development corp that promptly leveled some of the landscape to fill out a golf course, which as you can imagine was real popular with the locals, so in addition to being superannuated the viscount has to deal with being aristo-non-grato with his neighbors.

But then he doesn't really see much of them because Ballawinnie House is shut up for most of the year. The viscount doesn't stay there often and even when he does you're not welcome there, so just deal with it. This isn't like those other great houses where they open their arms to you and your AmEx and let you play I'm-a-British-lord for a weekend by shooting clay pigeons in the yard and eating fried blood for breakfast. Viscount Killwall doesn't want anything to do with you so just steer clear, okay? His security staff has a particularly vicious reputation in the area, and even though there are only about two of them for the entire billion-room mansion, you don't want to take your chances.

You might want to eyeball the house as you pass, though, as it's considered a pretty decent pile of bricks by people who go in for that sort of thing. It was built in 1680 by an architect from the Royal Society named Euripides Lash. (Doesn't it seem like everybody in 17th-century England had a totally bitchin' name?) It's built on the grounds of what used to be the ancient Castle Ballawinnie, which, if we're talking pile of bricks, is about all Castle Ballawinnie was. See, the castle wasn't burned down by angry peasants or bombed by the Luftwaffe or eaten away by rot and mildew, or any of the other fates that usually befall British castles. No, Castle Ballawinnie just . . . fell down one day. Blame it on a really bad construction job by some 12th-century architect who probably had his finger up his nose the entire time he was drawing the blueprints. (If they even had blueprints in the 12th century.) Anyway, when the place fell down the then lord of the manor (not yet a viscount) and his lady wife and all their kids were crushed to death, so the next brother down got to be the new lord and although he's the one who hired Euripides Lash and made the place something to look at today, he's also the one whose bloodline produced the present viscount, who won't let you go near it. That's history for you. Put it in your bong and smoke it.

Continuing along the A9 you'll find occasional mulberry trees which, in late summer, can keep you from getting too hungry while hitching . . .

INTERVIEW WITH VIOLA CHUTE
by E. Manfred Harry
(Excerpt)
Homophile, July 1993

HOMOPHILE: I want to thank you for taking the time to talk to *Homophile,* Viola.

VIOLA: Oh, I've enjoyed it.

HOMOPHILE: I'm sure your gay fans have enjoyed it even more. Any idea what's next for you?

VIOLA: Heavens. Hadn't thought that far ahead. I tend to live in the moment.

HOMOPHILE: You're not going to drop out of sight again, are you?

VIOLA: I hope not! I do rather love the limelight. But I suppose it's possible I could fall into another spell of husband-gathering and fortune-spending. (*laughs*)

HOMOPHILE: Well, we'll be watching you in any case. Before you go, I'd like to read you something written by the culture critic Paola Molinara—do you know her work?

VIOLA: No, sorry.

HOMOPHILE: She says: "The real value of our iconic film stars goes far beyond their onscreen roles. They continue to enrapture us offscreen as well, in the way that the demigods of antiquity and the saints of medieval Europe did; they sit between humanity and heaven. In them we see ourselves reflected, but also the gods." In the same essay, she also names you as being among those stars who "live life on an Olympic scale, eating, laughing, loving, grieving. No one wants to see Mamie van Doren pushing a perambulator or Joan Collins frying chicken or Viola Chute riding a bicycle. The current trend towards commonizing film stars, turning them from glorious icons into bourgeois artisans, is a disaster of the first rank, and will ruin more careers than it makes." Comment?

VIOLA: *(long pause)* I don't know *how* to ride a bicycle.

—ome in, come in. My name is Chester. This is my house . . . but then, I'm sure you knew that. You'd scarcely have taken the trouble to break in if you hadn't known all about me. Sit down. May I offer you a drink? . . . Not that you deserve it, but I'm going to have one, and I can't pour for myself without extending an offer to you. A pathology, if you will. Or simply the fascism of breeding.

I'm sorry if Billy was rough with you this morning, and that you've had to stay locked in the cupboard while I made the trip up from London. But that's what Billy's instructions are, when he finds an intruder in the house. And he *always* finds intruders, when there are intruders to be found. You see, my friend, what you and your ilk do not seem to anticipate—and why, I can never understand; I mean, knowing what I have here, do you think I would be *careless*?—is that even though my security staff is but two strong, the house is far from unprotected. As is, indeed, the entire estate. I have had installed the very latest in electronic surveillance and detection equipment. Oh, yes, I'm sure you were admirably quiet when you jimmied open that back door and crept across the kitchen; alas, you were dealing with sensors so finely tuned that to them, a housecat would have sounded like a brontosaurus. Still, don't feel bad; you'd blown your cover even before that. Billy and Nate were aware of you the moment you crossed the property line. Thanks to my electronic gates, you announced your coming like a herd of buffalo. Really, I'm amazed at the lack of sophistication exhibited by you young upstarts these days! In my time, a thief was a *professio*—

I'm sorry? . . . *Not* a thief?

Ah. I see.

I'm to believe you're a tourist, then? Looking for a golf ball gone rather badly awry?

I ask you, please, not to insult me. I have dealt with your ilk many times before and have heard every feeble lie, every plea . . . The idea that you . . . Look, even now you can't stop eying the painting that hangs over my shoulder. You're thinking it looks like a Rembrandt, but not any Rembrandt you've ever seen before. And that is, of course, because it *is* a Rembrandt no one has seen before. Not in a hundred and thirty-six years, at any rate. And it's exactly the kind of thing you were sent here to—

Oh, dear. This is rather disgusting. But I congratulate you on being original at least. You are, I am quite certain, the first errand boy of my experience to break down in tears upon capture.

. . . What am I going to *do* to you? What do you think? Send you back to your master, of course. Empty-handed. Who is it that you work for, boy? Hm? Out with it . . . I'll have the name from you, one way or another . . .

Geo . . . yes, go on . . .

Geo . . . for God's sake, man, pull yourself together!

. . . Georgia . . . Kirkby?

. . . I'm sorry. Do you mean Georgia Kirkby, the actress? . . . I had no idea she was a collector. How can she live so . . . *publicly* and not be found out? . . . Hm? . . . Boy? . . . Oh, not another squall! Really, I've seen Girl Guides with more iron in them.

Billy, fetch him a brandy. I don't care whether he wants one or not, he's having one.

. . . What's that? . . . You're here to . . . *what?*

Viola Chute? . . .

Helena? . . .

Unauthorized *biography*? . . .

Ah.

Ah-*hah*.

I think I begin to see what's happened here. You're not an errand boy at all, are you?

You're a writer, then. *A journalist.*

And indeed I begin to remember you, now. The unwelcome visitor who interrupted us at the Pierre . . . that was you, wasn't it?

Oh, dear.

I don't know why you should think that's going to help you. Makes it rather the worse for you, really. See, I could have counted on honor among thieves. Sent you packing with your tail between your legs and not had to worry about you saying a thing.

But now . . . I mean, you've come here *looking* for secrets to tell. And alas, in finding Viola's, you've discovered mine.

This explains the tape recording device, doesn't it? The one you've hidden under your jacket, that you activated the moment you walked in, thinking I wouldn't notice.

Well, never mind. You shan't be allowed to leave with it.

Let me think for a moment. I don't honestly know what to do about you . . .

Hm? . . . Yes, yes, of *course* Viola Chute worked for me. You already knew that, you said so yourself . . . What? . . . Why? . . . I must say, you're very inquisitive for someone whose immediate future is looking darker by the second. Have a care.

But as long as you asked . . . and as neither of us is going anywhere . . . very well. I'll tell you.

Don't bother adjusting the knobs on your device. I told you, you won't be leaving with it.

You can see I'm a collector. Since you're not what I thought you were, I suppose I must explain that when I say it, the word has a special significance. Since my youth, I have been interested in rare things . . . one-of-a-kind. I have always had a desire to own them, possess them . . . actually, it's more than that. Difficult to express, really. I've never attempted to explain myself to anyone before.

The long and the short of it is, I like to own things that no one else can ever see or touch. Things, fine things, that the vulgar world has not spoiled with its interest. The Rembrandt above us, for example. It came up for sale by a previous collector during the war. It is entirely possible that it might have passed into the hands of a legitimate buyer and been put on display. But no, I rescued it from the indignity of public scrutiny. And I must tell you, even now, the sight of your untrained eyes raking across its surface is just about more than I can take.

You've been through the house—well, some of it, anyway. You must have seen what I have here. Or perhaps I'm overestimating you. You're an American, so I suppose your knowledge of painting and sculpture goes no farther than your own juvenile watercolor smears and modeling-clay abortions. But believe me, in the halls of this house exists a collection, assembled lovingly over many decades, of Western masterpieces from the Middle Ages to the twilight of Impressionism—a collection that would, if it were appraised today, be valued at something close to a billion dollars.

The irony, of course, is that such an appraisal would reduce the worth of these works to almost nothing, in my eyes. To me, their value lies in their utter invisibility to the greater world. Most of these works have been missing for so long that their very existence is forgotten.

An added irony, alas, is that acquiring these paintings has nearly broken me, financially. I've had to sell off great stretches of my estate just to be able to afford them, and in turn to secure the house against their theft—an exceedingly expensive proposition, but exceedingly necessary, as well, as I can scarcely insure them in the usual manner.

But I'm getting away from the meat of your question.

There was a time, some twenty years ago, when my collection was first beginning to burgeon, that I was overtaken by a feeling of invincibility. I had made rather a lot of money through foreign investments, and was managing to add to my collection while keeping the house fully operational and staffed. I of course hired only the most ignorant servants I could find, those who would never look twice at any of the artworks around them.

Have you ever attempted something that was audacious in the extreme, and yet got away with it? . . . It's a heady feeling. It makes one foolhardy. And that's what happened to me. I began to seek other means of gratifying my obsession . . . this need to possess the rarest and most beautiful things alive, to remove them from circulation for my own private perusal.

It was at this time that I met Viola Chute at a party in Los Angeles. It was the kind of affair that bored me utterly, so I sat apart from the proceedings, watching with disdain. I was only there at the behest of a young man of my acquaintance, whose very great desire was to attend these sorts of soiree in as great a profusion as possible. Anyway, as I said, Viola was there. She looked ill and unkempt. I knew who she was, of course, and was shocked to see her looking so bereft of self-possession. There was an air of desperation about her, as well; I could see it in the way she approached people. I also noted with interest that whenever she did so, those approached turned away from her. It was only when she happened to pass my way that I noticed the stench of defeat about her. She was like a walking corpse, petrifying and putrefying. Los Angeles is a brutal town; I have never liked it, never. It had chewed up and spit out this woman, and she was too stunned by the experience yet to realize it.

And then it occurred to me: here was one of the world's great beauties. She had sunk to a level far beneath most people's ability or desire to notice. She had become invisible. She was like the Manet I have hanging in my bedroom, an uncatalogued masterpiece which, when one of my agents found it, was stashed behind the dustbin of an elderly madwoman in Brussels.

I engaged her in conversation. I flattered her beauty, praised her many performances. I pretended to her that my interest in women was other than academic. We split a bottle of Veuve Clicquot, and before we had finished it she had told me of the desolate sense of her affairs. The film community had rejected her, her career was in ruins . . . she laughed, made it sound as though these trials were something of a lark, to be waved away with a flick of her wrist. But I could sense the searing desperation in her. I knew this was a woman who would clutch at anything, any straw at all, that was offered her.

So I offered her a position on my staff. As my personal assistant. She bridled; I had pricked her pride. Then I told her that she could consider it a kind of retreat. The world would not know where she was, or even *who* she was. She would be incognito. We would invent a new identity for her. She could think of it as a kind of performance. Her duties would be light, she would live in one of the grandest houses in the Scots Highlands, and she would even take a salary. And when she had rested and recovered, she could return to her old life . . . ideally, having in the meantime inspired a wellspring of curiosity as to her whereabouts.

Of course, she said yes. I think if I told her she'd have to swim the Atlantic to get here, she'd still have agreed. She thought I was offering her a safe haven, a refuge where she could recover from the battering and the bruises she had suffered. And of course I had.

But once "Helena" returned here to Ballawinnie with me, I found that, as great a thrill as it was to have, at my beck and call, one of the most glamorous women of the age, the thrill was exponentially greater when I began to inflict on her little humiliations. Indignities. You're smirking, my friend. You understand what I mean, then? . . . Oh, protest all you like. I saw the look on your face.

She was my personal assistant, yes, but only in the manner of a valet. She shined my shoes; she ironed my shirts; she made my bed. Best of all, she dressed me in the morning and undressed me at night. Believe my, there was nothing erotic about it; it was as clear a demonstration of feudal prerogative as I have ever had the pleasure of experiencing. The great turning point came one night when she had disengaged my suspenders; my pants dropped around my ankles and I stepped out of them. At just the moment she was lowering herself to retrieve them, I broke wind. Loudly. Viola stopped for a moment, in mid-crouch. This was crucial. She had to consider whether she was going to continue in the employ of a man who had, to put it plainly, just farted in her face.

She picked up the pants and carried on. What else could she do? Where else could she go?

For seventeen months I debased that woman every day of my life, and enjoyed it. I *thought* I had destroyed her spirit. I had certainly wounded it. But I suppose I took it too far. She eventually fled. I don't think there was a single incident which prompted this; it was just the accumulation of so many.

I didn't hear of her for some months; then news trickled back to me that she was engaged at some mediocre level in her old trade. Performing guesswork on a television quiz show of some kind. I lost interest in her. My investments were beginning to sour; I was losing money. I had more crucial things to concern me.

But earlier this year, I became aware of her again. British television began airing episodes of a hideous melodrama in which she has a significant role. And the British press began running stories about her huge success in the part, and how it had reestablished her as a woman of achievement in America. I thought, well, here's a thing; I'm on the brink of penury, and Viola Chute is a wealthy woman.

And I thought what a good thing it would be to go to America and have a little chat with her.

So that's what I did. I found her in New York, and I demanded of her the sum of three-quarters of a million dollars, payable each month, in exchange for which I would not let it be known that she had, in her time of greatest need, taken a job as a household drudge. She of course told me that if I did any such thing, she would in turn tell all the world about my collection. Of course I called her bluff. I had by far the more to lose, but then, I knew Viola Chute. She would allow nothing to rob her of her newfound success.

Alas, her newfound success was soon lost. She mismanaged her career so badly that it fell apart during the short period I was in New York to see her. I left late last week, when it became clear that she would never be able to pay me even a fraction of what I asked.

I returned to London, which is where I remained until Billy rang me to tell of the intruder he'd caught in the house.

Now you've heard it all. I hope your curiosity is sated.

And I've decided what is to be done with you. First, you will hand me the tape recording device . . . Thank you. Now, Billy, I want you to take our young friend here and show him to the front gate . . . That's right, I'm letting you go. But Billy must escort you off the property, because it's very dark, and unless you know the lay of the land, anything might happen. Isn't that right, Billy? . . . It would be awful if our young friend here suffered some mischance on his way off the grounds. Wouldn't it, Billy? . . . I said, *wouldn't* it, Billy? . . . Yes, yes, I see you understand me now. You *will* act to safeguard our guest's welfare, won't you? . . . There, I knew I could count on you.

Goodbye then, my boy. Best of luck to you in your travels.

. . . The body of an unidentified man was found late last night on the perimeter of the Killwall estate. The man, who appears to have perished by strangulation, is said to be Caucasian and in his late thirties, but not a Killwall local. Police have questioned the staff of Ballawinnie House who have provided no clues. (Chester, Viscount Killwall has been in absentia since late June.) The body was discovered by passing cyclists Mr. Arthur MacNicholl and Miss Marigold Esskempe, on their way home from the St. George's gymkhana, where Miss Esskempe's team won the 500-meter relay. Congratulations, Marigold! . . .

"The night is bitter, the stars have lost their glitter . . . and all because of the call that got awaaay . . ." Hi, this is E. Manfred Harry. Don't hang up and leave me wailing in despair. Leave your name and number after the tone and I'll get back to you.

Mr. Harry, this is Georgia Kirkby. Hello? . . . Hello? . . . If you're there, do pick up . . . This is becoming extraordinarily tiresome. I know you must be back in Los Angeles by now, the charges to my credit card have stopped. Mr. Harry! . . . Mr. Harry! . . . Pick up! . . . Pick up! . . .

I have invested quite a bit of money in you, Mr. Harry. I am not accustomed to making bad investments. I will not tolerate the idea of taking a loss. Pick up! . . . Pick up!

Mr. Harry, I have your address. I know where you live. You *will* speak to me, and soon. I am not the kind of woman who is crossed with impunity.

Hello! . . . *Hello!* . . .

September 2, 1997

My darling Viola,

I know how and why we parted; I know how long ago it was,
and how much water has passed under the bridge since then.
But I've learned, to my inestimable advantage, that a man
must build the kind of world in which he wishes to live. And I
know, as well, that he cannot sit idly by while the woman he
loves is in dire straits.

I am coming for you, Viola. I am putting my affairs in order
and leaving behind this transitional life so that I might, with
whatever resources I have gathered in the past decade, prove
of some service to you. No one has ever replaced you in my
heart; no one, I know now, ever will.

I feel a special burden of responsibility in that the photos
which now so beleaguer you were stolen from my personal
collection, as you will no doubt have determined yourself, if
you've seen them. My apologies are heartfelt and abject. In the
months following my reelection defeat, I lost sufficient interest
in the running of my daily affairs to permit such blatant thiev-
ery to occur unchecked, and it is you, as usual, who now
suffers for my weaknesses.

Viola, I am a new man. I am stronger, wiser, more capable of
navigating the whims of fate. I will help you. I will protect you.

If you let me.

Your only
Dennis

MORGAN IN THE MORNING
Broadcast of September 3, 1997
KMAD-AM

. . . Aaaand we're back, Philadelphia! If you're just joining us, well, my guess is you're delighted to once again be hearing my masculine growl as you hang your woolly head over that first morning cup of joe. Yes, it's true, Morgan's back, after a two-week holiday in sunny Bermuda, and let me tell you, if you thought those two weeks of my estimable but pedestrian stand-in Jerry Bowen would never end, time passed entirely differently for yours truly; the two weeks flew by like a day and a half. Spent them baking on sun-drenched beaches, guzzling fruity alcoholic concoctions, and doing my bit for diplomatic relations between our own great country and the brown-skinned lasses of the island, whom I feel certain I have left with some fond, fond memories of Yankee initiative. And again, while you may have missed me terribly, subjected as you were to Jerry's competent but somewhat less than compelling attempts to fill my shoes, I found I didn't miss you at all, as I was able to keep track of absolutely everything stateside thanks to my trusty laptop and the magical, mystical World Wide Web. What an invention, I gotta tell you! Jerry's nodding in the booth. You've heard of the Internet, Jerry? . . . Jerry just made a nice backhand swing. No, Jerry, the Internet is not the thing you hit tennis balls over . . . He's knitting his brow. Let's let him figure it out on his own. What I'm saying is, the Internet . . . well, here's an example. I'm sitting on the deck of my villa, sipping a cold one as the sun goes down, when my friend Ira from Baltimore—great town, Baltimore—calls to tell me someone's found nude photos of Viola Chute. Now as we all know, this is a very classy, hot-looking lady, so naturally I am

263

intrigued. I ask Ira, who's publishing? When do we get to see them? And Ira gives me a Web address. In approximately four minutes, I am gazing on the photographs my friend in faraway America just got finished telling me about. And that is sensational. The world is getting so much smaller, isn't it? And hey, if that means I get immediate gratification in the matter of seeing Viola Chute *en déshabillé*—Jerry's frowning. That's *French*, Jerry—well, then, I'm all for a smaller world. Speaking of which, those were some photos, huh? *Yee-ow!* Now, let me just say about Viola Chute . . . here's a woman—and I mean a *woman*, a mature lady, not some dime-a-dozen cheerleader like we've all seen a million times over . . . and she's looking *fiiine*. In my opinion, every female in America ought to check out those shots and take hope from them. What is she . . . she's gotta be fifty. Fifty-something . . . does anyone know? . . . This is a fifty-something woman no teenage boy would turn away. This is, and Miss Chute will excuse me if I offend her dignity, I hope she'll accept it in the spirit that it's said . . . this is a *babe*. We've got a call. Hello, you're on the air.

Bob, it's Archie from Trenton.

All the way from Trenton! Lovely town. Morning to you, Archie.

I just checked my movie-star data base. There are two birthdays for Viola Chute. She's either fifty-two or fifty-five, depending.

Amazing. Either way, amazing. You seen those photos, Archie?

I made one into a screen saver.

So I take it you're a fan.

I'm a fan.

That makes two of us.

I never was before. I mean sure, she's a beautiful woman . . . but it wasn't till I saw these photos that . . . whoa. You know?

I know.

Listen, glad you're back, buddy. Jerry's all right and everything . . .

Say no more.

. . . but you da man.

Thanks, Archie. Another call here. Hello, you're on the air.

Bob, I'm so glad you're back!

Thank you. Whom do I having the pleasure of speaking to?

This is Jim Pouter, out in Bethlehem.

Lovely town, Bethlehem.

Thanks. I don't know, Bob, if you're aware of the flak Viola Chute has taken for those photos.

I've heard about it. Some blowhard in the Senate mouthing off.

That's right. Hiram Withers of Minnesota.

Right. Well, I'm so glad Senator Withers is on the job, aren't you? Our schools in crisis, the bottom dropping out of the inner cities, the national debt soaring . . . yeah, I'm glad Senator Withers is focusing on naked ladies. Thanks a lot, Senator Withers. And thank you, Minnesota, for electing this joker.

It's ridiculous. What harm does it do? Me looking at Viola Chute.

Exactly.

This is a beautiful woman.

Exactly.

A very, very beautiful woman.

Steady on, Jim.

It just makes my blood boil. I'm a single guy, Bob.

Don't rub it in, fella.

I come home from a hard day at work, if I want to sit back and spend a peaceful hour or so staring at something as beautiful as Viola Chute in the nude, who am I hurting?

I hear you, buddy. Thanks for calling. Listen, apparently Viola Chute has struck a chord with my listeners, and Jim has a point—there's nothing to be ashamed about there. So I tell you what, let's make this Viola Chute Defense Morning. Call in and voice your support. Let's send a message to the prigs and sourpusses in Washington that red-blooded American men don't need or want their asinine finger-wagging . . . Boy, howdy, look at those lines light up already! . . . Hello, you're on the air.

Hi, Bob, welcome back! This is Frank, out here in Colum-bus, Ohio.

Columbus, O-*hi*-o! God bless AM radio . . .

INVESTIGATION INTO PRODUCER'S DEATH CLOSED

Los Angeles Times
September 3, 1997

NEW YORK—Under pressure by the District Attorney's office to make an arrest or present a compelling reason to continue, the New York Police Department yesterday formally concluded its investigation into the August 7 death of television producer Alex Wylie. Traces of the chemical compound amyl nitrite had been found in the deceased's blood, and were believed to have contributed to his fatal cardiac arrest. Accordingly, the police had been seeking the party responsible for supplying him with the powerful inhalant, with the intention of pressing a charge of manslaughter.

Suspicion had been lingering on television actress Viola Chute, who was with Wylie in his hotel room at the time of his death. But Chute forced the District Attorney's hand by appearing on last night's edition of KYES's *Newsnight Magazine*, where she made a passionate case for her innocence. Chute denied providing Wylie the inhalant, but argued that even if she had, possession of amyl nitrite is not illegal in New York City, nor is there any certain evidence that it played a role in his cardiac arrest.

Wylie's widow, Jerri, who had been a vocal advocate for continuing the investigation, remains in seclusion at her home in Los Angeles and was unavailable for comment.

HOTEL PIERRE

September 3, 1997

Dear Mr. Lawley:

As per your request, this letter serves to acknowledge the receipt of the bank check you delivered to our office this morning, a photocopy of which is attached.

As you directed, we have applied the sum to the account of Ms. Viola Chute, which is now fully up to date. Your timely intervention in this delicate matter is greatly appreciated.

We look forward to seeing you and Ms. Chute at checkout this afternoon and wish you both a safe trip to Los Angeles.

Sincerely,
Georgette Klein
Manager

ACTRESS TRIUMPHS IN ASSAULT SUIT
Los Angeles Herald
September 5, 1997

Viola Chute, the television actress best known for her recurring role in UBN's *The Winds of Wyndhamville*, emerged victorious yesterday from a preliminary hearing on the 10 million dollar lawsuit brought against her by freelance photographer Berry Leyton.

Mr. Leyton had charged that in April of this year, Ms. Chute accosted him as he shot photographs of her while she vacationed in the British Virgin Islands, causing permanent damage to his eyesight. The actress, however, maintained that Mr. Leyton had trespassed on the gated property she was renting on the island of St. Lucia, and that she merely threw a mango at him. Mr. Leyton filed suit in May.

The case came before Judge Katie Szekeylhidi, who, at the request of Ms. Chute's attorney, Gretchen Ojan, dismissed it as being without merit. Mr. Leyton's attorney, Powers Keenlyside, told reporters outside the courtroom that he will appeal the ruling, but in the current climate it is doubted whether this will do him any good. According to Los Angeles legal commentator Arcady Killian, the August 31 death of Diana, Princess of Wales, which has been widely attributed to her car's reckless pursuit by motorcycling "paparazzi," has resulted in worldwide antagonism toward celebrity photojournalists. Indeed, Mr. Leyton was verbally assaulted by the crowd as he exited the courthouse, and cries of "Murderer" were heard— apparently a reference to the death of the princess.

In this climate, Ms. Chute's case, which many had considered in jeopardy, is believed to have been helped enormously by a piece of correspondence she read on KYES–New York's *Newsnight Magazine* on September 2: a short letter to her, written by the princess in August, wishing her good luck in her court case against "that terrible trespasser."

"Diana was a dear friend," said Ms. Chute on the broadcast, which was picked up by UBN affiliates nationwide, "and an angel of mercy to all the world. She recognized the appalling injustice of my predicament, and it was so like her to take the time to send a consoling note. It's beyond tragedy that she, who so sympathized with me in my battle against Berry Leyton, should lose so very much more to the same kind of vultures. When is someone—anyone—going to put a stop to this kind of thing?"

Late last night, Ms. Chute joined other television actors, including George Clooney and Fran Drescher, in a press conference in which they denounced the tactics of "the jackal press" and their role in the death of the princess.

Mr. Leyton was unavailable for comment.

FAX MEMO TO: Viola
FROM: Peter
SUBJECT: Enough already
DATE: 9/6/97

Think we've reached the expires-by date on our catfight. I've downsized the drama queen in me and got in touch with my inner agent. Can we go back to rapacious moneymaking now?

Got an offer on the table from a certain Holiday Books for a Viola Chute 14-month calendar—all nudes being the dealbreaker. But not like your website—we'll leave it the beaver. Instead enough cheesecake to turn Sara Lee vegan. Money's decent but I'm holding out for indecent. Meantime I'm Nancy Drewing Holiday to find out if they're the real deal or some desktop-publishing dweeb.

Also three guesses who's been serenading my voice mail. If one of your guesses is Kreiss and Asher, you win the bedroom set and minivan. Haven't returned serve yet: first I need your gut on returning to *Wyndhamville*. Can't promise that's their rap—seems unlikely after you batter-basted Kirkby's bottom. But the Boy Scouts say it best: Be prepared. And don't blow your Scoutmaster.

Con amore furioso—
P.

P.S. Oh BTW—I heard about your hissing match with Hippo. Shoot me some phone numbers and I'll ride a little roughshod.

SCA GIVES IN TO PRESSURE
Photographer's "Priestie" Award Revoked
Camera Arts
September 6, 1997

The Los Angeles–based Society for the Celluloid Arts has bowed to pressure from its members and rescinded this year's Merrill B. Priest Award, which had been intended for the Dallas-based paparazzo Berry Leyton. Citing Leyton's "aesthetic incompatibility with the Priest ideal," SCA spokeswoman Melanie Probst announced that the honor has been revoked and that no award will be given this year—the first such occurrence in the award's history.

The "Priestie" is awarded annually to an entertainment-industry photographer in recognition of "a lifetime of achievement in the area of celebrity iconography." The first recipient was Cecil Beaton, in 1954.

CONSTABULARY NOTES
County Killwall Despatch
September 6, 1997

. . . Police have announced that the staff of Ballawinnie House will be the focus of an investigation into the apparent murder of a Cornishman, Andrew Trebliss, whose body was discovered outside the grounds of the estate last week. An anonymous tip phoned into Scotland Yard provided the deceased's identification as well as the allegation that Chester, Viscount Killwall had personally ordered the young man's murder by a member of his security force, one William MacNeill. His lordship, currently in London, denies that he was even in residence on the night in question, though police have obtained affidavits from townspeople who claim to have seen him early the following day. Now that the victim's identity has been positively ascertained, the police say the next step is to be a search of Ballawinnie House for forensic evidence . . .

SUBJ: safe and sound in l.a.
DATE: 97-9-7 08:48:47 EST
FROM: emanfr@ysa.net
TO: nbcasem@bot.ubsm.edu

well what a long strange trip it's been. landed in nyc and spent two days face down on the bed at my friend's place too jet lagged to move. the 600 glasses of champagne i had on the flight might've had something to do with it. also just the whole ordeal in scotland. i still get the shakes. what can i say but thank you for listening to my wild raving when i called you that night at what i realize now must've been four in the morning your time. you're a good friend and true.

but how weird is it that my stalker not only didn't kill me but ended up saving my bacon. i don't know if i managed to tell you the whole story—i recall being a tad incoherent. anyway just for the record: i made it to chester's house which is named ballawinnie of course i immediately renamed it ballsandweenie. estate's enormous—acres and acres—so it was easy enough to get onto the grounds despite the front gate being locked up like fort knox. house looked empty so i broke in which was pretty easy—there was a service door that was so rotted i was able to just pry it open.

so there i am creeping around the place when all of a sudden wham something hits me over the head. i'm dazed someone drags me up a flight of stairs locks me in an empty closet—no jokes please. hours hours hours. finally i'm dragged out to meet guess who chester viscount killwall. no longer in nyc needless to say. deadly little man with a loony obsession—he collects extremely valuable artworks that the world doesn't even know exist. says he can't stand the idea of common people's eyes contaminating them. i want to ask what about the common people who painted them but decided it was safer to keep my trap shut. anyway i explain i'm no thief just viola's biographer but that only makes it worse for me. bastard takes my tape recorder and has his thug drag me outside to finish me off which i can't even begin to describe the terror. so paralyzed with fear i can't lift a finger in my own defense.

that's when andy intervenes god bless his psychotic little ass. seems he followed me to the highlands saw me go into ballsandweenie and waited for me to come out again even though it took all goddamn day. when i finally reappeared with the thug's arm clamped on my shoulder andy apparently misinterpreted this as us going off to the bushes to do the big nasty. all i know is suddenly he's jumping on the thug screaming and pummeling away—and there's about a nanosecond of confusion but that's all i need. i tear out of there so fast i don't even look where i'm going till i slam into a tree like a keystone kop. knock the shit out of myself but by then at least i'm well away down the road.

manage to make it to this little town where i call a cab take it to the train station get back to edinburgh by midnight. which is when i called you all hysterical thank you again for calming me down. then i checked out of my hotel without even spending the night and went straight to the airport where i traded in my ticket for the next flight to nyc. while i was waiting to board i made an anonymous call to the police and told them to go have a look up ballsandweenie way. all very inscrutable. saw later over the news wire they found andy dead there. that could've been me!!! they hadn't i.d.'d the body so when i got to nyc i called them again and gave them andy's name and address. least i could do for him really.

so anyway i'm down one stalker but i appear to have a replacement. there's like a thousand angry messages on my machine from georgia kirkby who's back in l.a. and threatening to come to my house. yikes. stalked by a two-time oscar winner next on jenny jones. i suppose i'll have to see her—i mean i have been living large on her dollar. and she never really canceled her credit card like she threatened to which makes me feel like a shit for using it so much in revenge. i guess i owe her huh. plus now that i'm back in l.a. i can't really avoid her.

that's right i'm back in l.a. as soon as i arrived in new york i went to the pierre to see viola and discovered she'd checked out. don't know how she got her bill paid but from what i can tell her career's miraculously on the upswing again so maybe she borrowed. you may ask why i even wanted to see the bitch after she was such a viper to me. well here's the thing—chester told me her terrible secret which is basically that she spent a year and a half scrubbing poo stains from his underpants. which is of course the only possible scandal for someone like viola—the mundane the tepid the drab. admitting this episode as part of her career would be like adding a teaspoon of motor oil to a bottle of champagne. make the whole thing just go flat.

so i figure i should at least warn her of the shit storm that's coming. see i've messed things up for her with chester. he must know i was the one who's sicced scotland yard on him and since he doesn't know exactly who i am he'll most likely take it out on viola. spill the beans about how she spent a year and a half in his employ dressed like ann b. davis. poor old girl just when she's getting back on her feet. i tried to get in to see her yesterday but she wouldn't answer my calls even though i kept leaving messages like urgent urgent red alert.

finally last night i just give up and go to her house. the door is answered by dominique her el salvadoran maid who stands just about a head shorter than the two harlequin great danes she brings with her—apparently because dominique herself is not imposing enough to prevent an intruder from pushing his way in. dominique—whose real name by the way is domenica but you know viola—dominique tells me miss chute she is out with the senor. i say what senor she says senor lawley. dennis lawley i ask si si. the ex senator ex fiance when the hell did he reenter the picture. so viola not only has her career back but she's getting laid regularly and now i kind of start to resent her after all—here's a woman who has everything yet who was perfectly willing to flounce out of manhattan leaving me stranded there.

but i rise above it and leave my card with dominique and on the back
i just write 3 words chester viscount killwall. i bet i hear from her now.

i'll let you know how it goes. meantime THANK YOU AGAIN.

hugs from the homefront
harry

p.s. oh yeah how's the foot still improving.

... Harry, angel! My *God,* how good to see you! ... *Mina! Sedgwick! DOWN!* ... Sorry, luv, they don't know it's just hugging, they think you're hurting me ... *I SAID DOWN!* ... Harry, Harry, I've been so *worried* ... I tried so hard to find you after we had that terrible row, but it's like you disappeared off the face of the earth ... I know Manhattan is a big island, but I thought I knew you well enough to figure out where you'd run off t— *MINA! NO!* ... Come in and have a drink till they calm down, Harry. It's *so* good to see you ... Is that a new tape recorder? What a tiny thing! Fit in the palm of your hand. Though I don't know why you've brought it, luv, the memoir's still off ... I didn't mean to fire you so unpleasantly, but the fact is, you're still fired. I've decided I still ... Ah! Dominique. *Deux coupes de champagne, s'il tu plait* ... I've decided it's too early to write my life story. So much of it left to live yet. Sorry, angel. But you'll get a big, fat kill fee from me today, I can promise you that ... Yes, things *have* improved enormously ... Oh, so you heard about Dennis? Clever Harry, I never could keep anything from you ... Yes, he *is* back, and this time for good. It's wonderful, angel ... Never *mind* if he's always been "the one." That's a silly way of thinking about re- lationships, and besides, it's none of your business ... No, you're *not* my biographer. I *fired* you, haven't you been listen- ing? ...

But hold on, Harry ... before we get too far off the subject, I've had some disturbing phone messages from ... well, I won't be coy. From Chester. Whom you apparently know about, despite all my precautions ... So it's true? I can see I've underestimated you. Anyway, I haven't returned his calls, but he's threatening to . . . Harry, what *do* you know about all this? . . . Ah, *merci bien,* Dominique . . . To your health, Harry, and safe return . . . Mmm . . . Now. Begin at the beginning. *Spill.*

. . . Harry, no! . . . You mean you were on to me from the *first?* Why didn't you just come out and confront me? . . . No, I suppose I wouldn't have, a*haaa*-ha . . .

She gave you *what?* . . . God! The little *bitch!* . . . I'd *wondered* where those Christmas cards had got to . . .

No, Harry, say you didn't . . . You didn't *really* go to the gorgon? . . . To *Kirkby?* . . . I ought to chuck you out right now . . .

She *what?* . . . Sent you *where?* . . . You were in *Illuggan?* . . . I can't believe I'm hearing this, Harry. The room is spinning . . .

The *brats?* . . . You spoke to *Regnal's* brats? . . . Both of them? . . . And you . . . you met *Beva?* . . . Harry, I . . . *Dominique! Refill, please . . . in fact, just bring the bottle!* . . . Go on, go on . . .

Dear God in heaven . . . All the way to Ballawinnie? I'm . . . I'm shocked, I had no idea, I . . .

He was there? Chester was *there?* . . . You can't mean it . . . He meant to have you killed? . . . Chester meant to have you *killed?* . . . I knew he was a cruel man, but I never . . .

Oh . . . So you know everything . . . All the sordid details . . . Well, no, you're correct, *not* so sordid . . . That's rather the problem, isn't it? . . .

Dominique . . . *Dominique* . . . fetch us *une autre bouteille,* there's a luv . . . I know it's just four o'clock, but I think we're both going to need it . . .

What now, then? You report to the gorgon what you've discovered? . . . What do you *mean,* it's up to me? It's scarcely that . . . I can't control Chester, can I, you've well and truly bolloxed me there . . . He'll reveal *everything,* don't you see, just to have revenge on us . . . I might be able to quiet him if I could pay him what he wants, but even if I'd got the million per episode for *Wyndhamville* I doubt I could've done it, the taxes would've been too stiff . . . I've really been fucked from the get-go, haven't I? . . .

I'm just surprised at this, Harry, at *all* of this . . . On one hand, I can't blame you, I was horrible to you, but on the other . . . well, you've always been so loyal. You even refused to buy those nude pictures of me . . . What? . . . Of *course* I know about those, I was the one trying to *sell* them to you . . . Don't look so shocked. I knew you were hungry for success in publishing and I thought it was worth a try offering them to you, maybe you'd rustle up the cash and get them into print. But no, you refused to have anything to do with them, which at the time I thought so touching, if a little annoying . . . Yes, I *did* want them in print, angel, but it had to seem like it was happening against my will. See, when my career started dis- solving I knew I had to do something desperate to save it, and, well, I had these photos Dennis took when we were on holiday in Xtapa. What can I say, he's into that kind of thing. But after he lost the election and went a little batty I had to walk out on him, and angel, in that situation I was *hardly* going to leave the photos in his possession. So I took them and kept them all these years. I thought they were just the shot in the arm my ca- reer needed, and look, I was right . . . What's that, luv? . . . Yes, yes, I know I told you I'd never do nudes, I told *everyone* I'd never do nudes. What was I supposed to say? "Why, yes, I'm looking forward to shoving my crotch at the camera?" It's just another kind of show, angel, and I've always been a show- man . . . No, I never believed it would ruin my career; I was just saving it for the time when it would do the most good. I mean, at my age, there's a kind of fuck-you aspect to baring it all, don't you think? . . . But it was going to take months to get them into print, angel, and things were falling apart so fast . . . Well, you can imagine how happy I was when I found an Internet buyer who was able to get them to the public imme- diately. And God bless Hiram Withers for being such a blowhard, because he told the whole country not only that the photos existed but exactly where to find them. He did me the most enormous favor, Harry, he really did. I was back to being scandalous, which is exactly where I needed to be . . . Even so, my bad girl reputation still needed an extra push, so I decided why not a *literal* push? And I went and shoved Georgia Kirkby into a layer cake . . . Did you hear about that? Tremendous fun! . . . You see, people were getting tired of nothing but assault and manslaughter stories about me; too unsavory, too unsettling. I had to give them something lighter to keep them amused. And it worked, didn't it? . . . Well, didn't it, Harry? . . . I said, *didn't* it? . . . Close your mouth, angel, you'll catch flies . . .

So it looked for a while like victorious Viola had her career back, her agent back, a calendar deal to replace the lost perfume deal . . . I was even getting overtures from *Wyndhamville,* though I've been playing hard to get. Plus, I beat the manslaughter charge and got the assault suit thrown out of court. That contemptible little hooligan photographer will think twice before he comes up against *me* again . . . What, Harry? . . . What do you mean? Luck had nothing to do with it! . . . The letter from the princess? . . . Yes, I suppose that *did* galvanize public opinion my way, but really, Harry, there was nothing lucky about *that* . . . Do I have to spell it out for you? . . . Harry, Harry, Harry. Diana *did* write me a note last month thanking me for contributing an item to one of her charity auctions. And she *did* tell me in Milan that she sympathized with me in my lawsuit. I just put the two together . . . Yes, Harry, if you must put it that way, I went on television and pretended to read words Princess Diana never wrote . . . What a question, Harry, of *course* I have no shame, ahaaaha . . . not very much, anyway. But really, no one manipulated the media more cunningly than Diana. And she'd have wanted some good to come out of her death . . . I'm *not* putting words in a dead woman's mouth. Don't be disgusting.

Anyway, it's all for naught if Chester chooses to drop his bomb, isn't it? The last thing I need right now is for him to give an interview where he reveals that the exotic temptress Viola Chute spent seventeen months in rubber-soled shoes rinsing snot out of his hankies and wiping up his loo. My reputation wouldn't survive it; people need to be *shocked* by me if I'm going to continue in the public eye, so how can I . . . Sorry, angel? What's that? . . . A *reverse* scandal? . . . Yes, that's exactly what this is! Clever of you to find a way to put it. But how can I fight it? It *happened,* after all . . . it's the *truth* . . .

Harry . . . what did you just say? . . .

Fight it with . . . a *lie?* . . .

My God, Harry. There may be hope for you yet.

Of course, of course, of *course.* I'll *lie.* I'll fight the reverse scandal with a *proper* one. I'll say that . . . that . . . oh, I don't know. Something close enough to the truth so that people who know a little of the story will buy it, but different enough in substance . . . hmm. I need time to work on this. Harry, you're a genius, but I've got to boot you out now. My wheels are spinning . . .

Sorry? . . . Kirkby? . . . Oh, yes. I'd forgotten about her . . . What *do* we do about her? . . . Give me a moment . . . How much of her money have you spent, anyway? . . . Just a rough figure, luv . . . *That* much? My God, the woman must really *loathe* me . . . and you have no idea how happy that makes me! A*haaa*-ha! . . . Hold on, I'm getting out my checkbook . . . I promised you a kill fee, didn't I? . . . Heeeere you are . . . annnnnnd . . . here's another check, covering the gorgon's expenses. You deposit this in your bank tomorrow, then write her out one of your own. Tell her you're paying her back and that this is sayonara . . . Of *course* she won't be happy, Harry. She'll be *livid* . . . You just do as I say, angel. Has Viola *ever* steered you wrong? . . . Well, yes, all right, but *this* time I haven't . . .

So long, then, luv . . . It really is *brilliant* you're back in my life . . .

FAX MEMO TO: Viola
FROM: Peter
SUBJECT: Welcome back Samantha
DATE: 9/8/97

It's parka time in hell. Kreiss and Asher have thumbs-upped your million per. As we speak Grand Duchess Samantha is being fitted into the current storyline like a dental bridge. Snag your senator and do some serious cork popping. Your first read-through is on Monday. Wear something nice.

Am I not an inimitable agent? Is this not the best of all possible worlds?

Con amore furioso—
P.

P.S. Following is some paperwork in re: Hippo. If it satisfies, then ratify.

"The night is bitter, the stars have lost their glitter . . . and all because of the call that got awaaay . . ." Hi, this is E. Manfred Harry. Don't hang up and leave me wailing in despair. Leave your name and number after the tone and I'll get back to you.

Mr. Harry, this is Georgia Kirkby. I received your correspondence this afternoon and I am examining the legal recourses available to me in this matter. It may come as a surprise to you to learn that in the state of California a verbal agreement is considered a contract, and is therefore binding. True, there was no witness to our agreement, but if it should come down to a matter of my word against yours, Mr. Harry, I ask you to consider which of us a jury of our peers would be more likely to credit.

My attorney's name is Matthew Tureck. Write it down. You may expect to hear from him.

Sayonara, indeed.

Glamorous Viola Chute, star of UBN's latenight soap *The Winds of Wyndhamville,* dropped a bombshell this week. From 1979 to 1982, the sexy siren revealed, she abandoned Hollywood to live in remote Scotland as the private plaything of a randy British lord!

"He swept me off my feet," Chute admitted to this reporter. "He was so cultured and so charming. And he had a mansion in the Scottish Highlands! I hated to give up my career, but Chester was irresistible—and he promised to pamper me like a queen!"

Chester, Viscount Killwall, is one of the most mysterious and eccentric members of the British aristocracy. "His home—Ballawinnie House—is filled with long-lost art treasures by the great masters," Viola reveals, "some of which the public doesn't even know exist! He has a passion for possessing priceless things."

While all of Hollywood wondered at her disappearance, Viola was installed in style at the rambling, art-filled mansion set amidst the grandeur of the Scottish countryside. "Believe me, I earned my keep!" she says with a laugh. "Chester was in his fifties at the time, but had the sexual appetite of a teenager. He kept me very busy!"

Eventually, however, the star began to tire of her life as a kept woman. "It sounds like a fairy tale, but in reality it was terribly dull. There was nothing to do and no one to see. I hoped I might fall in love with Chester, even marry him," she adds with a sigh; "but it's clear he always considered me just another item in his collection." Soon she found herself missing her days on the big screen. "I felt I had to come back to the life I was born for—and the fans whose love I can always count on."

Viola says with a frown that she has not seen or heard from her blue-blooded lover since. "He didn't like me leaving him," she says. "I suppose, for him, it was like one of his paintings getting down off the wall and running out the door."

Viola, who recently re-signed to the *Wyndhamville* role of virtuous Grand Duchess Samantha, says her character would never do anything quite so scandalous as run off with a wealthy suitor, titled or no. "She'd be tempted; but Samantha is a good girl. Viola Chute, I'm afraid, is a very naughty one."

VISCOUNT TAKEN ILL
County Killwall Despatch
September 15, 1997

Chester, Viscount Killwall suffered a stroke yesterday and is currently listed in critical condition in an unidentified London hospital.

His lordship has been somewhat beleaguered of late, what with the revelation of a long-suppressed and unsavory liaison with the actress Viola Chute following hard on the heels of an indictment for accessory to murder. A member of his security staff, William MacNeill, is currently in custody, charged with the actual slaying of a Cornishman, Andrew Trebliss, but tape-recorded evidence discovered by police within Ballawinnie House allegedly reveals that his lordship directed the crime. His lordship has defended himself by claiming that the man MacNeill slew was not the man being spoken of on the tape, but police are unconvinced.

Perhaps even more injurious to his lordship has been the attention now focused on his prized artworks, a curious collection of imaginative works rendered in the styles of the great masters. A representative from Sotheby's, called in by police to estimate the worth of the collection, valued it at roughly two hundred thousand pounds.

HIPPO TO RELEASE VIOLA CHUTE
DISCO ALBUM

Sounds & Stylus
September 16, 1997

Hippo Records has happily resolved its dispute with Viola Chute (see 8/30/97). The legendary actress, who had objected that an illictly recorded tape of her singing had been earmarked for inclusion on the label's third *A Song So Wrong* compilation, has signed an agreement to record a full album of "high camp" material based on her long career. The CD will include disco arrangements of songs from her films and stage work, as well as a vocal version of the theme from *The Winds of Wyndhamville* for which composer Jeremy Bashkin is writing specially commissioned lyrics.

As part of the agreement, the original bootleg cut (of Viola singing Cole Porter's "Love for Sale") will be included, but in a heavily sampled form mixed into a rap/dance arrangement. This revised cut will also serve as the disc's first single.

After six seasons as the long-suffering matriarch of the embattled Wyndham clan, Georgia Kirkby is calling it quits.

The two-time Academy Award winner turned sixty this year, and says she feels it. "I don't want to work so hard anymore," she confesses, "especially on something so ephemeral as television. I only agreed to play Jocasta Wyndham on the chance that the show might be a hit, which would mean money from residuals when it went into syndication. Well, I've done more than enough episodes to retire quite comfortably, so I'm turning in my russet wig and shoulder pads. I'm going to take some time off, get to know my grandson. Travel. Enjoy life."

Kirkby lowers her voice and adds that she "doesn't feel comfortable with the direction the show has headed recently, anyway." Might that be a veiled reference to last season's addition of Viola Chute as Grand Duchess Samantha? The two actresses' offscreen rivalry is well known, and Kirkby's retirement comes just a week after Chute concluded a grueling, bluff-calling contract negotiation by returning to the show for a reported salary of one million dollars per episode—making her one of the highest-paid talents in television. Kirkby lowers her eyelids and shakes her head. "No, that woman's return to the show, and her ridiculous salary, is a symptom of what I'm talking about, not the cause. But there's no point in discussing it."

Kirkby stresses that her retirement isn't permanent. "I hope to return to the stage sometime in the next few years," she says with enthusiasm brightening her eyes. "It's been so long since I've done anything artistically challenging. And my little summer adventure in New York"—where the actress joined the cast of her son-in-law's off-Broadway revue—"reminded me of how much I miss the theatre."

Kirkby's last episode of *The Winds of Wyndhamville* will air in January. Till then, she's keeping mum about how the writers are handling her departure. Does Jocasta die?

"No," she says firmly.

Remarry and move out of Wyndhamville?

"No."

Go to prison for murdering Grand Duchess Samantha?

An inadvertent grin slips onto her face.

"No. Alas."

JULIANNA MANN LITERARY AGENCY

NEW YORK ■ LOS ANGELES

September 16, 1997

Dear Harry,

How've you been? I've got some good news.

Attached you'll find a copy of a letter I received from a film production company in Australia. They'd like to option the rights to
Mincing in Urania—one of their principals is apparently a big fan.

Looks like a pretty decent offer—$10,000 for the first eighteen
months applicable to a purchase price of $120,000, with a re-
newal at the same price, nonapplicable. I can probably improve
on that; I've done a few of these before so I know the landscape.
You want me to go ahead and negotiate this? I'm guessing your
answer is yes, but call me anyway, we'll discuss.

Sincerely,
Julianna

From
THE WINDS OF WYNDHAMVILLE
EP 30076F—"Babe in the Woods"

EXT—SKY—TWILIGHT
The bad weather has worsened, turning into a powerful electrical storm. Drake Wyndham's helicopter is being buffeted by rain and wind, and threatened by arcs of lightning.

INT—HELICOPTER
Drake and Prescott are clinging to the seats in fear; the pilot is struggling with the controls.

> DRAKE
> *(shouting above the noise)*
What's our situation?

> PILOT
We're managing to hold on, sir. If I can just . . .

> DRAKE
. . . Just what? Answer me!

> PRESCOTT
For God's sake, Drake, let the man concentrate! We're in a desperate way here.

> DRAKE
I can see the way we are.

> PRESCOTT
I should never have agreed to this. I told you this was a bad time to go flying . . .

DRAKE

I wouldn't care if Krakatoa were erupting beneath us. This ghost or spirit or woods-creature—whatever it is—is upsetting the tenants of my resort community. We've had almost twen—

A huge peal of thunder drowns him out; he jumps at the sound of it, then recomposes himself.

DRAKE *(cont.)*

... almost twenty cancelled reservations now that news of this ... *thing* has gotten out. I'm going to get to the bottom of it and I'm going to do it *tonight.*

PRESCOTT

But it's just a foolish rumor, Drake. There *is* no woods spirit. In time, people will realize that, and the hysteria will subside.

DRAKE

We don't *have* time. We've invested too much in this place, what with construction, promotion, and fending off Summers St. Simon's legal challenges. If we don't at least break even this month, I'm going to have to—

A lightning bolt rips out of the sky and hits the helicopter just behind Drake's window.

DRAKE *(cont.)*

God almighty!

PRESCOTT

We're hit!

DRAKE

Pilot, what's our damage?

The pilot is fighting frantically for control of the chopper, which is now veering crazily. (Intercut with exterior scenes as needed.)

PILOT

I can't tell from where I . . . there's smoke, sir, I see smoke . . .

PRESCOTT

We're hit! My God, we're hit!

DRAKE

Get a hold of yourself, man!

PILOT

We're losing altitude, sir!

DRAKE

I order you not to lose altitude!

PILOT

Yes, sir . . . I'm trying, sir, but . . .

The chopper goes into a tailspin. Drake and Prescott scream. Fade to black.

EXT—FOREST FLOOR—MORNING
Fade up. Drake awakens on a bed of leaves. His head and right arm are bound with tattered cloth caked with blood. He blinks in confusion, then sits up and looks around.

POV DRAKE—*Prescott, also bandaged, is seated*

*cross-legged on the ground, near a fire. Next to him,
a figure crouches, draped in dirty burlap.*

ANGLE ON DRAKE—*Woozily, he gets up and walks
to the fire. In the background, we can see the smol-
dering wreck of the chopper some distance off.*

> DRAKE
>
> What's . . . what's going on?

> PRESCOTT
> *(slowly, calmly)*
>
> We crashed, Drake. Last night. The storm.

> DRAKE
> *(remembering)*
>
> The pilot . . . ?

> PRESCOTT
> *(shakes his head)*

> DRAKE
> *(sadly)*
>
> Damn.
> *(nodding at hooded figure)*
> And who's this?

> PRESCOTT
>
> Well, there are two ways to answer that question,
> Drake.

> DRAKE
>
> I don't have the patience for games, Prescott.

> PRESCOTT
>
> The first answer is . . . I'm fairly certain . . . that this
> is the forest spirit.

DRAKE

The one who's been spooking my guests?

PRESCOTT

The very same.

DRAKE
(to the hooded figure)

You're in for one hell of a lawsuit, fella.

The hooded figure cringes and draws the burlap closer around it.

PRESCOTT

For God's sake, Drake! She *saved* us!

DRAKE

She . . . ?

PRESCOTT

Yes. That's the second answer . . .

He reaches over and pulls the burlap hood away, dramatically unveiling . . . Grand Duchess Samantha! She's dirty and disheveled, but still beautiful. She jerks her head up, her eyes filled with fright.

DRAKE

My God! *Samantha!*

PRESCOTT

Yes, Drake. Your former fiancée.

DRAKE

But . . . but we thought you were dead!

PRESCOTT

Yes . . . from the fall off the bridge at Wyndham Canyon. I've told her that as well, Drake. She doesn't appear to understand what I'm saying.

DRAKE

You mean . . . ?

PRESCOTT

Amnesia. So total, she can't even remember how to speak.

DRAKE

So . . . all these weeks, she's been eking out a living in the woods, like some kind of animal?

PRESCOTT

Yes. And spooking any of the resort goers who happened to catch a glimpse of her.

DRAKE

But . . . that's fantastic!

PRESCOTT

Remember, Drake, this is a woman who spent years locked in a Communist prison. Her survival skills are very strong.

SAMANTHA

Drake . . .

PRESCOTT
(stunned)

She . . . she hasn't spoken up to now . . .

SAMANTHA
(struggling through the fog)
Drake . . . so kind . . . rescued me . . .

DRAKE
She seems to remember me, Prescott.

SAMANTHA
. . . took me . . . America . . . *marry me* . . .

She leaps up and flings herself into Drake's arms.

SAMANTHA *(cont.)*
Darling Drake . . . hold me . . . so confused . . .
(begins to sob)

DRAKE
(whispering)
My God, Prescott, she's . . . she's forgotten *every-thing!* The secrets, the betrayals . . . she thinks we're still engaged to be married!

PRESCOTT
You mean . . . she remembers nothing about Summers St. Simon?

DRAKE
(hissing)
Don't say that name! What if she heard you? Do you *want* her to remember him?

PRESCOTT
But Drake . . . surely she has the right to remember the details of her own life.

DRAKE

The "right" to her own life! . . . This is why I'm the chairman of Wyndham Industries and you're a lackey.

PRESCOTT

What are you saying, Drake?

DRAKE

Don't you see the advantage this gives us? . . . When he finds out we have Samantha, Summers St. Simon is *ours!*

PRESCOTT

But you wouldn't . . . you *couldn't* . . .

DRAKE

(to Samantha)

There, there, my darling . . . just let your beloved fiancé take care of you. You've been through a terrible ordeal, but you're going to be all right . . . just rest now, safe in my loving arms . . .

(smiles evilly at Prescott)

. . . I'll take care of *everything*.

Ms. Viola Chute
and
Mr. Dennis Lawley

warmly request your presence
on the occasion of their wedding

Sunday, October 31
Four o'clock p.m.
Shutters on the Beach
Santa Monica

Reception to follow

Regrets only
Dominique Herrera
310-555-1182

"The night is bitter, the stars have lost their glitter . . . and all because of the call that got awaaay . . ." Hi, this is E. Manfred Harry. Don't hang up and leave me wailing in despair. Leave your name and number after the tone and I'll get back to you.

. . . *ahuh ahuh* . . . Hello, Mr. Harry . . . *ahuh* . . . Very funny recording . . . Didn't know you were such a wit . . .

This is Edward Chute, I wonder if you remember me. Viola Chute's stepson? We met in London when you were researching her life. Afraid I was a bit snockered at the time; can't have made a very good impression.

I was delighted to get an invitation to Viola's wedding; very big of her to ask Judith and me. Judith isn't going, of course . . . says she can't believe I am. But it's high time we ended all the feuding in this family and knit together what tattered strands are left . . . my opinion, anyway. So yes, I shall be there, and I called Viola to say so. She tells me you had quite an adventure after we met, and what a hero you've been to her.

Listen, Mr. Harry . . . Harry . . . I suppose I must call you by your family name, Viola says you don't like your Christian one. I must tell you, then, Harry, I had something of a change of life after our meeting. I was . . . excuse my boldness, Harry . . . I was very taken with you. But of course in no condition to show it. I wanted so badly to be at my best, but as you know, that just wasn't . . . well, I blame only myself.

Anyway, after I left you, I fell down a flight of stairs in the hotel lobby. Caused myself an injury or two; ended up in hospital. Too bloody drunk to navigate a few meager steps. Although I swear to you it felt like I was pushed—as though I were being chastised for the chance I'd blown with you. Some incorporeal guardian shoving my face into the floor tile to make me see what a complete ass I'd been.

Well, I've had nary a drink since. A few cocktails, just to be social, but never another bender, not since that night. Made no end of difference to me, as well. I'm quite catching up to Judith in my shouldering of the family burden.

Listen . . . I've arranged to stay in Los Angeles for several days following the wedding. Could I possibly persuade you to have a drink with me during that time? . . . Or dinner? . . . I'd very much like a chance to provide the antidote to that terrible first impression. I've thought of you often since we met, Harry. Something about you . . . what can I say except it matters to me that you think well of me.

Hope I haven't made you blush. If I don't hear from you before then, I'll call you when I'm in town.

Ahuh . . . that greeting of yours. I'll be giggling all day. *Ahuh ahuh ahuh.*

Bye.

SUBJ: goin' to the chapel of love
DATE: 97-11-2 08:48:47 EST
FROM: emanfr@ysa.net
TO: nbcasem@bot.ubsm.edu

probably just as well you couldn't make it out here for viola's wedding. i ended up leaving the reception after about half an hour to do some serious snogging with edward chute in his rental car. yes it's true i have a boyfriend even if it's someone i thought was a big loser when i first met him. but then he knew he made a bad first impression and he's spent the weeks since pulling himself together so he could really sweep me off my feet this time. and let me tell you mission accomplished—he even changed his terrible hair. but i think i started to fall for him a little when he first contacted me about the wedding—see he actually laughed at my voice mail message which as you know triggers the gag reflex of just about everyone else on the planet. i knew if i left it on long enough i'd eventually meet someone with my sense of humor. i just never guessed it would be viola chute's stepson.

so look at me in love and successful. what with the kill fee for viola's memoirs and the film money i'm well not rich exactly but no longer on the brink of destitution. plus edward has a friend who runs an ad agency in london who owes him a favor and he's pretty sure he can get me a job there so we can be together. life is suddenly grand and i look at myself in the mirror and wonder who is this guy who has everything going his way he sure doesn't look like me. doesn't answer to my name either because sit down you'll be shocked i am allowing edward to call me elmer. i never admit that name to anybody but somehow he weaseled it out of me and he thinks it's adorable which it sort of is the way he says it ELL-muh.

anyway even though i'm on cloud 9 thanks to my own fab romance i did manage to pay attention to viola's ceremony so i could tell you in

detail what you missed. dennis looked very shaggable in his tux—
funny i never noticed how much taller he is than viola almost a head
and a half which sort of made me wonder how they manage in bed.
you'll have to excuse me that's the turn of my mind lately. he's kind of
a stud anyway—it's not the first time i've met him but it was the first
time i saw him all dressed up and hubba hubba. even despite his bad
seventies perm—whose idea was that.

viola of course looked sensational in a form-fitting cranberry dress by
vera wang. now that versace's toast i guess vera is her couturier of
choice—has to be a designer beginning with v remember. the dress
was cut just above the knee to show off the famous chute gams
though i confess when it comes to chute gams i think edward's are
better. the cap and veil were sensational a spray of mesh with one
long diaphanous strand cascading down her back to form a little train.
i wanted to step on it as she marched past not out of malice just
cause i was feeling giddy.

the ceremony was held on a deck outside the hotel with the ocean
in the background which should've been really stunning but you
know what the beach is like. there was viola with her big tall drink of
water libertarian senator hero plighting her troth and a few yards
away a dog taking a crap. they wrote their own vows which isn't as
embarrassing as it sounds mainly they just cut and pasted a bunch of
their favorite poetry. since viola doesn't have any favorite poetry i had
to help choose so of course it was heavy on rimbaud and baudelaire
which i thought would cause an unsettled stir in the crowd but again
this is l.a. so no one even blinked. i bet half weren't even listening.

dennis's best man was his brother from minnesota who is not quite
as good looking and surprisingly viola's maid of honor was angie ashe-
tippett—the actress hired to replace her on wyndhamville. apparently now that viola has rejoined the show she and angie have
become the fastest of friends which is undoubtedly another reason
gk left in such a huff—angie was supposed to be her protegee. speaking of which did i tell you gk finally called off her lawyer after bothering me for weeks. i guess she realized the only way she could actually

sue me would be to admit in public that she'd hired me to dig into viola's dirty laundry which of course no one of gk's lofty stature could ever bear to do. so i think i've heard the last of her knock wood.

besides angie the whole wyndhamville crowd was at the wedding of course. one of the producers sandy asher gave an amusing toast. he said he'd just recently learned how tough it was to negotiate with viola—he thought he could bluff her out of her million dollar salary demands by firing her from the show. he said he never had anyone call a bluff for that long—then he shook his head and said poor dennis i know exactly who'll be calling the shots on the wedding night. i don't know what was more amusing dennis blushing or the idea that anyone might believe viola and dennis were waiting for the wedding night.

i didn't get a chance to meet many of the other guests before i left but i did finally meet viola's daughter in the flesh. patricia hume you remember well she showed up wearing a brown suit that made her look like a prison matron. could probably be pretty if she tried but i'm willing to bet she refuses just to spite her mother. i expressed my surprise at seeing her there and she said i have always approved of dennis lawley he is a good influence on my mother's character. i had to ask myself does she have any idea who's influencing whom here. at dennis's bachelor party which was a totally disgusting affair but that's another story i got stone drunk and so did dennis. i ended up confronting him about viola stealing the nude pictures he took of her then using them on the internet and also her making up a letter from princess diana and oh just everything she's done. and dennis who is i remind you so ethical he'll put money in an expired parking meter to cover the time it takes him to pull out of it—he just shrugs and says well that's viola she's bigger than life i can't judge her i can only admire her strength. it's a cliche to say love is blind but so what it is and i'm glad of it. also i finally met her agent peter grace who it turns out is rather cute and a total homo despite which he is not even remotely interesting because he is SUCH an AGENT. if you were in the business you'd know what i mean. and i met her attorney gretchen ojan who was wearing this beautiful but strangely familiar emerald choker—i said hey isn't that viola's and she totally snarls back at me possession is nine tenths of the law. like whoa girl settle down have a percoset or three.

the reception was in one of the hotel's ballrooms but like i said edward and i ducked out early to relieve the pressure against our zippers. so yes just as well you didn't come as my guest because i'd have abandoned you without a second thought. you'd have ended up spending the entire event explaining photosynthesis to some barely sentient celebutante who was pretending to listen while really worrying about where she was going to score some x that night. honestly i've so had it with l.a. i can't wait to move to london. no actually i don't mean it i love this town i'm just trying to talk myself into being glad to leave it. i think it'll kill me to say goodbye. but hell how often in life do you find a boyfriend with an accent like michael york's and an intact foreskin i mean no contest right.

after the wedding viola and dennis headed off on their honeymoon the destination of which is a secret because of the tabloids but i'll tell you it's st. lucia. that's right the very place she got into so much trouble with that photographer. she figures it's the last place any paparazzo would ever look for her. i wish her every happiness i really do. this impossible infuriating self-infatuated woman has been a better friend to me than just about anyone this side of you.

miss you tremendously. will bring edward to meet you before i move abroad i promise.

hugs
harry

INTERVIEW WITH VIOLA CHUTE
By E. Manfred Harry
(Excerpt)
Homophile, July 1993

HOMOPHILE: Thanks again for talking to us, Viola. And thanks for being our favorite bitch goddess.

VIOLA: Oh, I'm not a bitch goddess, angel. Fame is the bitch goddess. I'm nothing but a humble acolyte. I am what she made me.

THE END

Plume books by the
"irresistibly funny"*
ROBERT RODI

*Quentin Crisp, author of *The Naked Civil Servant*